Keep Paris

..

Boston Brothers: A second chance series

Kelly Kay

Visit my website www.kellykayromance.com

Cover Design: Lori Jackson- LJ Designs
Editor: Aimee Walker : Aimee Walker Editorial Services
www.aimeewalkerproofreader.com
Copy Editor/Proofreader: Christine Wheary
https://cmwheary.com

Published by Decorated Cast Publishing, LLC

 Created with Vellum

To those who show up.
The ones who ever have my back.
You know who you are, because I've got yours. Love you. Thanks.

Quick note from Kelly

Hello Readers—

I'm thrilled you're here, but I wanted to give you a quick **content warning.**

There is a tense situation involving a near date assault. This book also discusses a past incidence of domestic violence. I hope I've dealt with the subject matter with respect and honesty. It's never my intention to be exploitative.

Know that, like with all of my books, a portion of the profits will go to a not-for-profit charity that reflects issues in my books. Just by reading this, you're helping the *Connections for Abused Women and their Children* - CAWC- in Chicago. Thank you. https://www.cawc.org/

Talk soon,

Kelly K

Also by Kelly Kay

FIVE FAMILIES VINEYARD ROMANCES

LaChappelle/Whittier Vineyard Trilogy

Crushing, Rootstock & Uncorked

Stafýlia Cellars Duet

Over A Barrel & Under The Bus

Gelbert Family Winery Standalones

Meritage: An Unexpected Blend

Residual Sugar

Coming Soon

Pietro Family pre order live

Langerford Cellars Book

CHITOWN LOVE STORIES

A Lyrical Romance Duet

Shock Mount & Crossfade

A Lyrical Spinoff Standalone

Present Tense

CARRIAGE HOUSE CHRONICLES

Funny, steamy, smart novellas for when you don't know what to read next. Released randomly throughout the year!

Follow Me - Now available

(Rockstar, second chance, forced proximity)

Sound Off - Enemies to Lovers, reverse grumpy sunshine, close proximity set in the music world

For the Rest of Us - Holiday

(M/M, holiday, marriage in crisis, one bed)

Something Good -

(Age gap, nanny, single dad, rockstar)

BOSTON BROTHERS: A second chance series

Keep Paris

Keep Philly - FREE novella (book 1.5)

Keep Vegas

Keep Tuscany - (pre-order live!)

EVIE & KELLY'S HOLIDAY DISASTERS

Hilarious Rom Com novellas with Evie Alexander

VOLUME ONE

Cupid Calamity

Cookout Carnage

Christmas Chaos

Part One
Première Partie
Ten Years Ago

LIZZIE

I'M ALREADY MORE CONTINENTAL. MY PARENTS INSISTED I GO ON this trip and I convinced my best friend's parents to let Kristin come as well. My senior year is kind of a joke since I basically could have graduated last fall. I've finished all my credits and I am currently number two in my class. I'll never beat Jennifer Liu. That bish has it on lock.

My high school hooked up with some travel group and offered twelve weeks in Paris for our spring semester. Intense study, culture, and because I speak fluent French, it's also AP credits. I want baguettes, architecture walks, to read French poetry on the steps of the Notre-Dame and to reread my favorite Lost Generation authors—in the cafés they loved. Words have always been my escape from my parents, peer pressure, or heartbreak.

Our group has twenty-three kids from various parts of the West Coast, my best friend Kristin and I are the only ones from Burlingame. She's, like, model tall with a wicked sense of sarcasm and short pixie hair that's braver than I ever could be. We've basically formed a gang with hysterical three girls from Reno. They ordered cocktails on the plane once we hit international waters. I hope I'm good at being part of a gang.

We're moving into our rooms at our dorm/hotel. There's a couple other groups from around the US and Australia. Maybe I can kiss an Aussie. I want to know if kissing gets better than a dude shoving his tongue into your mouth and wiggling. I'm eighteen and I've kissed my fair share of boys, but I keep waiting for it to be better.

The rooms have twin beds and the suite connects through a shared Jack and Jill bathroom. Because we're here for almost three months and my parents made sure I had my own space to study, but Kris is my suite-mate.

"AHHHHH. Holy shit, this is cool." Kristin does a spin and tosses her stuff anywhere she wants in her room. She has a ton of siblings, so to have her own space must feel decadent. "We could make a lounge out of one room, put the beds on the wall like couches."

I consider it for a second, then see her stuff everywhere and panic. "Let's see what it's like to have big rooms all to ourselves. Maybe later we can create a lounge."

"PERFECTO!"

"You know that's Italian, not French."

"C'est moi. Comme ci comme ca."

I smile at her. "I'm making one mega bed out of the two. I'll call down for king-size sheets."

I say, "Sounds good."

I head back into my room. I like things the way I like them. I unpack and arrange my toiletries around the closet sink. Kristin pops a beer as she comes into my room. I didn't know she had one.

"Where did that come from?"

"Reno girls. They want us down in their room when we're settled. You know, when you're done organizing. I swear, your fucking sweaters are folded like you work at the Gap."

"I dream of owning one of those folding boards."

She tosses her loofah sponge thing at me.

We make our way to Makenzie and Maggie's room. We don't have to be anywhere until dinner where all the students hear the rules and meet the teachers.

"Seriously, their room number is 666?" Kris's boisterous laugh fills the hallway as she knocks.

Makenzie flings the door open and French pop music comes spilling out. "I don't know what they're saying, but we're dancing our asses off to it."

They all have beer. Misty is smoking out the window and Kris joins her. I meekly take a beer and panic a little we'll get caught and kicked out.

Kris exhales. "Lighten up, Lizzie. You're fine." She knows me. I sway to the music. The lyrics are about partying and enjoying life. Ok. I get you, universe, message received. I toss back a sip and they cheer.

I'm dancing with Maggie and we're laughing hard when a phone ring cuts through our party. Fuck. It's management. It's the chaperons. We're so busted.

I turn off the radio and Makenzie bolts for the phone. Shit. I start pacing. I'm the only one terrified. Shit. My parents will kill me. All this money and opportunity and I throw it away within a few hours of being here. Shit. The institutional wall color is supposed to soothe me; it does not. Fuck you, pale yellow. Fuck you.

We all hold our breath as Makenzie answers. "Hello?"

We watch as her eyes widen.

"No." She answers a male voice. I never do anything, and here, the first time I let loose—busted. I'm never doing anything wrong again.

Then Makenzie smiles.

"Not possessed." We all exchange looks of curiosity and relief. "Why don't you come down here and meet my coven for yourself? Or maybe you want me to hex you?" Makenzie's fucking flirting.

"There's five of us... That's my lucky number, too."

I really, really hope it's not a chaperone. Christ. I don't know her well. Please let her not be an edu-chaser.

She hangs up and pulls on a pair of leggings. She was dancing in her underwear.

"What?" We're all staring at her. She grins and sits on the bed, moving her long jet-black hair out of her face. Then she applies red lipstick that's sitting on the nightstand. She tosses it to me.

"Tony and his friends are on their way down."

"Who's Tony?" Maggie asks.

Makenzie shrugs. "We'll find out."

DANNY

Been here four days, sober about twenty-five minutes. It's wicked pissah awesome. We convinced our parents we needed to come early to Paris. Why the fuck not? I haven't seen my parents in months because of my football scholarship at a snooty boys academy, and since I'm the star quarterback, and I'm fucking good, I haven't done shit with my grades all year. Charm and a good arm open all my doors. I'm waiting on the rest of my college offers but Penn State wants me bad. Duke wasn't willing to negotiate because my grades weren't stellar since I was born. Fuck them. I want a Big Ten or Pac-12 school. It would be fucking sweet to be the hometown hero in Boston but I'll play at the best program that wants me. Football is my path forward.

Tony, my suite-mate at Xavier Prep, is a fucking rich-ass party hound. He's from Boston too, but a very different Boston. He's never been down to Southie.

Tony's my tour guide through the world of money. Within an hour of landing in Paris, he had a pocket full of speed and a bag of coke. I don't touch that shit. Won't risk my scholarship or conditioning. He's that guy who always lands on his feet. I'm not that guy, so I stay clean.

I've known his parents since I played Pee Wee football All-City All-Stars with Tony's brother and started hanging around their house. They're kind and good parents. They paid for my plane ticket to Paris. They've been really fucking good to me. I told my mom the team paid so she didn't feel bad. I'll pay the back someday.

I've never let a training moment slide or slack off, despite what my father thinks. With the season over and my prospects good, Tony begged me to come on this trip. I don't need French credits, but three months bumming around Europe with his deep pockets sounded pretty fucking good. We might go to his house in Italy. His parents have a house in a foreign country. My parents have eaten at IHOP.

We're sitting around drinking and playing cards. I'm the shark and currently earning my spending money for the week. I've been regularly taking these assholes' extra cash for two years. My neighborhood and my Italian mother taught me a thing or two about tells. I learned early—you read the person, not the cards. Everyone has a tell. Mine's flicking my thumbs on my forefingers. Sometimes I have to sit on my hands.

Colton, my brilliant wide receiver and all around good fucking dude, calls my bluff. I toss the pot to him. He's from Boston but his dad is a Senator, so he splits his time between home and DC. We knew him from city sports but damn can he catch whatever the hell I throw. I love that he turned up at Xavier. Fucking love it. His folks have political money and power. He's a pussy cat though, who never lacks for company.

"You're slipping there, gangsta."

"Lulling you into a false sense of security until I take you for all your spending cash."

We're all playing except Tony is prank calling within the hotel. He's scaring the shit out of other kids or annoying the chaperones. No one can trace our calls on these museum piece phones. Most of this place is like a shrine to the '80s. We keep calling it a minimum security prison.

We turn our attention to Tony who leaps in the air yelling, "Jack-fucking-pot, gentlemen. Time to ride, my good men. Grab your armor and provisions, we have lands to conquer and worlds to bring to their knees. Hopefully with our dicks in their mouths." I roll my eyes. He loves a grand gesture. Last year during some medieval humanities unit we were the modern Knights of the Round Table. He dubbed himself king and we were all given a place at the table. He bought us chalices for Christmas and hung banners and flags with our "logo" on them. Other factions challenge us to soccer or flag football from time to time to try and take his "crown." He still has it.

His voice raises and returns to normal. "Up. Not kidding. Grab the beer." He starts clapping.

Colton pushes up from our makeshift poker table and groans. "Adventure?"

Tony puts his coat on and lifts his umbrella to the sky. "Onward to adventure, good chaps! The numbers are in our favor!" We all grab our coats and the beer cooler, and the elevator takes us down two floors. Not the adventure I'd thought.

"Come, the witches await."

He knocks on the door to room 666. A short, pretty girl with sparkling golden eyes and luscious long highlighted hair opens the door and says, "Tony?"

He smirks. "Are you the charming woman I spoke with?"

Another girl appears as the first opens the door wider. She's tall and skinny with straight dark hair and stunning dark eyes to match. They're both hot.

She looks Tony up and down and says, "Ok. I'll allow it. Come in. I'm Makenzie."

She winks at Tony and turns into the room as the first girl keeps the door open. Colton takes over door duty and smiles at her. She giggles at him as he winks. Colton is a man of few words, but that damn wink gets him laid every time. I'm the last one to file in, leaving Colton and sparkly eyes to themselves.

Tony and his female counterpart are in the middle of introductions as I remove my jacket. When I lift my face, it's like my O line isn't even there and I've been sacked. Breathless. Fuck me, she's gorgeous. I mean, like, otherworldly ethereal.

Her umber colored bangs unfurl over the lightest green eyes. Then she shifts her focus to me. Her eyes are saying things only I can understand and hear. Normally my attention would have already drifted to her legs, hips, and tits, but I can't look away from her face. My lips twitch into a smile that mirrors hers. Tony and the brunette point to her, but she doesn't look away from me as she speaks. We're in our own fucking world.

"I'm Lizzie."

Without prompting, I say, "Dan. Dan." She grins and it's as if all the stadium lights on a Friday night blaze to life.

"Hi, Dan Dan. That's funny, you know." Her face pales a bit, as if she's worried she's made fun of me.

"No, it's cool. Actually, everyone just calls me Dan."

She looks down and then back up, and her long-ass

eyelashes reveal her seriously stunning sea glass green eyes again. "I'm Lizzie Fox." She shakes her head because she's introduced herself twice, and I want to snap her up on my lap. Flustered Lizzie Fox is fucking hot.

"Dan Dan, Lizzie and Lizzie Fox?" I say.

She laughs. "Let's just go with Lizzie and Danny."

My stomach bottoms out as she chooses a name for me. Dan's the nickname everyone uses at school. I say, "Danny's good." I've never been Danny, but I can be Danny to her. Fuck, she's beautiful. She's hitting all the spots in my brain. And in my crotch.

Tony and Makenzie start catcalling, and it pulls our attention from each other. Tony raises his umbrella, but this time he points his long and annoying fake sword towards Lizzie, then over to me.

"Consider this union blessed by the king. Go forth, Knight Danson and fair maiden..."

Makenzie fills in for him, "The Lady Fox."

Lizzie protests, "Why does he get to be a knight and I have to be a fair maiden?"

The room looks at her. She shies away for a second, then the tall girl sitting next to her nudges her and whispers in her ear.

Her face is blooming red, but she says, "Why can't I be a knight?" It's flush with pink now and she's even more beautiful the more flustered she gets.

He bows to her, and her friend pushes her up. Lizzie curtseys. Then he nods and she kneels. He places his umbrella on each shoulder.

"Arise, fair knight, and go forth and make knightlets for me. So I may rule with an attractive army."

She huddles with her friend and shoots me a secret

smile. I move over and nudge Tony so he stops making her the center of attention.

He yells, "Guards! Guards! Remove the warrior from my sight." He turns towards the raven-haired hostess. "And you, good witch, your spell has landed upon me. Goodie Makenzie?"

She bites her lip. "You're fucking crazy. Can we just drink beer, or do we have to find mead or some shit?" Everyone laughs. And we all find places to sit.

I want Lizzie to sit near me, but she retreats to a chair in the corner. Colton's getting cozy with Maggie, whose bubbly giggle rises above the din.

I think I'd wrestle anyone who tried to sit near Lizzie. I glance back at her and she's looking at her feet. I can't see her tits, but I want to, yes sir, I do. My dick twitches and I arrange my jeans a bit. I mean, I get hard constantly, but this is different. There's no fucking way she didn't feel that shit between us, too.

Finally, she looks over and we're trapped by each other's gaze. Fuck me, she's so freaking pretty. Her neck is long and swan-like. I want to lick it wicked bad. I've never done that before, but I want to nip that neck. I've been so focused on not failing out of school and training. My only outlet from all of it is either fucking someone from the sister school—a townie—or drawing in my sketch pad. But at least I'm not at home with my less than ideal fucked-up dad situation.

I do want a part of this girl, though. Lizzie's smiling and all I can think is how dangerous her lips could be. I move across the room and ignore my teasing asshole suite-mates and sit next to her. I can already tell she's too good for me, but that won't stop me. No one has ever validated me with a look before. I don't feel less than, I feel more.

My voice comes out at half volume as she sidles up next to me. “Lizzie.”

She bites her lip. “Danny.”

And I never want to hear my name said by anyone else ever fucking again.

LIZZIE

He's so focused on me. I don't know where to look or put my hands. I keep reciting the most boring facts ever and wiggling my fingers.

I mentally glue down my hand in case he wants to hold it. I can't imagine he would. His jacket has athletic patches and he's big and strong and gorgeous. His dark brown hair is cut short but not crew cut short. And his eyes, well, I'm beside myself looking at them. I didn't know eyes could be like a blue-grey almost cadet blue. I'll bet his skin is soft. I'm so awkward and weird. There's no way he's into me. He's sitting here because all our friends paired off and it's a wingman situation.

We're staring straight ahead. Every part of me wants to scream to break the tension. I wish he'd say something. We're watching everyone drink and Tony pretending to joust to win Makenzie's hand.

Tony points to us. "Dan, can you run up and get more beer? I did not plan on the princesses... and our newly knighted Sir Lizzie consuming most of it." I smile. Then

Makenzie smacks him on the ass and he fake growls at her with a claw-like motion. She grins.

"Goodie Makenzie and I have business to attend to." He spins her in a flourish.

"You wish, King Arthur." He doesn't hesitate to pull her into his embrace.

"I do, fair maiden, I really do wish. I wish we were alone, and you could pull my sword from the stone, but for now, I shall woo you."

She winks at him. "Good luck with that. Crank the music, people, we're dancing."

I'm mentally freaking out because he's leaving the room. I'll be here by myself, hoping he comes back. This is totally Tony saving Danny from having to talk to me.

He extends his hand. "Wanna come with me?"

YES. I totally do. I'd kinda follow him anywhere. No one's ever looked at me the way he does. It's like my insides are a pinball machine with balls bouncing everywhere. He's got this smirk that makes certain parts of me glow.

"To get beer," he says with a leading voice. I forgot to answer.

"Oh. I'm an idiot. Yes." He's going to uninvite me now.

"Nah, you're cute." My face gets atomic red as I slip my hand in his. He's soft but has calluses that don't feel like they're from hard labor or writing. Must be from his sport. My hand is secure in his as he leads me to the elevator. I think this is what swooning feels like and I may need a fainting couch. I slyly put a finger to my pulse because my heart rate is going nuts. I want to make sure I'm not having a heart attack. My blood is crackling and my belly is going to explode with nervous knots.

The tension bubbles up and explodes out of me. "Did

you know there's a mummy named Belphegor who haunts the Louvre?"

He laughs and turns towards me. "What did you say?"

His eyes are, like, so intense I'm freaking out inside. OMFG his finger just brushed the back of my hand. My whole body is numb. I totally forgot he asked me a question.

"What?"

"What did you say about the Louvre?"

I look down because I can't keep staring at him. He's burning my retinas with his hotness. Through the curtain of my hair, I see a finger coming towards my chin. He places it under there and lifts my face to his.

"Don't hide. Look at me, Lizzie."

I've somehow slipped through a wormhole into a place where Lizzie is sexy and not competitive or awkwardly repelling cute boys. Oh my God.

I mumble my random fact again, "Did you know there's a mum—" I don't even get the sentence out and his lips are on mine. They're so soft, like fresh marshmallow Peeps—when they first come out of the package, before the air starts to harden them. His mouth is "fresh Peeps soft." He finishes the kiss and looks at me.

"Is that ok?"

I blurt out, "You kissing me is the most ok thing that's ever happened to me in my life." He smiles and his teeth are movie star perfect. Of course, they are. And here I am with my goofy arms hanging like sausages. My father says they're too gangly for my body. I push that thought away and focus on him.

"Then we should probably keep doing it." His lips curl and so do my toes.

"How long are you in Paris?" I ask.

"Eleven weeks and four days more. You?"

My entire body lights up. He's not leaving for an eternity. "Eleven weeks and six days. But we should keep kissing for eleven weeks and four days. And I'll take those last two days off."

"The ones when I'm not here?" He chuckles a bit. I think I might be successfully flirting. And I'm pretty good at it. And oddly, this gorgeous guy thinks I'm funny.

I nod. "Yes. That can be our break."

He laughs. He says, "Good, wouldn't want to think I could be replaced that quickly." He grabs my hips and I bite my cheek to keep from gasping. I instinctually put my arms around his neck. This kiss is stronger, and his tongue is, like, right on my lips, and I tighten up in panic. What if I'm shit at this?

"Relax, pretty Lizzie."

I have no filter. "How?" I've kissed boys. I want him to teach me how to kiss him. So that it's ours.

His fingers dust my jaw and his thumb feathers over my lower lip. "Open your mouth slightly next time and follow what I do."

"Why are you being like this with me?" It just slips out.

"You're killing me. You're gorgeous but have no idea that you're awkward and fascinating in all the right ways. You listen like you care what I'm saying. That's hot." He smiles.

"I do care what you're saying, but right now I'd super like to try that open mouth thing you mentioned. I've had bad luck with it in the past."

He pulls me closer. "Then consider me your good luck charm."

"This is happening. I mean, to me. This is amazing. J'ai

dû venir à Paris pour faire un bisou français, qu'y a-t-il à détester là-dedans?"

He smirks and says, "And I had to come to Paris to find the perfect girl to French kiss. So can we get to it already?"

"Oui, s'il vous plaît."

His mouth is gentle against mine and he teases the tip of his tongue on my bottom lip. I open slightly. At first, it's tickling and searching for mine. Then we get closer, and this is really hot. I let my tongue chase his in and out of his mouth. Then he does the same to me. And a noise comes out of me I've never heard before. A small gaspy, breathy moan, as if this is the most perfect thing. My moan doesn't lie.

He rubs his thumb on my cheekbone and says, "That was really sexy. Did you mean it to be?"

"Sure. Who knew I was sexy?" I try to joke, but he speaks just before his lips are on mine again.

"I did. The moment I saw you in that room."

The kiss goes on for most of the night and I can't even feel my body. It's floating in a state of bliss. Forget school, culture and religion. Screw geography, and my grades, college, and my career path; this is what I was born to do. Kiss Danny Danson.

DANNY

It took four days for her to become my preoccupation in France. Fuck school. It's all Lizzie, all the time. We spend all our free moments walking and hanging out. We've checked out our neighborhood or partied with our friends every day. And then we kiss. Then each night, after we say goodbye, I jerk off—a lot. I'm so wrapped up in her. Usually, my focus is making sure my back is always covered, both on and off the field. Maybe it's Paris and being so far away from my real life, or maybe it's her. It's the best feeling in the world to be free of those worries.

I blow off my afternoon thing and find her before she enters her seminar. She's dressed up in a purple dress with orange palm trees. Somehow this pattern is uniquely her. She's always so nervous about a million things, but underneath, she's this clever, strong human waiting to be unleashed. I feel it and hear it when I'm with her.

I get in her face and say, "Come with me."

She glares and sidesteps the door so others can enter, then whispers, "I have a lecture."

"So? You don't need class, but I do need you." She grins

and I can barely stand not kissing her. She ducks her head into the classroom.

I stand and wait for her. I toss my weight back and forth. I got my last college offers today and I have shit to sort out and she calms my head. I'm so fucking happy I get to make the commitment decision here, away from everyone, especially my dad.

I know what I want to do, and I know what my father wants me to do. And I know what the recruiting manager wants me to do. They're not the same thing. And I don't want to be that far from Ma. My older brother, Robbie, deferred his hockey scholarship to Minnesota for a year to train and watch over Ma while I'm at prep school. I want to step up so he can go in the fall.

My father divided his sons into three sports and drove us hard. He calls us his 401K. My little brother, Law, is a baseball savant and I'm a pretty great quarterback.

Lizzie puts her hand on my arm and I say, "Come on, genius."

She rolls her eyes. "I can't just walk away. It's not like college where we can pick and choose classes. There's attendance."

I cage her against the wall leaning in close. Her hair tickles my lips as I whisper, "Repeat after me: I'm sick."

She gasps. "I'm sick."

"And I need to go back to my room."

"And I need to go back to my room."

I put my forehead to hers. "And I need to kiss Danny as much as possible today or I'll die."

"Fine." Her giggle is really fucking cute.

"Hey, you were supposed to repeat that."

She says, "Repeat it yourself."

"I did that all night. Now I want you to do it." I waggle my eyebrows at her and she bursts out laughing.

She squirms a bit. "I'll come if you show me a piece of Paris you want to see. I don't mean your body."

I smile but make sure not to pressure her too much. "Don't do this if you're not feeling it."

She licks her lips and then grins. "I could maybe, I don't know, skip this one thing."

I can't wait to show her this place. I went the day we arrived. I was so antsy to see it.

"I'll be out front." I turn and hear her speak in perfect French.

"Excusez-moi, Madame, je suis malade et je dois retourner dans ma chambre."

She's staring all around us on the Metro then scribbles on a random piece of paper and shoves it back into her bag. She laces her fingers in mine. She smells a little like flowers and bubblegum.

I say, "I want to learn something new about you every day."

"It's been four days. How much can you really know when all we do is kiss? Though I'm not complaining." She smiles and I peck her lips quickly.

"I've learned four things."

She turns towards me in her seat. "And they are?" I stare at her, then take her hand. "Seriously?"

I say, "You use cinnamon toothpaste, which isn't that common, but I like it." She nods. "You've known Kris since you were in the third grade, and she moved next door to you." She smiles wider. "Your skin is the softest I've ever felt." She rolls her eyes.

She says, "And... what did you learn today?"

"Today's fun fact about Lizzie is..." I do a drum roll on my knees. Everyone stares and the elderly woman down to the right of us puts her hand over her heart. "You keep secrets."

"How did you figure that one out? Because I haven't told you any yet?"

I laugh and pull her back. "No, you don't keep other people's secrets, you keep your own. I want to hear every single one of them." She squeezes me.

"You want to know my secrets. You're going to have to give me one."

I grin, then tell her the thing that's weighing me down. "All my offers are in, and I don't know what the fuck to do."

"Offers?" Her brow lifts.

"College. Where I'm going to play football next year."

"Oh! How many?"

I look down sheepishly. It's a bigger deal than she'll understand, and I like that. "There are six solid schools, three amazing schools and two I-can't-believe-they-want-me schools."

"Where do you want to go?"

"My father wants me to go to Oregon, Texas A&M, UCLA. Or U of M like Brady did."

"Those are great schools. But I asked where you want to go, not your father." She smiles and it lights my insides on fire.

"I found out yesterday I got a full ride to Boston College. I really want to be at BC. I want to play for the team I rooted for as a kid. I want to be in my hometown and have my friends and family come see me. I want the town to be proud of the kid from Southie who made good."

I look away from her and she lets me. I also want to be where my Ma and Law can see me play, and I can make sure they're ok. He won't try anything if one of us is close. When we were kids, he could get away with all kinds of shit, but since Robbie and I train constantly and are stronger than he anticipated, he watches his fucking step now.

She takes my hand. "Sounds settled to me."

My father will rage. I'll give Robbie a heads up. I rake her into my arms and kiss the top of her head. I pull my phone out and email my recruiter and college manager. I have to go to some office to eSign the commitment, and he'll set up the actual signing here in Paris. Shit. I can't believe it's that easy or that I just did it.

"Are you always this decisive?" I ask.

She thinks for a second. "Not ever, I can't remember the last time a decision was mine. Except skipping that lecture." Her eyes are dancing.

She can tell me what that's about in time but my world of stress just lifted. I'm going to sling the ball for Boston College. HOLY SHIT. I can't fucking believe I'm going to be a Screaming Eagle.

I'm about to pull her towards me again when her phone rings. She frantically searches for it, like she'll be punished if she lets it go. She turns away from me and smiles at her phone.

"Hello!"

A man says, "Bonjour. Salut, mon petit menteur."

I sit straight up because he called her a little liar. She plasters on a super fake smile and glances over at me.

"Dad—"

Oh, shit. He knows she ditched. I put my hand on her knee. She flinches and moves away.

"Dad, why would you call me a liar?"

"En français."

"Papa, pourquoi me traites-tu de menteur?"

Her face scrunches up. I slide a little closer to support her. This is intense. I'm out of view of the phone, but she still scoots away from me. WTF.

He says, "Because, young lady, you promised you wouldn't slack off in France. You'd be the good student your mother and I trusted you to be. And you've already disappointed us by skipping class."

"I didn't really."

"I can see you're on the Metro." Why did she pick up FaceTime?

"I already passed that class, Dad. It's review. I could take the test today," she pleads with him and moves further away from me. I don't like any of this.

"En français!" His voice booms through the train, and everyone looks. Her eyes begin to glass over.

This guy needs to meet my pops. They'd probably hate each other, resulting in a bar fight brought on by my dad saying, "You think you're better than me?" I have a hunch her dad would reply, "Yes." But neither of them is correct.

She says nothing, and I can tell she wants to run away from me. That's not going to happen. I know a thing or two about fucking bullies.

"Oui, Monsieur. Mes excuses. Je ne suis pas nécessaire dans cette classe et j'ai un après-midi libre. Je me dirige vers."

She freaking apologized. The fucking class is an elective.

How she acts when she gets off this phone call will teach me a new thing about her. If she cries because she disappointed him, then I'm not sure she's the person I'm infatuated with. But if she's pissed about how she handled it, well, then she's exactly the girl I think she is.

I want to give her ammunition. We're not just blowing off education totally. I whisper, "Musée Picasso." Her face brightens, and so does my whole fucking day.

LIZZIE

HE'S TAKING ME SOMEWHERE WONDERFUL. AND HE'S NOT running from the freak getting yelled at by her father.

My father's always so disappointed. He's so sure of what he's doing and what everyone else should be. My mom must like being told what to be and how to speak, since she's stuck around. I love him, but I don't like his demanding tone, not when he's the one who forced me to come to France in the first place.

I've never lived in the moment until Danny kissed me out of nowhere. And now I'm addicted.

His voice is strong and he speaks in English. I know his French isn't as good as mine, so he probably wants the upper hand again. "Answer my question, little scholar. Where are you going that you think is more important than being in an academic environment?"

My gaze drifts to Danny. He's staring at me, but he's not angry or frustrated. His eyes are piercing, understanding, and sexy. And he wants to hold my hand and take me to exciting places. We have eleven weeks left. My brain has been trained to analyze things but I want to fall into confusion and Danny without thinking of consequences or deadlines. I stop my brain, look at my phone, and say, "Musée Picasso."

I'm not allowed to date. It "detracts from my studies and pursuit of excellence." My father is a stickler for the rules. But I'm choosing to believe those are United States rules. This is the Danny loophole.

There's a long pause. "It's not the Louvre, but it's still culture." Danny puts his fists up like he's going to fight my dad. "You were trained to study the classics but take excellent notes to create a study guide for Art History next year." He talks a bit more, and I don't tell him to stop. I wish I could. I will someday. He finishes his lecture and I hang up and shove my phone into my bag.

I turn away from Danny because I'm so full of rage it's leaking down my face. He reaches over and pulls my chin towards him. It's so unfair *he* gets to control me from another continent. Danny pulls me into his arms.

I say as I lean on his chest, trying to recover, "Are we really going to the Picasso Museum?"

"Oui."

I sit up and look at him. "Danny, I'm so sorry. This is so cool and I totally messed it up by answering my father's stupid FaceTime. But it's worse if I don't."

"It can get worse?"

I wince and say, "I'm so sorry. They're professors at Stanford and my father is an education snob. My whole life has been taking the next step before anyone else. Never-ending mantras in my house are extracurricular, extra credit, and extra assignments."

I look in his eyes and refuse to say my next thoughts. They've always pushed me to be extra. I just want to be enough. Danny makes me feel like I might be enough.

He lifts an eyebrow and smirks. "No need to apologize to me. Only Picasso."

His understanding spurs my emotions to bubble over to a place I never let speak. "I'm fucking pissed off. All the time. I hate second-guessing a good time because someone might find out. Or that I didn't stand up to him and say, 'I skipped class.' But fuck it. I'm eighteen. I live in Paris for now and what consequences could he bring?"

"Damn, girl. You're exactly who I thought you were. That's a good thing."

Danny doesn't hesitate to draw me into a deep kiss. It's lovely and chaste but meaningful. He pulls back a little and smiles, then says, "En français."

I giggle and drop my lower lip as he slides his tongue into my mouth for a perfect French kiss that lasts most of the ride. Every place he touches me, I want to tattoo the sensation on my brain. Usually, I'd stop and be polite. But maybe, well, maybe in Paris, I'm not polite. I'm the girl who gets things she *wants* instead of the things she's told she should have.

DANNY

THIS IS THE SECOND TIME I'VE BEEN HERE AND I'M STILL GOING TO need to come back. House Salé is grand and impressive, even without the art. Fuck, it's so beautiful, just like the girl on the end of my arm. We've walked for hours, but I want to show her something. Something that draws me in and fills me up.

We turn a corner and I guide her to the cases with my hand on her back. It's chilly here, and her burgundy sweater is scratchy and scrapes along my fingers, but the warmth from her back is awesome. Her sweater hangs below her puffer jacket sleeve. I can deal with some slight woolly irritation if I get to touch her.

I lean down as she's staring at the first Picasso notebook. His handwriting on display on postcards and notebooks fills me with inspiration. It's similar to mine, and if we're similar like this, perhaps I am an artist and not just a fucking jock on a scholarship.

"I'll tell you a secret if you tell me what you wrote on the Metro." I kiss her neck lightly and she shimmies, as if I gave her a chill. Like a sex chill. Fuck, I want to do that to her. Jesus, I need to get it together. I step back from her and breathe slowly in and out. I need to calm my dick down to a semi. I want to have sex with her, but I don't think she's ready. I won't rush her because I want to keep her.

I don't know what it is about her, but I go to sleep—if I'm able—thinking of her and rush to see her in the morning.

She pulls out the paper from her bag and hands it to me. I take it and sit on the bench.

It's scribbled notes: *Old lady, Parisian carpet bag, looks like she still rides the Metro to stay young or remember her youth. Everyone she loves is scattered around the world, and she looks for her lost loves all over the city. She is the city.*

My eyebrows lift. "You're a writer."

"No. I'm an observer, that's all."

She smiles up at me and kisses me quickly. It's the first time she's kissed me first. I glance at my watch. I want to mark the time and place in my memory when I fell for her for real. She's a secret artist, too.

"Your turn. What's another of your secrets? Mr. Jock. Football stud. Sexy star quarterback. Boston College royalty." I cringe and she notices. "I'm sorry. Was that wrong?"

I turn away and try to let it go, but she pulls me back. I say, "It's fine. I thought you saw more than that; that's all." Complete kick in the crotch, and for the first time since we met, my dick is totally deflated. "It's cool."

I stand up and drift down the room. I say, "Come on. We should get back." She gathers her stuff and scurries after me. My legs are long, so I'm well ahead of her. I need a second. I didn't know she liked me for that. Fuck. I head towards the exit, and when I reach the staircase, she catches up. She's huffing a little. I hitch my backpack and turn to let her go up the stairs first. She smiles weakly and pushes past me. Things are totally different now.

She's been quiet and respectful of my shit-ass attitude. Our thighs are touching but nothing else. I keep making a fist, releasing it, and breathing to calm down. I can't believe I fucking fell for it. I hoped she'd see how much the museum means to me. That there's more to me than a dumb, useless, shallow jock athlete. I didn't even get a chance to tell her that I draw. I use football to get laid occasionally, but she looked at me differently. Her hands are folded in her lap and she's staring down again.

She says in the smallest voice, "I don't know what I've done, but I'm so sorry."

I say without looking at her, "It's fine." We ride another two stops sitting in the uncomfortable silence. I stand and move around trying to shake it off. I want to go for a run but can't right now. I'm itchy in my skin but I exhale and sit back down.

She moves her hand tentatively towards mine. Then she retracts it. And when she does that, I realize I'm no better than my fucking father or hers. I made her feel shitty about something that's my fucking problem.

"No. I'm sorry. It's ok. I wanted to be more than a jock to you. But it's ok if you want to date a football player. It's fine."

She doesn't look up but says, "I like all of you." Then we're quiet again. It's fucking tense. I stay next to her but I need her to make the first move. I want her to choose me. Another stop, and she tries again to touch me. Two more stops and finally, she links her pinkie with mine. That's the right timing. I'm ready to be touched and she was brave enough to ignore my bullshit. I reach over with my other hand and lift her chin.

Her voice is small. "I know what it's like to feel as though you're something other than what people see. I want to see all of you."

I can't breathe right. It's like I took a hard hit in practice. No one has ever been that kind of intimate. I wrap around her and pull her close, and we ride the rest of the way like that. Just before our stop, I kiss the top of her head and say, "Thank you."

LIZZIE

I'm on my bed journaling. I haven't seen Danny much today, just for breakfast. Kris bursts into my room and flops onto my bed. "Whatcha doing?"

"Writing."

"Tell me it's for fun and not your dad. We're all going clubbing."

"Really? Where?"

"Some place Tony found." I sit up, pull up my knees, and rest my chin on them. "Can I play stylist?" she asks. She tucks a short hair behind her ear. It's what she wants to do in life and I'm her favorite test subject. I'll wash my face before we go out. I always do.

I shrug and she squeals.

I finish my champagne spritzer, and my head is light, but my makeup is heavy. I look pretty, but not myself.

"Pink or red for your lips?"

"Chapstick."

"Red it is." She opens her mouth slightly for me to mirror the position, then applies. It's been super warm the last couple of days, like winter disappeared suddenly. It's the beginning of March and I hope we can walk to the club.

"Cool. You're ready." There's a knock on the door and I realize Kris didn't get dressed up.

"Hey, are you not going out?'

"Nah, none of us are. Julian and I are hanging out. There's a poker game going on in Makenzie's room or something. We might wander down later."

"Then why am I dressed like slutty Barbie?"

"Sluts have more fun, don't you forget that." She whips open the door. Danny is standing there, dressed up in a white button-down and jeans. He's got vibrant flowers. I smile at him and he cocks his eyebrow.

"I see Kris got you ready for our date."

"Date?" My smile is immediate and huge.

"Yes. We've never had one. I thought it was time." My body bubbles with excitement. He's right. We've done loads of things together. We've explored so much of the city, drove to Belgium, and took the Chunnel to England for the day. But a date where he dresses up, picks me up, and it's just us—I guess we haven't.

We walk towards the elevators and he nudges me. "That's bright. You don't look like you."

"That's what I said! Kris said this is clubbing/date me, not regular me."

"I think regular you is pretty and so far, perfect." I blush, but he can't see it under all the tinted moisturizer.

"Stop. You don't have to say that."

He squares my shoulders to face him. "I can say you're pretty if you're pretty. If I find you the prettiest girl in any room. I'm allowed." I squirm a little and look down at my feet. He lifts my chin. "And I don't say anything because I have to. I try to mean everything I say."

I go up on my toes and kiss him. We take the elevator up, not down, and I'm confused. On the top floor, he pulls me towards a staircase. He flings open the door to the roof and Dave Matthews is playing from his computer. There's a blanket with candles.

I walk past him and put my hand over my mouth. We've spent ten times as much time together as other couples starting out. It's like we're on fast forward. My friend Sarah Crocket once told me when you have a boyfriend at camp, it's much more serious than real life because you're around each other ALL the time. I never went to camp but imagine this is what it's like. My heart is so full.

He says, "I'm insane about you. You're all I think about. I dream up ways to show you how I feel. Like this." I turn around and his lips curl into the sweetest, greatest smile in the world. "Lizzie, I'm fucking toast."

I laugh.

"I don't get it. You're a breakfast item? Ok. I'm scrambled eggs."

He shakes his head and says, "Then I'm over easy because I'm over and done with. I'm gone for you. I always thought I'd find someone to care about and want to be around, like, all the time. But I never thought I'd find them at eighteen. I keep waiting to not like something about you. I'm constantly evaluating if I'm delusional. No person can be this fantastic. Every second I want to be closer to you. It's like every moment I'm around you is better than the last. I like when we're not talking about anything, but we're close to each other. I don't understand how this happens in, like, three and a half weeks, but I know I also don't care to pick it apart."

He puts his hands up around his mouth to amplify his voice. I step closer to him as he literally screams from the rooftops. I grab his arm, laughing at him.

"I am fucking crazy for this girl! I can't get enough of her. Do you hear that, Paris? Lizzie Fox is fucking everything." He gestures all around as I look at the old buildings around us.

My entire body is warm and cold at the same time. It's confusing. I like him that much, too, but I'm afraid to admit it. I grab his arm to muffle his man-made megaphone.

I say, "Well, this is shaping up to be a good date."

He laughs.

He's breathing heavily after screaming how much he likes me. This is the dream. That they like you as much as you like them. It would be super creepy if I didn't feel the same way. I put my hand on his heart. And he covers it with his.

DANNY

She's standing there with her hand on my heart, in her dress that's sexy as hell and makeup, which is not. "Boy, I really went all-in there, didn't I?"

I scoop her into my arms where she fits perfectly. My arms were meant to do this and toss a football. I kiss the top of her head and she looks up at me. And like they always do, her eyes bring me back to center. When someone is about to hike me the ball, I let go. I let instinct take over. I don't overthink or worry about bad choices. In my mind, everything happens the way it's supposed to happen. Holding Lizzie, tossing a football, and drawing are the only times I've experienced something like that.

"Did I scare you?" I ask.

"Nah, I'm used to lunatics telling foreign cities how much they like me. It's clichéd," she says.

I tickle her side and she squirms, but I hold her in place as she lets an uproarious laugh explode over the city.

I wink and say, "Sorry, I'm so predictable."

I kiss her forehead and she goes up on her toes. She gets her face as close to me as she can, and I meet her halfway.

She whispers, "I like you, too. Too much, I'm afraid."

I step to her and say, "Impossible." I peck her lips and pull her to the other side of the roof. "Come here. Stand up here." I place her on the ledge. She's got a death grip on my arm.

She asks, "Now that we both like each other too much, you're going to kill me?"

I shrug, "It's the next logical step."

"Young Paris lovers suicide pact. So *been there, done that.*"

I laugh and turn her back around. Then I say without joking, "Trust me."

She's on edge. She must not be used to surprises. She tightly squeezes her eyes closed. "Ok."

"You'll need to look for the next surprise."

"How many surprises are there?"

"One more after this."

She nods and grins widely. I see that smile every time I sit with a pen and paper. Her cupid's bow lips, juicy and gorgeous, but aesthetically, they're perfect. I was drawing the other day—not her, just random figures. But every single mouth was hers. It's like I'm incapable of drawing others now that I've kissed hers.

"Now lean over to the right." I slide my arm around her waist and secure her to me.

"No."

"If I can hold on to a tiny ball while a 300-pound guy pounces on me, I can hold on to your curvy ass." She gasps a tiny bit.

"You like my ass, don't you?" she asks.

"Everyone likes your ass. It's the toast of Paris."

She bumps backward with her butt and it's right where I'm trying to conceal my mostly erect dick. Shit.

"Oh," she says and turns towards me.

I mumble, "Sorry. I have zero control over it." This is totally her show and oddly, I'm not even trying to convince her to do more. But I want to. I want to be with her, not because she's just some girl who will sleep with me, and that's how I know I'm falling hard.

She says, "Show me this thing."

I lean to the right, taking her with me. She extends her neck. She squeals, "Oh my. This is incredible. It's so much more beautiful like this. When you have to work for it. And with you."

We can see the tip of the Eiffel Tower all lit up. Tony told me about it. He and Makenzie come up here with some frequency. They're exhibitionists.

"Spectacular, right?" A breeze whips up, and her hair wraps around my face, but I'm not letting her go.

"Yes. Absolutely. So cool. Perfect. Stupendous. Marvelous. Get me the fuck down."

I pick her up with my arm still hooked around her waist and turn and place her on the ground.

She says, "I'm always astounded at how strong you are."

"Conditioned. I don't know about strong."

"I do."

I feather my lips over hers and she does that little gaspy thing, like she's surprised. She does it a lot and, truthfully, it's like a lightning rod to my dick. I want to be with Lizzie Fox. Like, really be with her.

She slides a hand into my hair and tugs a bit. Damn, that's new. My tongue responds by exploring her mouth as deeply as I can. My mind goes totally blank apart from how fucking good this all feels.

I grip the back of her head to pull her as close as possible. Her other hand rubs along my back and up to my neck. One of mine slides down and rests on top of her ass. I haven't touched it yet. It's barely been a month.

I've dated girls longer and knew them half as well. But I know if I cup her ass, she'd like it. It's like an instinct. I won't stop touching her once I start. I haven't even tried to touch those glorious boobs yet. I dream of what those tits look and taste like. But I'm afraid I'll screw up everything if I push too far. I need her to want it.

Foreplay hasn't been my thing because there's usually a time limit, like curfew, or we're in the back of a car. I'm usually more than ready to go. Don't get me wrong, I like my dick sucked, but I've never felt right going down on a girl. I want to take my time with Lizzie. I don't know how experienced she is, but her tongue does dangerous things to me.

She's moaning as she rocks into me a little, and I moan into her mouth. Fuck. I'm going to jizz my jeans if she doesn't stop. "Lizzie," I say with a shaky voice. And push her back a tiny bit. She backs away instantly.

"Oh my God. I'm so sorry. I don't know why I did that." She covers her face. I breathe in and out. I picture linemen in the showers. Big guys but not that fit.

"No. You misunderstand me."

She rushes to the blanket and starts to collect her things. I hear her muttering, "I'm so embarrassed."

"Don't ever be embarrassed. I'm so incredibly turned on by you. I have to take a breather so I don't lose it." She bites her bottom lip and I throw my head back and groan. "How are you this sexy?"

She shrugs. "I don't know how to be sexy. You must bring it out."

"Sit." She does as I say. I like that this stubborn and

private girl did as I asked. She crosses her legs and I sit opposite her. She's still looking away. I pull her chin up so we're staring at each other. "Never be embarrassed for something you want." She bats those lashes and grins. I see confidence return to her eyes.

She smirks. "Is the other surprise your penis?" I bust out laughing. I'm incredibly nervous, but I want to share this with her. I can't imagine holding anything back from her. I want to be all things to her right the fuck now. She's staring at the folder I handed her.

"Is this homework? I have a full schedule and can't take on anymore. You're going to have to do your own work." She's funny.

I inhale and hold my breath as she opens it. She doesn't say anything as she stares at it. She removes it from the little pocket and runs her fingers over the image. I can't tell what she's thinking or doing. I have no clue what to do. I shift and arrange things around me. I put my thumbs into my fist and pull them out again. She looks up, her eyes filled with tears.

"Are you ok? I'm sorry. Is that too weird?" She's staring at a pencil drawing I did of her. It's from the day we walked through the stamp market, the Carré Marigny, like Audrey Hepburn in the movie *Charade*. I'd never seen the movie, but Lizzie insisted it was a classic. So we walked around searching for a stamp vendor. I thought she was insane until that night when we watched her DVD of it on my laptop. She bought an exotic stamp for pennies, and I drew this picture.

She didn't stay the night, but I wanted to hold her all night and see what she looks like when she wakes up. I wanted to kiss her morning breath away and hide how hard my dick gets first thing in the morning.

She puts her hand on my forearm. "This is the most beautiful thing I've ever seen. Where did you get this?"

Oh shit. She thinks I had it commissioned.

Here goes nothing. "You know how you 'observe?'" I use air quotes. She rolls her eyes. "You write. I draw. Same skill, different sides of the coin. I observe, too."

"But it's so beautiful."

That breaks my heart a bit. She has no clue how fucking hot she is and how every person notices.

"Could you write a false observation?" I ask. She smiles a sweet, crooked smile. She shakes her head no. "I see you this beautiful."

"I don't know what to say."

"It's a present, say thank you."

"You're so talented. How did I not know? I'm sorry I wasn't paying attention. Is that why we visit Picasso's sketchbooks?"

"I was going to show you my sketchbook that day, then I freaked out over the jock thing. Then it was signing day, my dad blew up, and I hid it for a while."

She tackles me and now she's lying on top of me. She's staring at me with a new depth. I push her hair behind her ear.

"You know this a dicey position, missy."

She nods, then holds my face. "Let's not let your dad or my dad come between any conversation or moment again."

She kisses me. My mind is blank because the only thing in it is how she aligned her hips on top of me. My hands go to her ass. I can't stop them. Fuck it. She freezes for a moment then relaxes into it and kisses me deeper, sliding her tongue into my mouth. I knead her perfect curvy bubble ass. Her pelvis shifts and I need her to back away.

"Beautiful, amazing Lizzie. I can't believe I'm saying

this, but you need to get off me, or that hard-as-hell thing on your stomach will take over. My brain ceases to work when he's in charge." She rolls to the side and I follow. She props herself up on an elbow.

"I don't know what to do. How to not touch you," she says.

My brain almost pops out of my head. "That's exactly how I feel, but you have to set the limits, Lizzie. I'm following your lead. But it's getting really hard not to touch you in new places."

She sits up and draws her legs up. She leans over, takes one of the wet wipes I brought for the picnic we're not eating. She wipes off her heavy eye makeup. I sit up, leaning back on my palms, stretching my legs out. She's stunning under the sparkling lights as she returns to the girl I'm crazy about and not a girl who's trying to be someone else. I have no problem with makeup at all. But I can see it makes her uncomfortable. She morphs into my Lizzie as the wet nap becomes stained with black, beige, and green streaks. One last swipe of her lips and the garish shimmering red orange is gone.

"This? You want to touch this?"

"Are you trying to prove you're not attractive? Because it's not gonna fucking work. You're even more beautiful when you're comfortable in your skin."

She's so innocent and girly. She's cute and compact. And I can see her simmering sex kitten aching to come out. She's so sexy. Which is really a problem for me. Her rich milk chocolate hair is swaying along her shoulders as she looks at me and does this little fidget thing she does.

This is so much bigger than anything I've ever known. I mean, I care for my brothers and mom, but this is other level. I've liked girls, but it never felt inevitable.

LIZZIE

I'm not afraid of him or his penis. I've had sex before, but this feels weighty. He pulls me close and lays back down, my head on his chest, it feels like I'm supposed to be here. Like in my eighteen years of searching for my purpose, I find it right here. He puts one earphone in my ear and repositions me to lean on his arm so I can look up. And he puts on Dave Matthews. I used to like it ok, but now I love Dave Matthews. We watch the city of lights live up to its hype. His hand is lazily in my hair. "Stay" finishes, and he sits up on his elbow and looks down at me.

He traces my lips with his finger. I grin, and he leans down. "I like kissing you. A lot."

I want to experience everything with him. I've liked boys before, but my father always emphasized there will be time later. Maybe this is what he meant. This is later. I've already been accepted into college. I'm graduating. I have a best friend. Now it's time for him. I'm open and ready, and it's the best I've ever felt in my life.

It's like a spider web of tingles and thrills in my heart and low in my belly, every single time I'm with him, or even think about him. My heart beats a little faster, and the warmth of his hand is now a part of my permanent memories. I'm making room in my brain by dumping all the silly times I thought about boys or love. Oh my God, I'm thinking about that word. I know it's infatuation. I'm an intelligent girl and know it's a chemical reaction to him. But as I fall deeper under his spell, the science of it doesn't matter, only the tingles.

"I like kissing you a lot too." One hand rests on my hip, and he leans down. His full lips meet mine, and again, all the sensations shoot through me at once. Is it possible to feel everything at once? His tongue sweeps into my mouth, and I chase it back into his with mine.

He anchors my hip to the ground and leans over me. Then his fingers twitch. They're up a full inch onto the bare skin of my stomach. He's driving me insane while lightly tracing circles on my midriff. His big football mitts are so delicate on my skin.

Our kissing becomes intense and deeper. His hand feathers closer to where I want him. I arch a little into the kiss. Our teeth are in the way and keep clacking as he moves his head back and forth, searching for the perfect angle to devour me.

He's on my ribcage flirting with the idea I've dreamed of each time we're together. We've not done anything but kiss for the last twenty-six days. His hand is underneath my right breast and I pull my head back. I need to be bolder in this life. There can't be anything wrong with it if it's what I want. I grin at him, and his eyes are darker than usual. He's gazing at me in a new way. It's like I'm the answer to questions he has yet to ask in life. I want to be his answer.

My voice comes out as a whisper, "It's ok. I want you to."

All my anxieties and questions come to a sharp point and burst into being brave. I own all my feelings at once. I reassure him that this is what I want, too. "There's nothing you could do wrong by touching me. We're meant to do this. If we weren't, it wouldn't be so perfect."

I sit up and take my sweater off. The chill of spring and the heat of Danny make my nipples erect. I thought his eyes were dark before, but now he's like, all pupils. I wish I had nicer bras. This is a beige kind you buy off the little hanger at Target. Kris calls my bras "off-the-rack rack holders."

But I don't think he cares. I scoot onto my knees and face him. I drift my hand under his shirt. He sucks air through his teeth quickly as my cold fingers find his firm muscles. We go back to the Louvre as a class in a couple of days, and I want to compare his chest to some of those classical marble pieces.

I reach around and unhook my bra and remove it. I have no hesitation.

DANNY

I've been granted a fucking gift. I know my arm is supposed to be my gift, according to my dad, but these tits. Holy shit. They're staring at me, waiting. I'm kind of paralyzed, even though she gave me the go-ahead. I'm not sure I'll be able to stop once I start.

My voice is strained and comes out rougher than intended. "You're so beautiful. So fucking beautiful." I reach up and dust my thumb over her perfect and erect nipple. She smiles shyly and reaches her arms up and lets her nails drift over my chest as I remove my shirt. I let my gaze drift to all the new places she's revealed.

I'm drowning in her eyes, but I don't care. If I have her, I don't need air.

She grins. "You just going to stare at me all night?"

"Seems like a solid plan." Then I smirk and it's fucking on. I glide up her torso, leaving a path of goosebumps. I take both breasts in my hands as my lips push to hers. She gasps and pulls my head closer to hers. Her hands are gripping my hair tightly and it's fucking intense. I play, tweak, and rub her as my mouth drifts down her neck and chest.

She moans when I gently kiss around the peaked nipple. I've never taken this much time in that area. And usually, it's some kneading and onto the good stuff. But I want to make a career of this. I take her nipple between my lips. I groan, it's so good.

"Holy shit, that's amazing," she says as she throws back her head.

Can you major in nipple manipulation? What are the pre-recs to spending an eternity doing this to only her? I back up and she's all glowy.

She stretches, and they're slick with my worshiping. I dive back in and take a nipple roughly into my mouth, suck and explore with my tongue. My dick has never been this hard before, but I want her to feel good. I bend back down to give equal attention to both tits. And she's rocking her pelvis into me. I don't even want to ask if I can tear the rest of her clothes off. I've become some wild beast devouring her. I don't think I'm up to the task of properly worshiping her entire body yet. I need this to be really good for her and I'm pretty sure I've been an idiot in the past. Tasting her makes me more the person I want to be with every sweep of my tongue.

She has on a long skirt and the elastic is teasing me. I could reach down there. Or up her skirt. I make my way back up to her mouth and it's like this kiss has been lit on fire. Her hands touch every part of me within her reach. There's not an inch of bared skin I'm not obsessed with. It's another world. It's another universe. The hottest thing that's ever happened to me. We're skin to skin and everything in my fucking world could be blowing up as long as she's pressed against my chest.

We're totally focused on each other. The sounds of the city are white noise next to the banging of my heartbeat with hers. The lust is too loud to hear the roof door opening.

"Hé! Qu'est-ce que tu fous ici? Vous n'êtes pas autorisé ici." On instinct, I roll my body over Lizzie and tackle her to the blanket. Shit. Tony warned me you only have a two-hour window before the security sweep. I roll the edge of the blanket over her and pop up onto the balls of my feet.

"You can't be on the roof screwing yourselves," he yells in crass English.

Lizzie wraps herself like a burrito with only the top of her head visible. She's kicking me and whisper yelling, "Get me out of here! What if I get kicked out? That can't happen."

Oh shit. I can't get her kicked out of the program. There's no way she'd ever talk to me, let alone taste her, again. I swipe my shirt and pull it over my head as I walk towards the red-faced man.

LIZZIE

OH MY FUCKING GOD. I'M IN PARIS WITH A DREAMY JOCK artist who likes me, and I'm ruined. This is the worst thing that's ever happened to me, like, right after the best thing. I'm still warm and pulsing all over from his touch. I rub my thighs together, trying to make it stop.

This guy probably saw my boob in his mouth. That French security guard is questioning my morals. But what is morality? Is it a construct created to keep me in my place and be a so-called "good girl?" Or is it the code I'm supposed to set my compass to? I need to read and research this. First, I need out of the fucking blanket so I can hide from everything and everyone.

This is my punishment for wanting a man to suck my boobs. Sex has always been fast, confusing, and poking, and I know it was going to be different this time. I've only ever come when I'm alone, but I was damn close before *Pierre Blart: Mall Cop* interrupted. Danny is tongue-talented.

I'm terrified this incident will go on my permanent record and jeopardize my Stanford scholarship. My father will kill me, and then I'll just be dead. But at least I got to be felt up correctly before I die.

Danny approaches the man. I roll over in my cocoon and smoosh my boobs to the ground. I can't believe I'm topless with two men within fifteen feet of me. This isn't quite what I expected of France. But it is French-like.

Danny says, "Sincères excuses, Monsieur. Nous partirons immédiatement. Mais je dois demander une touche d'intimité pour mon invité."

He asked for privacy for his guest. He's taking care of me. My dad tells me what to do, but Danny is actually thinking about what I need. But now I have to hide forever because that guy heard me make porno sounds. I'm an R-rated movie sound machine.

He puts his hand out. He's a handshake guy, the kind that owns his shit. My head is battling with my heart and my lady bits. I mean, something happened here. I wanted to do everything to his body. Danny hurries back and kneels.

"I haven't known you for years, but I know exactly what's going through your head. I wish it wouldn't. It's written all over your face. You're ok. I'm sorry this happened. Not what we did, just beefy Jacques interrupting us."

He helps me unravel and sit up. I cover myself, and he frowns as I turn away from him.

"Lizzie, don't ever hide from me. Every day is more - I care about you more and I want to care for you more. Please don't let this embarrass you."

Turns out, he does know me. My responsible nature is beating its drum through my brain, and I can't turn back. It's a train with only one track. I exhale to steady my heart.

"Lizzie, talk to me."

"I, um. I think we need to take a moment. Slow down." I

have to slip away. This is too much for me. I feel like we have to cool off.

He stands up and starts walking in a circle and windmilling his arms around. I scramble for my shoes and fold the blanket. He walks over, pulls it from me, and throws it on the ground. Then I'm in his arms as he slams me to his chest.

"Don't do this, Lizzie." He holds me close. And despite my guilt and fears for my future, I can't help but relax into him.

He says, "Don't pull back from me. We're not in trouble. He just said don't come up here again. That's it. Everything we do together means something. Please. Lizzie. Don't distance yourself from me. I'm not sure I can take it."

Tears fall down my cheeks. I can't let my dad down or ruin our plans. I need to talk to my mom to help sort through this. I have too many emotions sometimes, and they hit me at once. I hold him tighter. My words squeak out.

"I have to. I'm a mess. Give me a day."

He kisses my forehead. "Lizzie. I'll do anything you need. I'll give you time and space. I'll be right here for you. I can't explain it, but it's like I don't know how to be anything but yours." I sigh into him. I don't know how to tell him yet that I think I might be his as well, but that's impossible.

"Lizzie, trust yourself if you can't trust me."

He's touched me almost every second we've been around each other. My knee, an elbow, thighs sitting next to each other, boobs to tongue. Innocent and not-so-innocent touches, but always in contact. It's been twenty-six days and it feels like two years. The intensity of what I'm feeling is suffocating me even as it breathes new life into me.

I say, "It's too much." I step away and wrap my arms around my stomach.

He says quietly, "Where does that leave us?"

I want to run away with him right now. But that's not what smart girls do. They don't throw away opportunities. They don't go after things that make waves, according to my father.

"I'm sorry. I'm so sorry. He's not going to report us, is he?"

Danny cocks his head. "No. He's not. I said that. I talked him out of a report. But who cares if he did, Lizzie? You're all set for college. It's not like this is criminal activity."

Tears burst from my eyes. "I can't get kicked out."

He puts a hand on my shoulder, and I let him. "They're not kicking you out. Don't worry so much. I'll always take care of you."

My body fills with a glow I've never experienced before. But I push it down.

I say, "Always. You're talking a scary increment of time."

He steps to me. "Whether this is something or ends up being nothing. I know there won't be a time in my life I won't care about you. And that's scary to me, too, but it's how I feel."

I'm a coward, and scared of all things that aren't books and words. I bolt down six flights of stairs. I pull my clubbing skirt up so I can run faster. I whip open my door and fling myself on my bed. I listen for twenty minutes, waiting for a knock. I asked him for time and he listened. I'm not sure how I feel about that. I'm not sure of anything.

DANNY

I CAN'T SETTLE MY BRAIN. I'VE WORKED OUT NON-STOP AND IT'S not helping. It's the sixth day since the roof. I don't even give a shit about the sex stuff. I miss her. I'm off my axis. I can't seem to keep my feet on the ground. I drank with the guys and some of her friends. Hilarious night, but I lost in poker because my head was elsewhere. I want her to sort her shit out, but I'm not even sure what's she sorting.

She hasn't ignored me, but we haven't been alone or connected. She sits across from me at lunch and smiles in the hallways. It's like I'm itchy and can't scratch. I'm terrified I've become an obsessed stalker because she's all I think about. I took a pass from afternoon classes and forced myself outside. I'm letting her dictate what happens. I won't push myself on anyone.

I've sketched thousands of pictures of her. When she left, I stared at that fucking door for an hour. Stunned how my life flipped so fast. Today's obsessive thought is *how do I get by without her*. I'm nobody's fucking fool. I won't embarrass myself by wanting a girl who doesn't like me back. Even though it's deeper than that.

I'll never forget that moment when she looked at me, and I could feel us slip into a relationship. We were an "us."

The idea of an "us" was always temporary until I kissed Lizzie Fox. My brothers and I were always pitched against each other. My teammates in Pop Warner, Pee Wee, and high school became my brothers, and even that was taken away when I was thrust into boarding school to get a leg up on on the other Southie kids who could sling a ball.

Some of those muthafuckers are better than me, but my father is craftier and swindled this New Jersey prep school into a scholarship so I could be seen by better colleges. I'm grateful to the bastard for only that because without this school I wouldn't have met her.

My father unloaded on me again about wasting opportunities by picking Boston College. I hope he rots on his dingy-ass bar stool down at Whitey's Pub watching me play instead of being invited to the stadium. I kick some stones in front of me, and one of them zings off a garbage can and startles a giant dog.

I jog a little bit to get down to my favorite stretch of the Seine. If people weren't speaking French, it could be Boston. I miss home today. My ma always says home is a whisper you should hold close. She grew up in the Italian neighborhoods in the North End but gave it up for the Irish man who charmed her way too young and moved her down to his area of Boston. She doesn't talk much about her family but we were spoon-fed her heritage. All three of us can make spectacular cannoli and quote her many idioms as if they're gospel. I think Lizzie might be my whisper.

My feet have brought me to my version of church. I've sat through all the Catholic stuff, but when I walked through these doors, I finally had a religious epiphany.

I shuffle in and wave. "Bonjour, Sallie et Barnabe. Allay."

Sallie gestures to me. "Et comment allez-vous aujourd'hui, monsieur Danson? Venir dessiner à nouveau notre escalier?" I laugh as they ask if I'm going to do the exact thing I came here to do. Draw a staircase.

I reply with my traditional snark, "If I don't do it, who will?" They wave me through and I scan the membership card I bought with poker winnings. I head to Level 1 – Richelieu Wing. Lefuel Staircase of the Louvre. Many people sit and stare at the Daru Staircase leading to Nike of Samothrace. It's stunning, but my favorite has less hype. I find it more beautiful because of all the angles. The smell of art always sets me right. I've been here every day since the roof. Before that, I only came every other day, but it wasn't to observe steps, it was to bask in the paintings. Now I need the steady and measured structure of form and function. I pull out my sketchpad and stare at the intersecting staircases, arches, and columns.

I'm practicing line drawing because every fucking figure I draw is her. Fuck, I have to get this under control. I sit down, cross my legs, lean against the wall, and stare at the marble staircases. The sun hits them in the exact same spot as the last couple of days. I open my pad, diving into the sound of a pencil scratching on thick paper.

I get lost in the light. Security stops by, checking my progress, and gives me a thumbs-up. The Tuesday guy shares his snack, usually an apple, or a bag of cookies. The left gallery fills with kids I recognize, including this prick who calls himself Thumper. He fucking hates my crew because we stopped him from hitting on our friends. He's slime and his French is shit.

I put my stuff away before he sees me or discovers what

I'm doing. I don't tell a lot of people I draw and paint, it's just for me. Football is for everyone. I'm walking away when I hear her laughing. My body floods with adrenaline and joy. I can't leave now.

Her hair is up and her jeans are rolled. She's wearing this flowy paisley blouse that sinches at her waist. She's scribbling in a notebook I bought for her. Maybe she's thinking about me. I look too long through the archway. She catches me and I see her gasp.

LIZZIE

He's here. My heart flips when our eyes connect through the galleries. Our docent is talking, and I'm not paying attention. I haven't paid attention to anything for days. My mom told me not to worry so much and that I could use more silliness and fun in my life. I should let go and kiss this boy. But she doesn't realize how much I like him. And I think feeling this intense is going to mess up everything I've worked for. That's what I was thinking for the first three days apart.

Then something shifted inside and for the last three days, I've been plotting how to tell him I miss him. It's awkward when we see each other. I know I'm making it so and right now, he's staring at me like I'm as beautiful as the art. And he's wrong because he is! He gives me a little chin lift and turns away. My heart aches a bit more.

I wish he could read my mind. *Please don't go.* I know what I said, but I don't know how to unsay it. Every time I try to text him, it comes out sounding dorky, so I delete it. I'm the least cool human being ever. I've cried every day. How do you tell someone you pushed away that you want them back? What if he's taken this week and, like, moved on? I'm terrified he might read my text while making out with someone else. What would that look like? The thought squirms and turns my stomach. I would die if he were with anyone else. I stare at the archway, hoping he's here alone. This is awful.

My focus snaps to the docent and the asshole's arm that just slid around my shoulders. I wiggle away and open my backpack to get away from Thumper. He keeps saying shit like, "Now that you dumped the meathead jock, it's time to get on my..."

He winks instead of saying the word cock. Ugh. He's the worst. I slammed the door in his face last night. He wasn't happy, but he wouldn't leave me alone. He leans down while I'm rifling through my bag.

"Let's break off from the group. Come on, good girl, time to mess with a bad boy."

"Ew. Stop." I bristle.

"You say that, but you don't mean it."

I whisper, "I do. I mean it. Stop."

"Mme Fox, veuillez faire attention."

I hate being yelled at.

I apologize and move away from him and towards the Rococo gallery. I can't concentrate since I've seen Danny. I want to fix this, which gives me an excuse to shake off Thumper.

LIZZIE: Hey.

I'm so stupid. I don't talk to him for a week, after moaning with my nipples on his tongue, and now the only thing I can come up with is "hey." I groan at how dumb I am.

He answers immediately. At least I know he's not

making out with anyone right now. I wonder why he's here. He has class.

DANNY: Hey!

Well, that's unhelpful. Did he miss me? Has he already moved on? Will I have to nurse heartbreak in Paris alone? We got so close to something, and I fucked it up. How do I say that without saying that? I'm walking and looking at my phone, and I don't realize I've completely lost the group. Great, now I'll flunk Art History next year.

I try again.

LIZZIE: What are you doing here?

I scurry into the next gallery and fucking run smack into Thumper. He's staring at The Death of Sardanapalus. Of course, he is. Lots of naked women. He sees me and points to the painting.

"Boobs."

Oh God.

"Where is Madame Jeanea?"

He walks into my space. This part of the museum is closed for our school today. There are six classes here today, but currently, it's empty.

"I'm here. Let me see if your tits are as good as hers." He motions to the painting. He's gross and kind of predatory. He pushes into my space and I back up. Warning bells rattle in all my nerves, but I'm not sure what I can do.

"You haven't talked to that asshole all week. What's the deal?"

I'm backed into a corner when my phone dings.

DANNY: If you ever want to know what I'm doing here, I'd be happy to show you. I was trying to give you space.

My chin is to my chest as I stare at my phone, elated he answered. I'm hoping my lack of eye contact gives this asshole the message to leave, because I don't have an escape route he can't block. I put my phone in the front pocket of my jeans.

My voice is stronger than ever before. "Back off, Thumper."

He lifts his other arm and his nail touches my cheek.

"That's no way to act. I mean, we're in a public place. You're perfectly safe. And I see the way you look at me. I get it. And you can totally get it, if you go with it."

I pull my face away from him. "GO AWAY. Get the fuck away from me." I slap his face and he licks his lip. I know we're in a public place, but I'm still scared. He grins and grabs my arm hard, and I can't pull away.

"Let me take you where I want, then I'll go away." He licks my cheek. Holy shit. This is fucking dangerous. I'm in an actual dangerous situation, and I let it happen because I didn't think it was anything. Why didn't I tell someone he was harassing me or wouldn't leave my doorway last night? Stupid me didn't want to make waves, as my father would call them. I didn't want to bother anyone. I kept thinking, *It's all in your mind. He's not really risky. Don't overreact. You'll only cause problems for everyone. Don't be a drama queen.*

I've been conditioned not to be rude. That's bullshit and now I'm too late with this epiphany. I should have trusted myself the moment I was creeped out. I should've screamed it from the rooftops.

"NO." I twist my arm away from his, but his grip intensifies as he pulls me towards a door. I don't know where it leads. I see a security guard.

"Help! Aider!" I yell. "Ce n'est pas quelqu'un de sympathique."

Thumper squeezes hard and laughs. He responds to the security guard who's moving towards us. I keep yelling in French that he's not a friendly person.

"Non. Ma copine est confuse. Nous nous sommes disputés et je veux m'excuser." He nods. He believed Thumper, not me. He said we're a couple and had a fight. This is happening. He's practically dragging me now.

"You're going to rape me?" Well, I'm making waves now. Wow, I just said that. I pull my arm, but it won't budge from his grip.

"If you like it, it's not rape."

Holy shit.

I'm braver in the face of being a victim. "Pretty sure I won't like it. And if I say no, it's rape." I spit at him and he grins. "Rumor has it you fuck like a hamster."

"Bitch." He keeps moving, dragging me, and I look away.

Before I even have good sex, I'm getting raped. I'm not processing things correctly.

Suddenly I'm free and I hear a sickening thud and the crack of a nose breaking. My arm is splashed with blood. I almost fall to the floor, but someone catches me before I can collapse completely. I look into the face of the one who said he'd always take care of me.

He scoops me up and places me on a bench. Then Danny levels him to the ground with another swift but powerful punch. The guard who disregarded me is white as a sheet.

Madame Jeanea finds us and screams for more security. "Are you ok? Are you ok? HELP! Anyone. Come quickly. Help! Take him!" I want to sink into the floor. I want this to be about someone and something else.

"Piece of shit," Danny spits out as Thumper curls up into a ball surrounded by guards. She digs her hands into Thumper's arm and he tries to get away as the guard who believed him roughly grabs him.

"Are you sure you're ok, Mmm Fox? Are you hurt?"

"My arm hurts a little but I'm fine. He just scared me."

She squeezes my shoulder. "We need a statement, when you're ready." She wraps me in a blanket that security handed her. Then she points to Thumper. "I want him out of here. You're expelled!"

She turns to Danny. "And you. Consider this your reprimand for fighting." She winks at him. "Take your time. Take care of her."

She pulls me to her and I stiffen up. Security is holding people away from me but everyone is staring.

Thumper is ranting about what his father will do. His nose is gushing and he keeps pointing at me. I shiver with all the scary what-ifs running through my head. And Madame Jeanae walks off to deal with it all.

There are too many people around. I panic. I try leaving and he puts his hand on my arm.

"Are you ok?"

I don't know how to answer, so I break apart in front of people. I'm crying about Thumper, missing him, and that I might flunk Art History. He shelters me and pulls me out of the fray. He's shielding me and I sob for minutes on end. It all flows through me and onto my cheeks.

And then I look into his blue-grey eyes and say, "Hi." I don't know what to say.

He's concerned and shakes me a gently. "I need you to answer me. Are you hurt?" I shake my head. "Can I hold you?"

I blubber out, "For as long as you want."

Then I'm in his arms. He buries his face in my neck and hair. And I sob. He keeps comforting me and leads me out of the room into a stunning white marble stairwell. It's peaceful. People, paramedics, and teachers keep coming up to us, and he shields them from interfering with my breakdown.

He leans over me and I whisper in between sobs, "I didn't know how to get back to you. I didn't know how to talk to you and tell you I'm sorry. I was stupid and overreacted. I didn't know how to reach out."

He strokes my hair and keeps shushing me. Then he whispers back, "I didn't go anywhere. I was waiting until you needed me. You needed to choose us for yourself." My heart bursts.

He repeats while kissing my head, "You're ok. I got you. I'm here."

I sit up and realize we're alone except for one security guard who Danny nods at, but he doesn't go anywhere. The guard says, "Est-ce votre cœur?"

Danny smiles and says, "Oui. This is my heart."

I sway a little at his words. I speak in French, "And he's my heart. Nice to meet you."

I look at him. "You'll never need to find me again. I'll always be right here."

He says, "You promise?"

"I do." I really do.

Then he says, "I'm not going anywhere. We'll talk to them when you're ready. I only saw the end of it as I wandered around waiting for you to text again."

"You were waiting for me."

He turns me towards him and his cadet blues spark with sincerity. "I realized something over this past week. It's insane, but I'd wait forever for you, Lizzie. I wasn't kidding when I said my heart belongs to you. I tried to pull back or stop it, but you're like a piece I didn't know was missing."

Tears start again but for a very different reason.

"Are you ok?"

I stammer, "I think, I mean, I don't know for sure because I don't know if this is it or not..."

"Cut to the point, Lizzie." He smirks at me and I melt.

"All the thinking of you and feeling better about myself when I'm around you. I stood up to Thumper. I'm more Lizzie than I've ever been. I'm learning that I'm stronger and it's all because I love you."

"Lizzie. I love you so much, too. So fucking much. So much I've wanted to say it since the moment I held you."

"I love you, Danny."

"I want to be the Danny reflected in your eyes. I want to be that guy. I know it's so fast, but I think this is how it's supposed to happen. I want to make you fall apart in hysterics when you go on a rant. I don't just want to sleep with you, but protect you, share with you, tell you everything about me and listen to any fucking thing you want to say. I will listen to you for as long as you'll let me."

I grin at this man who has suddenly become the most important thing in my life. It's all the more desperate because we were apart and because of what almost happened. Turns out, I don't want to experience anything I don't tell him about.

I say, "Shit. Are we this all-in?"

"I'm undeniably there. Lizzie, I love you. And even if we can't make it a lifetime, I know I'll never feel like this again about anyone else."

I snuggle closer to him, knowing no one will believe us. I'm safe, accepted, and loved. I'm also sure I'll mess it up somehow. But not today.

DANNY

I'm finishing a math assignment when Tony bursts into our room.

"Where the fuck ya been? Inside Ms. Bay Area?"

I shake my head.

"Dude, you didn't hit that yet?" He tosses a sweaty shirt onto the pile in his corner. He still doesn't get that he has to do his own laundry.

I swivel my chair and cross my arms. "Look who's playing, big man? You fucked anyone but Makenzie since you've been here?"

He crosses the room, takes a massive swig of water, and speaks through the drink. I sit on my bed and face him.

"No need. That chick is everyfuckingthing." I turn to watch him flop onto his bed. He gestures to my bed. "We did it there last night. Watch out for the wet spot." I toss a pencil at him and he ducks.

I smile. "So, we're all domesticated and shit now?"

I haven't left Lizzie's side in two weeks. Her dad went apeshit over Thumper. He tried to pull her, then threatened to shut the program down. Her mom calmed his shit down, thank fuck. I don't know what I would've done. Probably followed her to California.

Tony sips again. "Gotta hydrate, gorgeous is meeting me here in twenty. So, finish up your school shit there, Danny Boy." Tony loves my football nickname. The crowd sings "Danny Boy" at the other team when I play. It's kinda poetic, now that the name Danny has a whole other level of meaning for me. Tony rolls his hand in front of him, as if that will hurry me along.

I laugh, grab a couple of shirts and jeans, and shove them in my bag to head to Lizzie's room. We haven't spent a night apart since the museum incident. Then I close my laptop.

"Halt!"

I stop and turn to my king. "Yes, my liege?"

He bounds off his bed and gets in my face. "Have you not fucked Lizzie because you love her? Are you a boy in love with that feisty fair maiden?"

"You knighted her."

"So I did. A feisty knight, then? Answer the question."

I inhale and exhale. Then I say, "Yeah, I do. And yes, I texted your brother."

Where Tony's the good time guy, his older brother is ride or die steady. Neither of them are fucked-up about their parents' money and are like family to me.

Tony puts his arm on my shoulder. "You should have told me first. I'm better looking than him." He flashes his eyebrows.

"Fuck off. You were buried in Makenzie, wasn't time to catch you up."

He leaps on the bed and bounces up and down. He runs

his hand over his shorn platinum hair and smirks. "Get out. She'll be here soon and she'll want polite chit-chat with you. I can't have that. I have a plan. Let's grab dinner on the parents tomorrow after my daily ravaging of my favorite witch."

I shrug and say, "I'll ask her."

"You don't ask. You do." I glare at him. "Ok. If you're still trying to get some, maybe don't make too many demands that don't involve stripping her."

I take a stance with him and he puts his hands up.

"I apologize. No more talking about Lizzie's privates."

"Dude, I fucking swear I'll kill you."

His demeanor shifts. His voice is softer and reflects his brother's a bit instead of bold, brash Tony. "Sorry, man. Seriously. You're hung up."

"I'm going to ask her to follow me to BC today." I've thought about it a lot. I don't think we'll survive long distance and I'm committed to Boston. She shouldn't say yes, but I hope she will.

"We'll all be in Boston. Huzzah! Makenzie thinks she might head to Northeastern." He pulls me into a hug.

"Whoa, dude. Like to be with you?"

"Nah. It's not like that. She was thinking of going there anyway. She knows we're not, you know."

"No, what?"

"Like you and Lizzie. Or Colton and Maggie." I get it. I mean, I'm going to spend the rest of my life with Lizzie, but Colton and Maggie are another level of mushy love.

Tony blows me off a bit. "And, like, I have to dig into all the family shit. Not like I have time for anything other than a good time after this. She knows. I think she knows. It'll be fine. Maybe we'll hook up in Boston." The player doesn't want to admit he actually likes a girl. Nice. But there is a lot of pressure on him, so I get it.

Tony's destiny is his father's communications company. But I want to take art, finance, and marketing shit, so I can get a job after football. Or who the hell knows, maybe I'll be like Brady. Lizzie and I can retire when we're forty. Holy shit. I had a non-sexual fantasy. A domestic wicked whipped one.

I wave and flip Tony off and head out. As the door closes I hear him singing, "She'll be coming round my cock, when she comes. She'll be coming round my cock..."

The first night I slept in her room, after walking home from the Louvre, just as we fell asleep, she whispered something. Not sure she meant me to hear it.

"I'm going to trust myself. He makes me stronger."

Turns out, she makes me those things, too.

We have seven weeks left, and I'm beside myself with the idea of losing her. It's clouding the present as I focus on our future.

I push open her door and inhale her scent, cataloging it for the too many nights of FaceTime ahead of us. Her face lights up; I drop my things and rush to her like it's been days, not hours. We planned most of this day apart to see if we could do it. Not doing that again.

I slide my tongue over her lower lip. She throws herself at me as if this is our everyday domestic life without an expiration date. When we go home, we still have school, graduation, and living with our parents. It's going to be so fucking weird walking away from all this freedom and time together.

We volley our tongues, then she grins while I'm kissing her. Gripping her ass, I can't stop thinking about how I got her off with my hand last night.

"What?" I say, pulling back.

"Nothing. Just love you. And love being loved by you." Her smile is so wide.

I say, "Well, that's about the sappiest thing I've ever heard."

I move to pick up my stuff from the floor. She tugs at me and says, "Come on. Let's go explore." We run down the street so we're not spotted, in case someone wants to come along. As the days wind down, we've become selfish with our time.

"There's something I want to talk to you about."

"The answer is yes." She smiles.

My eyes bug out of my head. "Yes to what?"

"My answer to you is always yes."

I test that theory. "Wanna steal some gold?"

"Yes."

"Shave your head?" I tug at her ponytail.

"Sure."

"Wash my workout clothes?"

"Hell, yes."

I kiss her roughly, desperate for her little moan.

"I'm tired of being timid. I'm tired of fucking hiding behind people, words, and books. And rules. Christ, am I sick of playing by the rules. My answer to everything is yes. Especially to you."

"Well, now I have a different question... but we'll get to that later." I know we're close to having sex, but I think that was my green light. Now I don't want to go explore anything, I just want to go back to her room and shut us inside for a week.

There's a wicked grin on her face as she licks her lips and says, "The answer will be the same. Yes." Green light. My dick perks up as I pull her down the street, grasping her tightly so I don't turn around and haul her into bed.

LIZZIE

I LOVE WHEN HE RUBS HIS THUMB ON THE BACK OF MY HAND. THE sidewalks are sparkly in the sun where the locals have rinsed off the winter crud that invades the city's beauty. We turn down a street and it's different than where we're staying. We're on the Left Bank walking through the 5th arrondissement and my mind drifts to all the romantic things I've always conjured about Paris. We look like our future, walking together in a metropolitan paradise.

I planned this Lost Generation walk around Gertrude Stein's Paris. I want to drift up to the 6th and find lunch around the Zadkine Museum. He was this funky sculptor and I think Danny would like.

We walk by Hemingway's apartment and I imagine he's up there writing *The Sun Also Rises*. I wouldn't like to meet him—he was a misogynistic asshole—but he wrote a hell of a sentence. I imagine him explaining the blood and gore of Pamplona to Matisse as he draws in the dying light. Ezra Pound pouring them all another drink. I mentioned Huxley and his connection to Paris, and Danny countered with

Picasso and T.S. Eliot. No one else has ever understood my fascination with found family like he does.

When we go home, we have to go back to being the people they expect. But here we can be our own artist/writer collective of two. Here we can dream and be lost in love, and everyone is happy for us.

I turn onto Rue de St. Germain and 6th. He's sucking down a café au lait and I'm sipping a white hot chocolate. The cobblestones and buildings are rich with history and potential. We're surrounded by people, not students, and it helps with our illusion of being older and in control of our lives.

He pulls me to him. "This is wicked awesome."

"I know, right?" I say back.

"It's exactly how I picture us in a few years." His voice is excitable. He runs his free hand through his now longer raven hair. His light eyes sparkle and my entire body feels like it's fizzing.

"Me too!"

He spins me around and I end up in his arms. We must look like the vision of young love that we are. "I'd live here. First place I can imagine living outside of Boston."

He kisses me lightly. I inhale his slightly woodsy, citrusy smell. He smells like everything I've ever wanted in a boyfriend.

I say, "Let's live here. We can get café jobs, wander the city, and make it ours."

He pulls me closer and his lips slide to my neck. I love it. I dig my nails into his hair. We've hard core fooled around but it's time to be completely his and have him be completely mine.

"Funny you should mention running away..." He kisses

me quickly, then we interlace our fingers again and stroll forward.

He clears his throat, "How certain are you about Stanford?"

I squeal because I had the same thought. My parents teach at Stanford and I had my doubts about being so close to them. As employees they only got half tuition for me and I earned the other half but I don't want it.

I push him back a little. "Mind reader!" With a broad smile, he leans towards me and kisses me, and people curse in the melodic language as they sidestep our PDA.

I tell him what I've learned. "I researched—Stanford doesn't need a quarterback."

He laughs hard. "But I think I can get into Boston College late admission. There's a work-study program. I'd have a pretty good shot at getting a full ride for my sophomore year based on my academics and need. Of course, I'll have to get a good job, like an office job, to make up the rest of it, but..."

He picks me up and spins me around. "I'll get a job, too, and help with your tuition in off-season. We can share my meal plan. You eat, like, nothing." He swallows hard. "You would do that for me?"

"It's for me. I'm selfish."

He laughs, then smirks at me. God, I love that sly little smile. "You could use a little more of that attitude."

I say, "Get used to it. It's the new me. 'Paris me' goes after things she wants."

"Then we get a place together. I have to stay in the team dorms for football season. But spring, I shack up with my super-amazing, brainiac girlfriend."

I'm bouncing up on the balls of my feet as we make plans.

He says, "Are you sure? BC is awesome, but it might not have the specific academic things you need like Stanford."

I did this research, too. "Don't underestimate me. Harvard doesn't do late admissions, but I can apply for a transfer after first semester."

He shrugs. "Sure. Just transfer to Harvard. It's so easy."

I bump his hip. "Dude, I'm kind of a genius. Wow. Sorry." I slap my hand over my mouth.

He pulls it off quickly. "No, sir. A knight like you never apologizes for any amazing part of you. Shout it loud to the world. No one else will do it for you. Be the genius."

"I'm not used to bragging."

"Not bragging if it's the truth. I want you to open your mouth, firecracker. Be as proud of you as I am. I see your fire. I'm fucking great at football and drawing. And I can house, like, two to five steak grinders in a sitting. Now I have a fourth thing I'm wicked great at—loving you. And I don't want that to end. I fucking love you."

What I feel is so much brighter than anything that's ever touched my world. He gives me permission to stop asking for permission. I'm withdrawing from Stanford and registering for BC today.

His kiss frazzles my nerve endings.

He groans and pulls away. "Jesus, Lizzie. I'm hard all the time." He bends over in front of me, breathing in and out slowly. I bite my lip and stare at my stunning boyfriend.

Just then a man fumbles his phone and Danny twists his body in a complicated way and catches it. We both stare at him and he shrugs.

I think he needs to hear this, too. "Don't ever apologize for how spectacular you are."

"I just caught a phone."

"Like an airbender moving through space and time,

knowing exactly where to plant your feet or outstretch your arms. I can't wait to see you play."

He steps back to me. "Oh yeah?"

"Yeah. I don't want to brag, but I was on middle school cheer until my parents thought it might hurt my studies."

His eyebrows go up. "And here I thought I was so far from a cliché, dating a brain instead of cheerleader."

"Star quarterback deserves every cliché, right?"

He kisses me again, blocking the sidewalk while people curse us.

We break apart and giggle. Then he looks down the street and his breath hitches. He pulls me down the block towards a very chic woman with a tight chignon and chic lime green suit exiting a stunning home with the red sign. The mix of old and new architecture is the push-pull of Paris. I feel like I am the city sometimes. I am that mix. The sign reads: *Journée portes ouvertes.* Open House. It's old beige plaster smoothed over stone.

She disregards us. I squeeze his hand to pull him away. I'm not sure what the hell he's doing.

DANNY

My Ma used to do this with us all the time when we were younger. We'd go to a neighborhood we could never afford and saunter around open houses as if we were buyers. Then, she'd take on a different personality and pretend to have a different life for a moment. We'd all play along. I want a different life than the one I'm returning to, so I will imagine it here with her.

"Pardonnez-moi, maman. Nous nous demandions si nous pouvions encore regarder autour de nous? Nos parents américains veulent nous acheter un petit appartement français pour notre adeau de fiançailles. Et celle-ci a son cœur sur celui-ci."

Her eyes widen as I lie, telling the woman we're engaged, and our American parents want to buy us a Paris apartment. And my fiancé wants this one. She looks at her watch. I nudge Lizzie a bit. She needs to play along.

She stumbles through her response, pretending she's a rich brat. She even stamps her foot a bit. The realtor explains that they were closing up.

"Oui. C'est celui-là, chérie. Je ne serai jamais heureux dans la vie sans cet appartement. Tu piges!"

I bite the inside of my lip as she grips my fingers in a death hold, so we don't laugh at what she just said: "Yes. This is the one, darling. I won't ever be happy in life without this apartment. Get it!"

The woman's response is immediate. "Très bien. Nous avons fini pour la journée, mais mon assistant est toujours à l'étage. Donnez-lui vos informations. Et je t'appellerai. Je dois courir."

"Merci. Très bien." She pushes past the woman. It's the bravest I've seen her so far. It's sexy and addictive. I glance at the woman and assure her we'll just be a minute and that she can be pushy, but I love her. We're supposed to register our names with the assistant on the third floor. I step inside as the realtor leaves.

There are large black-and-white tiles in a harlequin pattern on the floors and high white columns surrounding us. The ceilings must be twenty feet in this expansive entryway. There's a door for the first floor apartment but we head up.

"Let's go, my spoiled fiancée." I pull her close to the wall and begin slinking up the bright white marble staircase.

"What are you do—"

I cover her mouth quickly. She licks my hand and I stifle a giggle. Every detail of this building is old and restored. There's nothing this old in Boston and it makes me feel like I'm witness to history.

We skate quietly around the second floor, where apartment number two is all closed up. We round the next staircase and hear assistant upstairs. The walls are a lush grey and the landings are rich with exotic dark patterned carpeting that looks like it's out of a magazine. It's probably the fanciest fucking place I've ever been.

I want to play house.

I peek around the doorway at the top of the third floor. It opens into this elaborate hallway and there's another staircase up. We need to get there. But the door is directly across from a large open kitchen and the woman is clacking away on marble floors past a giant-ass red stove. She's putting things away in a glass closet. It takes me a moment to realize it's the refrigerator. She can walk into the fucking fridge. The stark white walls soar up and meet with decorative molding.

I shoo Lizzie down the hall, out of sight, and point to the staircase. She's panicked and I motion with my chin to go up. She takes off running and the woosh of her movement jostles a curtain. I drop to the ground hoping the woman can't see over the giant island she's standing behind. I army crawl over to the side of the large open archway, then stand and run up the stairs two at a time.

I stop cold when I realize this was probably an artist's studio at one time. The ceiling is glass and metal, and open to the sky. The light comes from behind a cloud and a beam of sunshine highlights the subtle auburn in her dark hair. It gleams in the room and the whole thing takes my breath away.

She whispers, "This is fucking amazing. I never want to leave this room. This is the reason to have a building like this. Think of what we could create up here. I'll bet even the dust bunnies have something to say. Do you feel it?"

I kiss her like I need her to fucking sustain me. Her tongue touches mine and I breathe in her scent. I pull back before I bend her over the crimson couch in the corner. The exposed beams are so cool. You can see the other buildings, streets, and the tops of the Paris I've always dreamed of.

"Downstairs is like Audrey Hepburn's apartment in *Charade*."

My fingers start tingling and flicking. I want to draw her. She pulls my hand to her mouth and kisses it. "You need a pencil, don't you?"

"How do you know me this well?"

"Well, we are engaged."

How I wish that were true. "You and this light are the most beautiful things I've ever seen." I take her hair down and she bows her head towards her feet. I lift her chin. "Take in every moment, every compliment." We hear a crash and swearing downstairs.

"Ok, we have to get out of here." She moves towards the staircase. I pull her back to me.

"We belong here somehow. It's ours. Forget your rules and our families. Tonight, let's be these people. Artists in love with a shit-ton of money in Paris. Play with me."

Lizzie's eyes light up. We can hear the woman ascend the staircase. There's no closets, only an armoire. We climb in and I crouch and smoosh my body to fit. She holds the door closed and we try not to move as we hear her arrange furniture. Then we hear her texting. We're holding our breath and I'm going to break through the back of this fucking thing. My whole body is one big fucking cramp. I'm sweating through the pain, then the woman flicks off the lights and goes downstairs. Lizzie opens the armoire then lands on top of me as we fall out. I wrap my arms around her with the sunlight as our only light. This is my Paris. She's my Paris.

LIZZIE

"OH. SORRY." HE HOLDS ME IN PLACES AS I TRY TO SCRAMBLE OFF of him.

"It's fine." He kisses me. I lean to the side, so he'll let me slide to the ground. We've got to get out of here. But instead of getting up and leaving, I sink into his kiss. It's a mystery why it's so good. His tongue flicks in and out, and I sigh. He backs away, kissing my jaw and neck. I want him to make me weightless.

"Let me up." He instantly removes his hands from me. "I want to see this place."

He laughs, leaps to his feet, and scoops me up. He carries me to the velvet chaise lounge in the corner, and I'm on fire. I keep rubbing my thighs together, desperate for relief. I tingle all the time so I have to tell him somehow.

He walks in a circle and stands in the middle of this stunning room. The sun is starting to set and the orange is lighting up this room filled with glowing light. His loving gaze never leaves me as he explores the space.

"I could paint a million pieces of art in a place like this."

"You should." He rolls his eyes at me. I sit up on my

knees. "I'm serious. It's our house, why shouldn't you make this room into your studio? I'll write in the corner."

He laughs. I jump up and say, "We should probably go make sure all the rooms in our house are in order."

He pulls me close and holds me. "This is our first home. We do need to treat it with care, so it cares for us."

"That's the dumbest thing I've ever heard."

"My ma says it."

"And how's that working out? Does your house care for your Mom?" I laugh at my own joke and he gets a little quiet. "Shit. Danny. I'm sorry. I didn't mean it like that. I'm so sorry." I forgot his home isn't always happy. He'll never fuck me now. I hate the taste of my foot in my mouth.

"No worries. Let's go explore our house."

I follow him as he flicks some switches. The main floor of this apartment is massive and stunning. We're standing in the kitchen; it's industrial, yet vintage. I'm sure some of the fixtures are original. It's so charming and perfect. It opens to the living room. There's a mix of old and new. I love the exposed brick and the massive windows you could stand in. The arches are grand and decorated with intricate scrolling. But the beams have been covered with galvanized steel in the kitchen.

"What's for dinner, honey?" he says and hoists me up on the kitchen counter. We attack each other's lips as I wrap my legs loosely around him. He moans and kisses me deeper. Our teeth are scraping and I could eat him up.

I gasp. "Dinner later. We haven't explored all the rooms. I'm especially interested in one in particular."

"REALLY?" He puts his hands on his head and steps back. I lick my lips. I think that might be sexy. I don't want him to have to jerk off anymore. I want to help. I want to be a part of all of it.

He leans against the sink across the kitchen from me. "Please, for all that's holy, say it's the bedroom and not the laundry room." I laugh and nod.

He smiles. "You need to know this isn't going to last long. But I promise to make it up to you."

"I know you will. I trust you." He rushes to me and I scoot to the end of the counter and dry hump him. He's so big. He's gasping as I'm rubbing and I've started a fire I'm not sure will ever be put out. He pulls back suddenly.

"I haven't waited for this moment just to come in my jeans. Come on, my beautiful girl. I'm going to need to see all of you."

He picks me up and cradles me as he carries me off towards the bedrooms. He uses my feet to push open a door. It's an office.

"Nope. I need a bed, like, now." He laughs and tries the next door. "Need to use the bathroom?"

"I'm all good." I giggle. I love him so. This is everything I'll ever need. Him to adore me and believe in me. And make me this turned on—that's pretty great, too.

The third door's a charm. He growls as the door slowly creaks open. Soft white sheer curtains fall from the twelve-foot windows and the four-poster bed. The bed is black and shiny, with fancy hotel windowpane bedding. And then the stunning and chic room fades, and all I see is him.

He's on top of me and already lifting my shirt. All the bullshit in my life—rule-following, guilt over wanting this—falls away.

He kisses my stomach as his fingers reach the front snap of my bra. He opens it, and his hands find my breasts as he leans up to my mouth. I've been conditioned that it's wrong to think and want it. That it's function, not fun. Such bullshit I've been swallowing.

I moan into his touch. I can't be close enough to him. He takes his shirt off and I glide my hands over his cut torso. It's hard and soft, and familiar, like it's mine now. I own it. He pulls us to standing and I wiggle out of my capris surprising him with my new lace thong. It's the most scandalous thing I've ever done. He backs away from me and stares.

"Those didn't come from home." I bite my lip. "Fuck, you look good."

He takes me back in his arms and kneads my ass. He pulls me closer to him. He growls in my ear and then tosses me onto the bed.

He kisses me and moves up slightly, settling between my legs, and I wrap mine around him. He's so serious and utterly open to me, as if I can see forever in those slate blues.

"Love isn't strong enough."

I'm a flush of emotion. "I know." I buck my hips a little.

He says, "So, you're done with the mushy love stuff?"

"Yeah. I think it's time we were naked. I want to see your cock." It's the boldest I've ever been in my life, and the look in his eyes is worth it.

"Jesus, don't start dirty talking. I won't even make it inside you, gorgeous."

He leaps up and within seconds, he's completely naked. I've never seen him in this kind of light. I can see every vein and ridge on his dick. He reaches for it as he notices me watching and offers himself to me. I grip him and I've touched him before, of course, but this is hotter. He puts his hands on his hips and throws his head back and the harder he gets the bolder I become.

He guides me the way he likes it, sexy instructions instead of demands. He's like steel, but there's a softness to it. The tip leaks and he groans. I slide my hand over it and he moves a little into my fist. I like it.

"You done exploring? I can't take much more." I smile and nod. Then I lay back down on this decadent bed.

He pulls my pink lace thong off. He stares, and for a moment, I start to close my legs. I don't know what to make of him staring at that part of me.

"No. Stop. This is gorgeous." It's the first time we've been totally naked with lights on and without a time limit.

"You look like fantastic sin in our home." He grabs a condom from the back pocket of his discarded jeans and I laugh at him.

"You travel around with that?"

He shows me he has a couple with him. He jumps on the bed and spreads my legs. I'm up on my elbows watching him.

"Um, with you around, hell yeah. I wasn't going to miss this chance since the moment I walked into room 666. And lucky for you, I'm a forward thinker, or we'd have to stop before we started here in our home."

He pushes me down to the bed so he can kiss the hell out of me. I grip his back and pull him closer.

"Can I touch you?" He always asks. But this time it has more weight. "Lizzie, I want you to come before I enter you, if I can fucking wait, but I'll try. I read it won't hurt as much if you're already blissed out."

"You're so big, I'm sure blissed out is a good thing," I say, biting my lip.

"Trust me. I also think making you come is going to be my major in college."

"Football? Art?" I lick my lips.

"Hobbies, next to the importance of this." He slides

between us and his fingers swipe my pussy. He groans. "You're really wet. That's hot."

"It is?"

"Trust me. Hot as fucking hell. Because it means you want me as much as I want you."

I slam my lips to his and it's rough and sloppy. Our tongues can barely be contained as he finds my clit. He swirls his fingertips around it and the pressure is too much. No one has ever touched me like this. I don't feel guilt or shame, just a ball of excitement tightening low in my core as he starts caressing me faster. Then his hand goes lower and he skates over where I want him most. He grinds his body down a little, so his dick puts pressure on my clit and inserts a finger into me. My whole body coils. It pinches a little, then I relax into it as he kisses me harder. He's made me come like this before and I'm a huge fan of it.

"That's good."

He kisses me and says, "I want to try something. You game?"

"Don't stop!"

He laughs. "Trust me. I couldn't if I tried."

He moves down my body. I've done the other things before, but what I think is about to happen is freaking me out in the best way. I've watched porn that Kristin found. I've seen this and longed to try it. He kisses my inner thigh so slowly.

I hiss, "Yes." I tremble at his tongue snaking up my leg. Oh my God, this is happening. His fingers keep exploring while he kisses my clit. I gasp. "This. Is. The best day ever."

He raises up and smirks. "Watch."

"You want me to?"

"I think you want to. You're a secret sex goddess who likes watching. You're an observer, right?" I prop myself up and watch him go back down on me. Holy hot. He's right. I don't think I can handle this. It's so overwhelming. It's too much. He flicks it, and I moan and shove myself further into him.

I gasp, "You're good at that."

"Thanks. I've never done it before. Never felt like it with others. But you taste so fucking right."

His finger wiggles inside me and I gasp. Then a second finger begins to stretch me out. I wait for the good part when the pinch goes away. It takes longer this time. Then he sucks on me and I lose all thoughts of pain. He moves in and out of me with his hand, and his tongue is circling all the bits of me, and I flop down. I can't watch this stunning boy do this to me anymore. I get lost in all the sensations and I'm gone over the top with pleasure.

"I like it here. Right there. Wow." I'm climbing this hill and fuck if I don't want to fall down. "Oh. God. Right there, Danny. Right there. I have to come."

He lifts his head for a second. "That's the point." Then he's back on me. I feel his teeth for a second and it's all so right. And then everything in me tenses up, and I'm coiled tight like a spring. He moves his fingers out of me and back in, and I scream his name. I explode and my body does some kind of a convulsion thing. He keeps doing what he's doing with his tongue. He's caressing my leg in a calming manner as his fingers have stilled inside of me. My whole being is pulsing and I'm pretty sure there's no greater feeling in the world than what just happened.

I'm breathing heavily, exhaling in rhythm. I didn't even realize he was sitting up, watching me.

"Christ, that was fun." He wipes his mouth and cheeks, then leans down to me. "You ok?"

I'm not sure I can accurately express how perfect he is. "Yes. Are you?"

He lays down and lines himself up. "I've never been better. You ready, my love?"

I put my arms over my head in a big stretch and grin at him. He laces his fingers in mine on either side of my head. Then he kisses me softly as he slides inside of me.

My eyes get wide. "You're bigger than your fingers." He pulls back a little. "But it's so good."

"It's so tight and good. Do you know you're a sex kitten?"

I say too loudly because I have no control, "I am?"

He pushes back into me and groans loudly. "Fuck. You're perfect." He kisses me and pushes in further.

"You're so long."

"Curse or blessing?"

I blurt out, "BOTH."

He kisses me again, sliding his tongue against mine, and I wonder if this is what I taste like. Then I'm thinking of nothing. He's not moving, just sliding slowly inside me. I'm so full. I don't think I can breathe. It pinches and I wince.

He's alarmed, but I reassure him. "Keep going." Out to the tip, then back inside me, and suddenly it's like my body opens up to him. We revel in the moment as it becomes perfect and gasp together.

"Christ, I'm almost done with just this. Fuck. I've wanted this for so long. Someone so perfect."

"I am?"

He says, "You are. I'm going to move now. Try and match my movements."

"I know how to do this."

"Prove it." He thrusts into me and we both moan. I counter his movements. This is all more than someone doing it to me. I'm part of it. Again, my body knows what to do. I raise my pelvis and he slides a little deeper and starts thrusting harder. It's so good. He goes faster and faster. We both start sweating and he raises himself up, straight-armed. We're staring at each other and his face pulls into a strange look.

"Fuck. Fuck. I can't stop it." I keep thrusting and lifting into him as fast as he's moving. My clit so happy with the intense friction.

"Don't stop yourself," I say.

"Fuck. Lizzie. Lizzie. Oh fucking God. This is so good. FUCK." And then I feel him jerk inside of me. My own good time is still building, but this moment is for him. He throws his head back and I can see where we're joined together. He growls my name, then stills. Then his eyes pop open.

"That was fucking amazing." He lays his head down on my chest to catch his breath. He says, "You're so incredible. At this and everything. I love you more than anything I'll ever do. You're my firecracker sex-kitten."

He pulls out of me as he groans. I feel like a house with no owner.

Empty.

DANNY

It's like I've never actually ejaculated in my life. As if I've been doing it wrong all this time. I kiss her nose and run to find the bathroom. I wash up and bring a cloth back for her.

She rolls over onto her side, away from me. I cross to the other side of the bed and lean down. And I realize she didn't come. I'm like a selfish prick. Shit.

"Hey." I move her hair out of her face. "You ok?"

Her lips curl up in a slow, satisfying way. I show her the washcloth. "Do you need this?"

She whispers, "In a minute. I have to go to the bathroom. But I'm ok."

"Just ok?" I ask tentatively.

"I'm transformed."

She skips to the bathroom and a giant smile breaks out on my face. I yell after her, "You are? Because I'm pretty sure you didn't, um... you know, during sex."

"Come." She peeks her head out of the bathroom as she says this.

I'm shocked she's talking like this outside of the actual sex act. "Yeah. Come."

She finishes up and leaps back into the bed. I roll her onto her back and climb next to her and share a pillow.

She says, "I didn't, but it was so wonderful. I didn't know the actual sex part could feel good."

I lean against the headboard and pull her onto my puffed up chest. I slowly tickle her back. She curls in snug.

I say, "I think I like this part the best."

She laughs. "Liar."

"True. How are you that good?"

"You unleashed me. In more ways than one and I don't want to go back." Wetness trickles down my abs. I pull her up and see she's crying.

"Are you sad?"

"Not from the sex but that I have to miss it."

"I love that."

She's so earnest. "Will you teach me how to do that to you?"

"You need no lessons on how to have sex. I'll have to work on lasting longer. I couldn't even contain myself but I'm sure I could rally for another go right now."

"Maybe, but I mean how to taste you." Jack-mutha-fucking-pot. I'm never letting her go or letting anyone else know she's flawless.

"It would be my honor and privilege to teach you to blow me. I can't believe you just said that."

"Me neither! But I want to know it all, and all with you."

"Good thing we have a long time to figure it out." She flings herself on top and straddles my hips. "Careful. I'm not sure I can handle the sight of you here." I rub my thumb over her still erect nipple.

"In a minute. First, do you really want me to come to Boston?"

"Are you having second thoughts?"

"No! I never wanted to go to Stanford but there wasn't really an alternative."

"I want you to do this for you, not just for me. Cuz I'm not worth all that."

"Yes, you are. And we *so* are."

I turn away from her. It's too much. The way she's gazing at me makes me think I could be worthy of her.

"I've never wanted anything more in my life than you with me in Boston. You can wear my jersey and cheer on the sidelines. I'll come to your classes and cheer for you. Every time you take a test, I'll show up in my Lizzie Fox jersey."

"What's your number?"

"14"

"Then that's my number, too."

I pull her closer and she rocks on my cock a bit. Shit.

"Are you sore?" I smooth my palms up and down her arms.

"Nothing I can't handle."

"In that case, perhaps I can teach you a little something."

"I'm an adept learner." She grinds down. "I pick up hard concepts quickly." I groan as she wiggles again.

"Then possibly we do a little practical application." She licks her lips. "Yes. That's a good start. Lick them again. Good. Shit." She moves down my body and I realize having a genius sex kitten around me might be the best reward in my life. She's never seen me play or... holy shit, I've lost my train of thought. She's kissing my abs and grabbing the base of my shaft.

"What next?"

"For now, why you don't just freestyle." I grin.

"On it." She flat tongues my dick from shaft to tip, and I'm gone. Seriously, Danny has left the building. I don't know who I'm going to be at her side, but I know I'll never be the same after tonight.

"Hurry! We gotta go," she yells, and I appear in the archway from the living room as she madly wipes down the counters.

"We didn't even touch that counter. You don't need to clean up. The bed is made and perfect. I even folded the toilet paper back in that fucked-up triangle."

"Should we vacuum?"

"It's our house, you ok with a few crumbs?" I love teasing her. I grab her around the waist and take the paper towel from her. "Stop. They're not going to figure out it was us if they discover anything. The only thing they'll notice is we ate all the cheese and crackers."

She giggles. "Let's go." It's six thirty in the morning and we have to run before the realtors arrive. But I'm a little sad to be leaving our slice of paradise. "I felt like a person here, not like a high school kid. Like this was our life." She sighs and looks around.

I say, "I feel the same."

"But it's so pretty. Can you maybe find a spare million or so and buy it for us? We could ask Tony." She hangs off my neck as I move us towards the exit.

I grin down at her. "How about this? When I get drafted into the NFL, I'll spend half of my signing bonus on securing our perfect fuck palace."

She laughs. "Why half?"

"The other half goes to my mother. Brothers' draft pact."

We make our way to the first floor; we're almost home

free when the door to the first-floor apartment squeaks open, and a tall man points at us.

"Qui es-tu? Vous n'êtes pas d'ici." Oh shit. We do not belong here.

She yells back as we bolt out the door, "Qui es-tu? Vous n'êtes pas d'ici."

I howl with laughter as we run at top speed around the corner and into a park. I leap down the little wall to get to the Seine walkway and help her down, too. I can't believe she asked him, "Who are you and why are you in our house?"

We catch our breath while winding through the 6th. We cross over the Seine and wander towards some open-air shops setting up near Notre-Dame. They're huge tourist traps to grab anyone who wants to see it. They're also set up in front of the Eiffel Tower because no one leaves Paris without seeing both.

I love that our Paris is different. The curvy little streets and smaller shops. The bistros and cafés that don't mind if you spend the afternoon drawing. She lets go of my hand and walks towards a vendor who's setting up. I hang back and stare at our surrounding all slightly coated in mist and dew. It's warmer today, still chilly, but it's getting too late to pretend we have plenty of time.

She bounds up and presents me with a small black Eiffel Tower key chain and displays her matching pink one. She closes my hand around it.

"For the keys to our house. When you get the signing bonus. I promise to get a job that pulls my own weight, but for now, I'm going to have to rely on that sweet, sweet NHL..."

"NFL. Football. Not hockey."

She nods at my correction. "NFL cash."

I kiss her and the sun rises a little higher in the sky. Fuck. I'm a sap. This is too fucking perfect.

I rest my forearms on her shoulders. I squeeze her tight and dream of how soon we can come back.

I say, "I love you."

She kisses me lightly. "How soon can we do it again?" She winks, and I pick her up and throw her over my shoulder. She's laughing. "You're going to carry me all the way back to our dorm?"

I two-finger whistle.

"Nope. I'm splurging on a cab. There's not enough time to do all the things I'm thinking about, so we need to save every minute we can."

LIZZIE

I CAN TELL YOU THE EXACT NUMBER OF MINUTES I'VE SPENT without him. But it's all bearable knowing we'll be together next year and from then on. It's been five long weeks but I'm getting pretty good at phone sex. Never thought I'd say that.

I've steered clear of my father. I don't want him to know about Danny yet. I haven't had the courage to tell them about Boston College. I want to wait until there's nothing they can do about it. My father keeps saying I've changed and he can't wait for me to settle back into the sweet, smart girl he raised. He does it half-joking, but the one time I told him I didn't want to go to a lecture on hieroglyphics because I wanted to hang with Kris, he grounded me. Kris snuck in through my window and we hung out anyway.

She's decided to go to Whittier College in Southern California. I'll miss her so much next year. She told me I had to write to her with paper and pen because then it's real not electronic. I float through my days living for my phone. My father monitors my usage, but I told him I'm discussing plans for next year with my roommate. Prom is tomorrow, and I'm all prickles of anticipation.

DANNY: This all sucks. Can I call you?

LIZZIE: No. I'm watching TV with my parents. That B+ I got in chemistry sent my father into a tailspin.

I curl my feet underneath my legs. I casually pretend I'm paying attention. I've perfected one-handed texting without looking at the screen.

DANNY: But you're still valedictorian, right? Crushed your rival?

LIZZIE: Duh. By .04.

DANNY: I'm getting some city award for football.

LIZZIE: And you played in New Jersey for the last two years?

DANNY: Yeah. Makes no kind of sense, but Boston loves a hometown hero.

LIZZIE: You're MY hero. I guess I can share you with Boston.

DANNY: It's so fucking strange not being around you all the time. Like we got a taste of what it's gonna be like, and now we have to go back to being kids.

LIZZIE: Tomorrow.

DANNY: And we'll have the whole night. Do we have to go to prom?

LIZZIE: YES! My dress is so pretty.

DANNY: I'm sure, but can I admire it on the floor? Did you tell your dad about prom yet?

LIZZIE: Mom says we keep it on the DL. She thinks I'm staying at Kris's after. And you're staying at a family friend's house.

DANNY: Can't we tell them the truth? My ma is all on board with you.

LIZZIE: My mom only does what my father wants. And so, this is a big deal, me going to Prom. I'm thinking of telling him I'm going with a group of girls.

DANNY: Firecracker, when are you telling him about Stanford?

LIZZIE: Soon.

DANNY: Sunday morning. Let's all sit down. You introduce me, and we tell them our plans. And that you're already talking to Harvard about the second semester of your freshman year. That you have it all under control, and you're still going to set the world on fire even if it's from Boston.

LIZZIE: I'm scared.

DANNY: I got you. Always. You're stronger than you've been told.

LIZZIE: So are you. Did you show your mom your Paris drawings?

DANNY: Good ole Pops, burnt the ones I gave her. But I drew more of you to show her. She said you're pretty.

LIZZIE: I'm so sorry Your dad can suck it. But I can't wait to meet her.

DANNY: She can't wait to cook for you. Wants to know if you prefer sausage or meatballs.

"Lizzie, are you paying attention?" My father's voice is sharp.

"Of course, Dad." I laugh at him and panic. I don't want Danny to worry. But I also don't want my dad to take my phone away.

"Kris is in crisis," I reply.

My mom says sweetly while she yawns, "When isn't she?" Even she's bored by this documentary on bees.

"She got a bad haircut and doesn't want to go to prom now." Oh, shit. I brought up the P-word by accident. Well, I'm in it now. I breathe in and my entire body fills with steel. I got this. I'm verging on excited to stand up for myself. I'm starting to live for this adrenaline rush. Perhaps I'm a thrill junkie.

My father pauses the TV and crosses his legs, then turns to me. He's got that Grand Inquisitor look.

I cross my arms. "What? What are you angling for, Daddy?" My phone vibrates.

DANNY: Are you there?

He clears his throat. I put up a finger. "Seriously, hold on, Dad. Let me tell her I'll call her later." Oh, God. This is too close.

LIZZIE: I LOVE YOU. I do so much. You're perfect, and I love you. I'll call. I promise. I have to go. My dad is on my ass and is about to ask about prom.

DANNY: Be bold. Love you too.

I turn towards my father. "What's up?"

"Apparently, you had something at the dry cleaners." He picks lint off of his sweater and then scowls at me. My mother shrinks for a moment.

I sit up straight and channel Danny. I'll let his confidence fill me until I find my own.

"It's my prom dress." My mother's eyebrows go up. I think they both thought I'd deny it. No more hiding I have my own life.

She turns to my dad. "We were going to surprise you once it was altered but the day got away from us. It's a lovely dress. It was a little too low cut, so we added a piece of lace to the bust." He frowns.

"Dad, it's prom. It's not like I'm going to be graded."

"It's hard for me to swallow you went behind my back. It's an archaic ritual I thought was beneath you. I expected more from you." I hate him. Because he gets to give the thumbs-up or down.

"I'm excited to go," I say, lifting my chin.

"Are you going with Kris?" *Technically, yes, we are.*

"Yes, and spending the night after." I fidget with my shirt.

"I'm calling her parents." *Go ahead, her parents don't care if we're out all night.*

Mom's tone shifts. "Seriously? The girl's never given you one reason to doubt her. We're lucky she's this wonderful. She's been sleeping at Kris's house once a week since third grade. The girls will be separated next year. Let her have this." My mother holds my chin and smiles at me.

My father snaps, "She's only this way because I knew what she needed. And I'm not so sure another night with that girl is a good idea. Her moral code is questionable."

I blurt out as if I'm a dog let off the chain, "She's my best friend in the entire world for my whole life. Do not say that about her."

He looks stunned that I raised my voice. I'm a bit stunned, as well. Too late to go back. It might not be the best time to tell him I have a date and we'll be having lots of sex, then I'm moving across the country to live with him. Should I bring that up now? Nah. Maybe not.

My mother says, "It's decided already. She's going to this rite of passage. Kris, her date, and Lizzie and hers. I think it's fine."

"And who asked you to think?" He steps in front of my mother and she shrinks and sits at his words. I hate that.

She says, "Stop it, Eli."

I erupt, "DAD!"

His voice is even keel and controlling. "I need to know everything going on in my house. You know this is not how this works. I don't want you to jeopardize all we've worked to achieve." He turns to my mom. "Who do you think is good enough for our daughter? I assure you, whatever piece of trash the two of you bring in my house won't be your intellectual equal."

I present him in his best light, which isn't hard. "A good Catholic boy I met on the Paris trip named Danny Danson. He's a star athlete and has a full scholarship to Boston College next year."

He scoffs, "Are you kidding? A jock?" I don't tell him he's coming from a different coast.

"He and his best friend are coming here to go to the prom with us." Part of that's true.

Then my mom adds, "And then the boys are staying with family friends. It's all fine."

My father stands and puts his hands on his hips. "It's fine, is it? I guess it's all sorted, then." His tone is cruel. I can't have him talk to Mom like that when it's my fault.

I stand and face him. "Dad. It *is* fine. I'm eighteen."

"You're still a child under my roof."

"I'll get to make all my own decisions next year when I'm not under your roof."

He laughs but it's cold and creepy. He's cracking and the monster is leaking out. He keeps him locked up most of the time, but I see the look in his eyes and it's time for the monster to surface. I'm ready.

"You can think that. I'll be right on campus. I'll see everything that goes on. I'll know all. I've never steered you wrong, smart girl. You don't need to lie and cheat. That's your mother's game."

"DAD! Leave Mom alone. I did this. My choices. I asked for her help."

He rounds on me while my mother straightens up in the corner. He won't hurt us, but he'll remind us of who's in charge.

"You and your flighty mother would be nowhere

without me. Your mother would be humping it at a community college if I hadn't found her and molded her into the perfect scholastically superior history teacher. And you, well, I've seen what girls in your generation are like; I'm constantly stunned you've accomplished anything with that scattered brain of yours. Boys are not the answer. No prom. This weekend we'll tour Stanford. You have an appointment with your adviser to discuss what you should be doing this summer to get ahead. And we'll spend the night at your grandmother's on Saturday."

My body lights up with a fire I've never let out. But it's there. I may be punished for the rest of my life. What else can he do to me? I secured a scholarship to Boston College. I've saved plenty of money for fall and a plane ticket to Boston. I'll pack a bag and go to Kris's tonight. He can't make me come home unless he makes a scene, and he won't do that because then the world will know he's not a nice guy.

My mother's crying as my father cleans up our dishes from our bland healthy snack. A voice comes out of my body that scares the hell out of me but shocks the fuck out of him.

"Not one more second. NO."

He towers over me and I'm not intimidated one bit. "What? What else could you possibly say in that tone of voice? You've become a classless, belligerent, ordinary teenager. I let you out of my sight for three months, and now you need to be reminded how things work around here. Next year you'll report to my office every day after your classes, and we'll review your work and notes like we do now. You will be superior again."

"NO. All of this is NO. And you know what, I'M NOT

GOING TO STANFORD. AND I AM GOING TO PROM. Deal with it, Dad."

My father stumbles. I am the girl Danny thought I could be.

"What are you talking about? Young lady, that's not a tone you take with me."

I sputter back, "Why not?" He's in my face. I'm not afraid for the first time in my life. He has no power over me anymore. My phone vibrates like Danny knew I needed him.

"Why what?" he yells.

"Why can't I talk to you like that? You taught me to stand up to bullies with counter arguments and dazzling vocabulary. You taught me to be a critical and careful thinker. You raised me to be a responsible and mature adult who can make thoughtful and important decisions. That's exactly what I'm doing. I'm going to prom with Danny. And in the fall, I'm flying my adult ass to Boston for college. There's nothing to weigh in about. Nothing to debate or get up to speed on. It's happening. I've withdrawn from Stanford, returned the money and enrolled elsewhere. Consider this all the waves you've ever warned me not to make."

He screams louder than I've ever heard him. And somehow, I don't react. I am steel and determination.

"I FORBID YOU FROM LEAVING THIS HOUSE. You'll miss graduation if I say you do. You'll go nowhere without me or your useless mother. Who apparently can't stop you from rebelling. But I'm involved now. And I'm the one in charge. Go to your room."

"Cool, that's where I wanted to go anyway."

"Leave your phone."

"No. You've made me pay for it since I was eleven by working odd jobs, babysitting, and walking dogs. I own it.

It's mine. There's NOTHING you can take away from me anymore."

"You're on our plan," he says smugly.

"And I can get myself off it. I'm eighteen, Dad. You have exactly zero authority over me."

"What the hell happened to you in Paris?"

"Everything."

I shove my charger, computer, and some clothes into a bag.

LIZZIE: Scary shit went down. I'm coming over NOW.

KRIS: Shit. What's up?

LIZZIE: He knows about everything.

KRIS: CRAP. I'll get the Oreos.

I shove all my clothes and my prom stuff into the bag as fast as I can.

LIZZIE: He knows about Boston College.

DANNY: Wow. Are you ok?

LIZZIE: I think I am. But only because of you.

DANNY: Do you still want me to come this weekend? I can wait. Is it still a good idea? It's just prom. I don't want to cause problems with him. Seems a little intense now for me to be there. And there's always the possibility that I'll tear him apart to protect you. Not sure I trust myself.

LIZZIE: I NEED YOU. I'm headed to Kris's house. He's yelling at my mom downstairs. He's possessed. I hope my mom's ok. Shit. Maybe I should stay. I don't want her to get yelled at.

DANNY: Go to Kris's house tonight. I get it about saving your mom. Trust me. Get out of there. This is all so complicated. Is this the best plan? I don't want to screw anything up for you.

LIZZIE: Yes. It is. I'll work all of this out with him. He's still my dad, and I do love him. I just want him to see me as an adult. ILY

DANNY: Ok. Fine. Cool. I can't wait to see you. ILY2

I'll be safe at Kris's house and now I need to see him even more.

I wipe my tears again and stare at my phone. Still no messages or missed calls. I haven't moved in hours because I can't believe what is happening. No one's heard from him. I spread the blue satin over the bed again. The dress matches the color of his eyes. There are flowers wilting on the dresser to my left. I cross my legs. I stare at my matching shoes. Where is he? Why won't he answer me? I've been worried, angry, and now I'm moving into devastated.

I call one more time and I'm connected again to an automatic voice mail.

"Danny? It's me. Prom ended. I'm still at the hotel. Did you miss your plane? It says it landed six hours ago. I didn't go because I waited for you. Where are you?" I burst into sobs. My makeup and dress are ruined. "I don't understand this. Why didn't you come? I can't take this. Where are you? Are you ok? Can you tell me why? Did something horrible happen, please let me know at least that."

My texts won't go through and I think he blocked me. They all bounce back. Kris called Tony and he hung up on her. I sent her away so she could be with her date. I still have hope he's showing up, but every second is making it harder to believe.

I curl up on the bed to try and stop the pain. I hope he's ok. Maybe he'll show up in the middle of the night. There's a knock at the door and I race to open it. My tears instantly dry, heart beating out of my chest. I was wrong. He's here. Thank God.

I whip the door open. My dad fills the doorframe.

"Leave, please." This can't be happening, Danny loved me yesterday. I move to shut the door on my father but he places his hand on my forearm.

His voice is soft and kind. "Don't close the door. I didn't come here to yell at you, sweetheart."

I don't understand.

He steps inside and I stare at him. My dress is swooshing as I move around the room like a gentle breeze. He gives me a couple of sheets of paper. It's an email from ddanson@gmail.com .

Dear Mr. Fox,

I'm writing to you out of respect. Your daughter and I were involved in Paris for the entire program. I cared for her, but now that we're back in the real world, my priorities and feelings have shifted. She's expecting me tonight, but I can't bring myself to make it there. It was cruel to stand her up, but I couldn't take the time to fly across the country to tell her this. I realize I'm a coward, but I couldn't face telling her this in person since she's become so emotional. Her plans and expectations of me are too great. I have an athletic career to think about, and can't be tied down with distractions. She won't listen and I don't know how to make her understand. I can't have her here in Boston. Let her know I wish her the best, but our time together must come to an end.

Sincerely,

Danny Danson

I fall to the ground. I scream at my father, "NOW leave! Get out! Leave me alone! This isn't real. He would have called." Danny loved me yesterday. I'm sobbing, and my father kisses my head and he leaves quietly. The door shuts and I'm trapped alone with a pain that's so intense I may never recover. I recheck my silent phone. I call and get that same automated message. I crumple into a ball, trying to make it hurt less.

I'm going to have to reinvent myself in order to survive the pain.

Part Two

Deuxième Partie

Present Day (aka...ten years later)

BETTE

"I hate that guy. I hate him more than flan. And flan is disgusting. Flan is failed cake."

"There's no flour in flan." My closest friend and colleague, Sophie, shakes her fabulous beachy waves over her shoulders. She helped me become who I wanted to be in life, helped me push through. Well, she did, and *the night that shall not be named*. She's a genius graphic designer. Infinitely better than that smug fucking Beantown asshole.

I hate all of Boston there's not a stitch of it that brings me joy. He's there and, well, I have a bad history with men and Boston.

Sophie waves her stylus in the air. She needs to get back to work so we can bury this fucker. "What did he say today?"

"It's like the guy doesn't know our positions at this agency are absolutely equal. And he's not condescending because I'm a woman, he's like this with everyone. I want to destroy him. I want to scorch the earth and have someone lay his body at my feet. Then I want to wear that blue dress that Daenerys had on after she emerged from the fire with those baby dragons."

"She was naked."

"Well, in my story, I'm wearing the dress. I look better in blue than naked."

"I'm sure that's not true."

"Do you want me to strip right now?" I ask while presenting myself and thrusting my hips towards her.

"I really don't think that will goose productivity, but if you think it will help, that's your path," she says offhandedly. "It's not like we have to see him. Or have ever seen him. Ignore him."

We've shared an office since I was named Senior Project Manager and Creative Director in Chicago. I've only had to deal with Assface directly since I was promoted two years ago. Before that he was an occasional nuisance. He's the 'me' in the Boston office and we just stole a client because our work is better. He's not taking it well.

The Eva/Rinaldi Ad Agency or E/R A is currently huge. If you bought anything in the last year, I guarantee my agency convinced you to do so. The owners are super quirky, and all creatives are in teams of two, called the lyrics and book approach, like Broadway musicals. One editorial and one artistic comprise each team. I'm the words and Sophie's the pictures. Assface in Boston is the art to his partner's words.

E/R A is collapsing all their branches into one to focus less on the housewife market and more on "Real Housewife" luxury market. There's only one VP Creative Director job in New York to snag. Eva and Rinaldi have set up an insane competition to prove we deserve the top job.

Sophie only takes me seriously when I put my hands on her armrest. Which I'm doing right now.

"First off, he said, 'You're doing some passably good

stuff at the regional level.' Then all morning, I've been fielding calls from the Athens, Georgia Chamber of Commerce telling me I'd won their 'Athens—Where Adventure Awaits!' campaign."

Sophie laughs hard because it means he pitched it behind my back. Our agency doesn't do local work.

In our two-year history of pranking each other, I admit, this is a good one. Our war started with him dropping me from our first joint client call. I still don't know how he did it, but we've been escalating ever since. Fucker.

"You need to get laid. Maybe fall in love because it's been a freaking decade."

"Go suck a dragon egg. Work is my focus and I have been laid."

"Not enough."

"True that."

This is who I became after *the night that shall not be named.* The only way to survive the pain was to transform into someone else. I gave up worrying something bad could happen because it already had. The worst thing I could imagine—Danny disappearing from my life—pushed me over a line I've never crossed back over.

When I emerged from my funk a year later my philosophy was engrained in my brain. I stepped out of everyone's shadow to control my destiny so I never relied on anyone else.

Sophie tosses a pack of accordian Post-its across our office. It arches like a paper slinky in faux celebration. "Congrats on Georgia!"

I look back to Sophie. "And get this, asshole thought that wasn't enough. I have four messages from the Tall Clubs International Foundation."

"What the hell is that?"

"It's literally a foundation for supporting tall kids. I mean, that's great and all, but they asked if I was still interested in the receptionist position because they heard I'd be looking for work soon."

Her mouth drops open. "That little fucker. I imagine his dick is super tiny and he needs to lord his power over strong women on the climb." She pauses and gives me a look. I'm bouncing up on the balls of my feet and twisting my thumbs. "What? You're too excited by something." She grins.

"It's so stupid. But I hacked into his Burbs soda project and added a graphic of a middle finger into the logo and a tiny eggplant with an arrow pointing to his name underneath."

"Get the fuck out! Did you email it to him?"

"I sent it to all the printers in the Boston office."

"Was it the IT dude I fucked a couple years ago at the Christmas party?" I nod. "Bette, that's brilliant. Password please, we'll need it for future sabotage."

"*IhateBette14*."

My tone turns from the high of fucking over that annoying man to a reality check. "Soph, there's a thing I have to tell you." She shifts in her chair, then moves from behind the monitor. When she sees my face, she stands and heads to our worn fluffy cherry blossom covered couch. We've had it for four years, it's our good luck cherry.

"This is a couch conversation." She's fourteen years older than me, but I never sense that. She's a mother but not maternal or patronizing at all. She sweeps her feet underneath her legs on the couch. I'm going to get the fucking brass ring job in New York. My dearest wish is for Boston to go fuck himself straight to hell. Perhaps Satan's in the market for a creative director. I hope I get to fire him.

"We're moving to New York." I'm not giving her a choice. Since my best friend passed, she's it for me and I'm not doing this job or life without her.

"Fuck. They're closing the office, aren't they?"

I nod.

She says, "I don't want more responsibility. Can I stay at this level and move to New York?"

"I guess, but why not?" I shrug, not sure where she's going with this.

"Would it cut into my 'me' time?"

I shove her a little. "Me time?"

"Pussy parties."

I roll my eyes. "We have six months until the offices are consolidated. Come with me."

I hold her hand and squeeze. She's the only person in the world I completely trust and that's a sobering statement. Mom can't be trusted because she's still unraveling her life since my dad died.

"And you're so sure you're going to get this job?"

"Duh," I say.

Her lips curl up. "Hell, yeah. I've already fucked all the men in Chicago. I could use a change of dickery." I laugh.

She leans forward. "Let's bury teeny peen and his very quiet sidekick." She's referring to Dax, the words to asshole Hayden Corelli's pictures.

"Eva and Rinaldi set this intense competition, basically."

"Of course they did."

"We have to create a 360 campaign in two months. And we don't know the product yet."

"Two months? That's a fucking short curly haired timeline." I grimace. "What? Stop it, prude. Why is this so complicated?"

"You've met Eva and Rinaldi. In Roman times they would have run the gladiator pits. Mostly to wear elaborate gold outfits, but they live for competition as well."

They pay exceedingly well and they're not assholes, just tilted, so I'm fine with their brand of chaos. But Eva and Rinaldi are over the top bizarre and insanely successful. We're not sure if they're brother and sister or married. It's a toss-up. They always wear matching outfits and speak in vaguely European accents, but rumor has it they're from Tampa.

Sophie says, "Game fucking on, I got your back. I'm suited up, bring on the lions."

"Or like in *Game of Thrones*, we'd be jousting, and you'd be forging my lance."

"Did you even watch the show?" Sophie sighs.

Of course I did but I'm always preoccupied when I watch TV. I get the gist. "You'd be my Dinklage, Tyrion Lannister."

"I drink and know things. I'll take it." Sophie turns away.

"I thought it was drink and forge things. That he was the secret guy forge master. With the space rings. You know, one ring to rule them all."

Sophie stands up and her face is almost red. "So much of that was no. Are you thinking of Dinklage in *Avengers: Endgame*, where he made the new hammer thing for Thor? With a twist of *The Lord of Rings* thrown in there? Dinklage wasn't in that."

"Sure. Sure. I'm a bad geek. I don't hold those details. All hail those who can remember and glorify those details."

"Stop watching fantasy, it's confusing for everyone around you."

I shoot her a finger gun. I'm better with books.

I wink at her and respond to upper management that we're staying on. Bring on the pitches, bitches!

As she walks out I yell,

"Fetch me a timeturner, Sassenach!"

She flips me off and yells as she enters the hallway, "Just, no."

HAYDEN

I PUSH MY DARK HAIR OUT OF MY FACE. I GO THROUGH PHASES AND right now I want to be shielded so I grew it long. I roll up my sleeves and mosey back to my desk. I've been sitting with HR learning how to let people go. My world is going to implode around here. My partner, Dax, waves from his desk as I pass by. We have adjoining offices so we can work together easily. But I'm the Senior Project Manager and Creative Director so I get to pass out the pink slips.

I've got to let Dax know what's about to go down with pitches and our ascent to New York. It's more of a formality. No one can hold a candle to what we do in this company except that Chicago thorn in my side. But we can best her.

My artistry in graphic design is fantastic, and the woman she works with is great, but I'm younger and hungrier, and we have such different styles. So I'll keep her on, but Bette's out. No room for her annoying ass in my department.

I'm walking through the halls, trying to muster my big dick energy before I head into the boss's office to weasel intel on the upcoming secret project.

There's snickering behind my back. I turn around and it stops. This is never good. I grab a Nerf gun off the arsenal wall outside the break room and shoot a round into the cubicles.

"Did I sit in something? What's funny? Don't make me take a hostage." No one says anything from the bullpen. Dax is holding a piece of paper, leaning on his doorframe, smiling. My assistant, Monica, walks by and I grab her and put the Nerf gun to her stomach.

"No suh, Hayden. It's just a stupid freakin drawing. Get over it," she says in her pert little Boston accent.

"What drawing? Someone tell me or I let her have it. Your lunch orders will be all messed up." Everyone's laughing with me now, the way I like it. With me, not at me. I love giving surprises but I like to have all the information. Can't stand a thing done behind my back.

Dax flips the page, showing me our Burbs cola mock-up. I shuffle Monica over towards Dax without removing the Nerf gun from her side to get a better look. Everyone's laughing. I yank the paper from Dax.

Instead of the logo in the center of the soda can, it's a one-finger salute. And placed below the logo is a small eggplant. My name is underneath the emoji penis and it reads: *To scale drawing.*

I laugh so people won't know it bothers me. "Fine. I've been a little wrapped up lately, who did this? Everybody have a copy?" They all raise a one.

Monica giggles. "It went to every printah in the building."

My face falls. "What witchcraft are you talking?"

Dax shakes his head and sits down. He's a reserved fella who loves writing words more than using them.

"Interns! Where you at?" Three overdressed local

college kids stand. The rest of us are in t-shirts, hoodies and joggers most days. I wear a button-down and jeans usually, but they're always in business formal attire, as if it's some archaic ritual handed down from their parents.

"Collect all the copies. I don't care whose office, gather them all. Monica will provide you with the list of printers from IT."

Monica groans. She hates IT. She slept with one of the geeks years ago and he always brings her strange tiny sculptures made of old wire casings.

I pull her aside. "Monica, my perfect and efficient assistant, can you call IT and find out who did this? Where did the print command originate from?"

"Yes, suh." She walks away and puts her middle finger in the air.

"Do you have answers? Who gets late night scut work?" My money's on the vidiots. Three dudes who create our video and social media content. They think they're hysterical—I find them mildly amusing. But depending on how many people have seen this stupid prank, it might be damaging.

IT is in my office, on my laptop when I return from the bathroom.

"Got it."

"Who?"

Monica peers in, sees her suitor, and turns tail to Dax's office. The IT guy swivels my laptop to me. "Not from here."

"Are you sure? Like someone hacked our system?" Jesus. So many protocols and paperwork for a dark breech. Shit. I hate paperwork. A lot.

"No. Someone printed from your IP address. You can

print to any printer in our network if you have the right password. I suggest you change yours."

"I'm so confused. And trust me, there's no way anyone knows my password."

He pushes my laptop towards me and points to a location on a map. "It pinged off a laptop in this network."

No fucking way.

"Chicago? Holy fuck. Can you tell if it's the fucking annoying woman?" I'm irritated but impressed.

"If you mean Bette Miller, then yes." The IT guy tucks his shirt in and stands up.

I'm fucking floored. My latest prank was external, but this was seen by the people we work with and possibly my fucking COO out of Boston. Fuck my life.

Rage fills me and I explode. "MONICA!" She runs in. "Do you know how much I fucking hate that woman?"

"I do."

"Did you tell her my password?"

"Because she and I talk all the time. No. But *IhateBette14* isn't hawd to figure out if she's got an IT guy on her end who cribbed your password." She puts her hands on her hips.

I punch pillows so they slam against windows. I pick up the discarded Nerf gun and fire off a twenty-dart round, spraying the window between my office and Dax's while screaming, "SHE WILL PAY FOR WHAT SHE'S DONE."

I cannot believe her. This is a professional woman. Someone I'm supposed to respect, and she shoves my name on an eggplant emoji. What the fuck? I'll apologize to the building while setting the bus on fire as she rolls under it.

Bette Miller's the worst, most irritating human on the planet. No one has ever gotten under my skin the way she does, and I've never even met her in real life. It's been all phone calls and emails, so I've never seen this witchy woman. She always uses a stupid avatar for Zoom and somehow has avoided social media. Granted, I have lurker accounts, so you can't find me, either, but it pisses me the hell off she's doing it, too. There's no way someone in this business doesn't have socials. My reasons for hiding are personal. Why ya hiding, Bette? She's a ghost and I'm done being haunted.

Dax opens the door and stares at me. "Are you done, *Die Hard*? It's funny. I give her props." I have one dart left and hit Dax square between the eyes.

He stands there in silence. I eventually laugh and say, "You should probably get back to work."

"And you should probably curb the carnage and plot your next move."

I drop the gun and rub my hands together like Monty Burns from *The Simpsons*. "Excellent. Excellent. Smithers, release the hounds!"

Dax yells to the bullpen, "Interns, scatter!" The interns scurry out of sight to collect all the stupid eggplant papers. One of them, who's on dart duty this week, collects the spent ammo and reloads the guns.

I sit at my computer and change my password. I hope to God she figures it out.

GamefuckingonBette14.

BETTE

"THEN HE HAD THE AUDACITY TO FUCKING STEP TO ME ON THE regional directors call, mansplaining my job." I slam the rest of my wine, then glance at Paul. He's so uncomplicated with his predictable IPA and chicken order. No matter how it's cooked, ole predictable Paul can be counted on for a chicken dish. I smile at him and he does not return my grin. That's not good.

He hasn't touched his chicken. Paul loves chicken. He sits back and sips his beer, then puts it down slowly. I wave to the waiter for more wine. I think I'm going to need it. Paul slowly turns his wrist to see his watch, then he looks up at me.

"Thirty-seven minutes."

"Until we have sexy times?" My voice lilts up at the end of my sentence in an exaggerated tone, trying to change whatever subject he's settled on.

"Of my day devoted to hearing about him."

I wince. He's asked me not to obsess over work or Hayden Corelli. I can't help it. I give a lot of blow jobs to make up for the shop talk. I don't think it's going to work tonight.

He reaches for my hand and pats it. It's weird. Not romantic, but like a stranger consoling you. He continues, "I want to hear about your day. But when my entire dinner conversation consists of 'uh huh' and 'wow,' it's a bit much, Bette."

It's not a new relationship, but it's not old, either. It's just a relationship.

I make a silly face and pull my shoulders up. "I'm sorry?"

"The thing is, you're not. You love your job too much. And your obsession with Hayden Corelli—Christ, Bette. I shouldn't know the man's name. He's not even in your office. You have more of a relationship with him than me. And I'm the one holding your hand. I'm here, but your head is almost always with him."

"Not true." God, I hope it's not true. "I hate him. I like you." It's a little true, probably.

He squeezes my hand, then lets go. "This isn't working."

This would be better with wine. I wonder when I checked out of this relationship. I didn't even notice this time. None of them have staying power. Ok, Bette, focus up. You must pay attention and ignore wine. He's saying things he thinks are important. *Don't fucking look.* My eyes dart to the waiter and he notices instantly.

"Did you hear me?"

My eyes snap back. I lie, "Absolutely." He's bland chicken babbling, no one could ever pay attention to everything he's saying. I'm awful.

"No, you were focused on wine. I mean so little to you?"

"Paul. I think you thought this was more than I did."

No man has ever has had that spark. I keep hoping I'll feel it again. But each guy, like Paul, is nice enough but not enough.

Danny lives at the bottom of all my relationships. I've tried to shake it. I've been to therapy and certainly talked it out with Kris until she passed away. Hell, I still talk to Kris about it. I randomly write to her or talk into the ether so I can feel her around still.

Danny's three fucking months set the tone for my love life. Two people finding a connection deeper than they could understand. A desperate and glorious love that guided me to be a better and worse person.

I can't find Christopher Danny Danson since the fall of his senior year of college. I always thought once I healed, I'd look him up and ask what happened. But he's simply gone without a trace. I haven't healed so it's probably for the best he's hiding.

I'm moving to New York. I'll leave all the boring chicken men in Chicago and find someone who makes my soul rumble again.

Paul's still talking. "You have a drawer at my place. It's been almost eight months. We're on a path."

He crumples his napkin on his plate and the edges begin to stain as it takes on the chicken piccata sauce. I stare at it slowly creeping up the white napkin until he pushes his chair back a touch to cross his chicken legs. Oh shit, I never noticed. He has chicken legs and only orders chicken. He's mad at his poultry legs and taking it out on real chickens.

"BETTE." That's a lot of volume from him. And the other diners are now all up in our business. "Even now, as I break up with you, I'm not your focus. You owe me something."

I take a big gulp. Why must I always have to make it ok to break up with me? I'd tell him the truth, but no one believes me. Hell, I got married to run from the truth. The ex-husband got married for the fun of it. A few months in we both realized our life was a joke. He's happy now while I still labor under a heartache that feels fresh. In my attempt to become someone else, free of my past completely, I kept the ex's last name. It felt right.

"YOU'RE DOING IT AGAIN. You're looking through me. I'm right here, Bette."

I thought Paul would be a better break up, I'm a little disappointed in him. He's pounding on his chest and the whole thing really is inconvenient.

I slurp some wine and purse my lips. "Paul. I'm sorry. Perhaps I wasn't clear enough when I said I never had my heart to give. I gave it away a long time ago. Was totally serious about that. It was not a challenge but a fact." It sounds like a line but it's true.

His eyes bug out of his head. But I'm giving him a peg to hang the breakup on. Blame me, dude. I do.

"Bette, look at me, please." His tone has shifted to concern and I'm instantly annoyed he's treating me like a victim. I'd like him to stay 'angry breakup' Paul. That was easier. "Are you going to be ok?"

"About this?" I gesture between us. "Yeah. I'll get through it." I fake sentiment.

"Are you really jaded? You hid it well."

"I don't hate the idea of love, I'm just unable to feel it." And look at that, I'm honest with him.

"But will you be ok?"

I don't hesitate. "I don't think so, but what're you gonna do?"

"You should get some closure, that will help," he says, as if he's trying to solve me. So long, Paul with the pleasant apartment and regular guys night out.

I drain the Syrah and lie, "I enjoyed the sex quite a bit." His foreplay was better than his missionary.

"Call me if you ever need to talk."

"Like a 'let's still be friends' thing?" Poor delusional Chicken Paul. He's sweet and always takes out the garbage.

He says, "We were only ever friends with benefits." He's only slightly wrong; we were acquaintances with benefits. After being dropped by the love of my life and losing my best friend to cancer, I keep my circle pretty tight. Sorry, Paul, my dance card is full up on friends. I have the one and that's all I can handle.

I place whatever cash I have on the table and walk away. I think I'm walking away with some dignity, but then Paul calls after me and I turn slightly to see him.

"This is eleven dollars in ones and a parking ticket. And this is a dry-cleaning receipt." I contemplate snagging the receipt back; they're sticklers about claiming with the ticket. The restaurant is staring. It's ok. I didn't love that skirt.

I reach my hand towards him and say in a dramatic fashion, "Take it. I've given you everything I have. Seriously, it's all I have." I hustle to the sidewalk, down another boyfriend and no closer to finding love—again.

Goodbye Paul. I'll miss having something to do. It's only nine.

On my way home E/R A texts to announce that our pitch is dog food. Arco Dog Food wants a slick rebrand of its one-hundred-year-old product. I'll go home, drink more wine and try to think like a dog. At least it's something to do. Work is always there for me.

I pull on a headband to get my long bangs out of my face. My hair is so straight it just sticks up in the air when I do this. It's cut into a long shaggy bob, so headbands don't work so well. But who cares? It's not like I have anywhere to go. I have to get a new Chicken Paul. The thought of finding someone who zaps my nervous system and zings my heart and brain is a bit too much to ask for. I just want to go to dinner.

I sit in the cozy big brown chair in the corner. It's hideous, but it was my dad's. It was in his office on the Stanford campus for years and it's where he wrote his dissertation. He used to take me to work when I was little, and I'd read and write in this chair. It's my best memory of him. When he died four years ago, it's the only thing I wanted of his.

I'm writing copy by hand with a sharpened pencil. It's a crisp new one and I think that matters when you need a crisp new idea. I sip my white hot chocolate. Most people find it repulsive, but the first sip of each cup takes me back there for a split second. I needed to feel connected with Paris for a moment tonight. Most days, you can keep Paris. It's full of too much old bullshit. But then there are days like this when I need to revisit the good, the flood of happiness, even for a whisper of a moment.

This week was awful. Asshole Hayden retaliated by telling everyone what I did and therefore appeared superior. Then the fucker changed all the fonts in my documents and in all correspondence online to Comic Sans 14pt type.

I'm locked out of changes. I constantly look like I'm inviting people to an eight-year-old's birthday party in 1997. And as much as I hate him, it's really funny.

I inhale the scent of my drink and try to wash Assface away. I have plans for him, but for now, I need to focus on dog food. Dog food and how much I love it. I don't know dogs. We always had cats and now I'm panicking a little I'll lose my dream job because my mother is allergic. It's not my fault we didn't have a schnauzer.

"I don't know dogs, but Arco does. Don't worry, Arco has your back. We put the time in, so you don't have to. We have a hundred years of history at your disposal." No, don't say disposal. "We have a hundred years of experience at your back. We got you. We take away the worry." It's right there on the tip of my tongue. I'll work it out. I need to beat him.

HAYDEN

I USE HER EGGPLANT AS MY AVATAR FOR THE ZOOM MEETING. SHE does, too, but with her name in the middle of it, in the much-maligned font Comic Sans. I love that my little revenge is wrapped up in hers. It's funny.

In my mind, she has curves for days. Maybe because all my fantasy women end up looking like a grown-up version of something I had in my youth. I've never used a picture of me and never been live on a Zoom because she hasn't. I'll mirror her *The Art of War* tactics all fucking day. Bring it! I have plans for a deeper retaliation than changing her fonts.

But we do have to play it cool while we're evaluated for what I'm calling "The Condensation." We're on a regional directors call and the meeting is endless. So much droning about shit we already know.

Bill puts his hand up like it's fucking school. He's the Canadian. "Sorry. So, there's two separate campaigns?" he asks.

Shenika, the loud and hilarious woman from Atlanta, answers him. I like her and will definitely keep her when I get the job.

She says, "Bill. Jesus. You have the same info the rest of us have. One campaign from your Vancouver team for this Arco Dog Food. One from each of us. We all pitch in a Survivor-like death match and half the teams survive to pitch another day. And the rest hope to keep a job of some sort."

I laugh a little too loudly.

And, of course, Bette jumps on me. "Did you just laugh at Shenika? How professional of you. Or were you laughing at Bill for misunderstanding the assignment? Way to go, school bully. Go scoff in a corner of the playground, the rest of us are here to work."

Bill smiles and I want to crush her. Every once in a while, her voice transports me to fantasy but most of the time her haughty tone drives me fucking insane. There's a timbre to it that I get lost in and forget she's a horrible human for a second. Her voice is, and it pains me to admit, comforting. And occasionally, sexy.

Shenika says, "I was making a joke, but your point is well taken, Bette."

"I'm sorry if I offended anyone." I post a middle finger in the chat to Bette. I've never reached out like this before. I don't know how to take it back, so it's staring at me as I wait to see if she replies.

A mouth and a poop emoji—eat shit—is volleyed back. Glad she didn't fucking report me. I lean back in my chair and grab a Nerf. I volley a round off to the new targets hanging near the edge of my office. They're all her name. I snap a picture of them and send it to her.

Michelle, from San Fran, is going off on how much he hates this shit. I agree, but this is a monitored call, idiot. The New York version of us is exempt from this circus. She was automatically promoted to EVP. The San Francisco guy is also trashing her. Seems ill-advised.

Bill chimes in with something so painful, "Let's all be on the same page. I think we should read over the memos together."

I tune out. I'm so bored.

I type quickly.

You're not really this fucking concerned about Bill?

She responds instantly. Interesting.

No. But Curt and Michelle Michelle are digging their graves pretty deep.

I respond, *Michelle Michelle?*

Listen to her, whenever she makes a point, she says it twice, emphasizing a different word the second time. Like—THIS is important. This IS important.

She just trashed a coworker with humor and observation. She's like a little onion with many layers. I spend too much time imaging what she looks like for someone I hate. Today her hair is red in my mind.

Do you have an idea yet?

She responds, *How dumb do you think I am? And is that my name in those targets? The picture is blurry like most of your overblown work.*

"Jesus, this woman!" Fuck. Just when I think we're getting along she slips in a dig. Irksome.

Dax comes in and leans in the doorframe. "What woman?"

"Her."

"Your epic nemesis?" I nod and my boy whips down a target and rips it in half. I laugh.

"We're chatting."

"Whoa, really?" Dax does a little dance as if he's excited by this.

"Why not? Stop your jig, we're trading barbs at the moment. She's not as witty as I'd hoped."

"You hoped she was something? Let me see." He peeks over my shoulder. "Actually, she's pretty quick."

I shake my head and hurl my empty plastic gun at him. "Go think of something brilliant, so we can take this fucking game in one match. No second round. Got me? Dog food—that's what you live and breathe right now." He salutes me and disappears. The best part of Dax being my best friend is he keeps his comments short, but I know he's got my back.

Does this mean I win? she types.

Not even close.

There you are.

I type quickly. *Admin is going over the rules. I muted. You?*

The moment Curt started a sentence with, "Well, up in the Frisco office..." No one in that wonderful city says "Frisco."

Ha.

Oh shit they asked you for last year's budget numbers.

On it. THX.

She responds, *Propping you up to cut you down another day.*

She is wittier than I give her credit for most days. I respond while droning on about budgets, *I look forward to it.*

The colossal waste of time call ends and I stand and stretch a bit. Too much time at my desk. I toss my yoga mat on the ground and do a couple of poses, holding them almost perfect. What I really need is some time down at the boxing gym, knocking the shit out of the heavy bag. I have a date tonight. I'd rather be with the heavy bag. That's not a good sign. Doesn't bode well for... shit.

I yell from Warrior II pose, "MONICA. MONICA! WHAT'S HER NAME?" I don't like the name. I remember that. She works in the district attorney's office and she's hot.

An intern, not Monica, looks into my office. She pulls up her iPad. "Her name is Leslie Sherman, goes by Lee."

"I'm calling her Leslie. Or babe. Not Lee. Where's Monica?"

"Vermont. Her niece is in a play. She's the second lead in Glengarry Glen Ross."

"How old is she?"

"Eleven."

"School play?"

"It's a progressive school" She's way too excited to tell me this information. My phone rings and as she scurries off to get it, I fire off a text to Monica.

HAYDEN: How important is this niece? More important than me and the date whose name I can't remember? You took my memory to Vermont.

My phone rings and I hop up from the floor. I assume it's Monica, since the intern put it right through.

I say, "There's no going to Vermont. Did I ok this? Not in the middle of war. You get your skinny butt back here so we can attack the enemy on all fronts. I need to know what's going on in Chicago at all times. My assistant does not take time off when I need her."

A voice that's definitely not Monica's knocks the wind out of me a bit. "I do keep a tight grip on your assistant's whereabouts, and my ass. Nothing happens in my city without going through me. That's why you don't actually know what's going on. Did you want to come by and kiss the ring?"

"Fuck me. Miller?"

"You couldn't handle me." I laugh at her balls. She continues, "Yes, it's me. I'm calling with an olive branch."

Her voice is deep and rich. I imagine it gets throaty when she has sex.

"What's your angle?" I flick my thumb from behind my index finger.

"No angle. We have so much to focus on and I want the piece of my brain back that's constantly either coming up with ways to torture you or bracing for your next move."

I flop back into my chair and sip a very cold cup of coffee. Seriously, who the hell let Monica go away? The devil has a point, though.

She asks, "Are you there?"

"Here. Sorry, struggling with cold coffee because my admin had to go to the theater."

"Culture never hurt anyone."

"It's hurting me in this war."

"I'll send some air support."

I ask, "Are you always this quick?"

"Yes, I make sure to speak like I'm in a Billy Wilder movie at all times. It's exhausting, but in the end, it's worth it," she quips.

I pace around my office and stare at Dax. He cocks an eyebrow and I point to the targets with the harpy's name and back to the phone.

I say, "I'll brush up on my snappy comebacks and screwball comedy banter."

"No need, you won't be around long enough." Again, ruining our vibe with digging at me.

"Christ, woman." She laughs and I scrub a hand over my stubbly face.

"No, just Bette."

She's so fucking quick.

"What's the reason for this maddening phone call

that's accomplished next to nothing?" I say, ready to throw my phone across the room.

"Next to nothing?" She quips.

"I'm now aware you talk in circles." I'm exasperated trying to keep up with her.

"Also, your intern mentioned her name is Leslie, and she goes by Lee."

I grunt into the phone. "She told you about my date? What the fuck is with this one?"

"No clue. I think she thought I was your assistant."

"Aren't you?"

She growls and I like it.

"Was it your next pitch you needed an assist on? Sorry, I'm booked." Too fucking quick. No one is this smart.

I fire back, "Do you go home and practice patter at night?"

She doesn't hesitate. "When I'm not busy creating work superior to yours."

"Now, we're getting personal. You know as well as I do your work is good, but ours is great."

The banter stops cold. There's too much silence. I overstepped.

"This was a stupid idea to call you. Never mind. This was hopeless. Have a lovely evening with Lee." The phone goes dead.

I yell as the interns enter Dax's office. "She fucking hung up on me! What the fuck was that? She called to taunt me, mock my dating life, and then she hung up."

Dax enters and leans against the doorframe. "Sounds as if she's accomplished her goal."

I fire off a round at her targets. Then I walk quietly over to my couch and grab a pillow to scream into. She drives me fucking crazy. She's the flip side of a good romantic crush. She's a nasty preoccupation. I pace and Dax laughs.

He says, "Hey, I think I cracked this, but I need you to focus. I'm actually going to use those art skills of yours this time."

I roar, "Intern number three. The one covering for my theater-loving assistant! Please come in here."

Her head peeks in. "June."

"June what?" I shrug. It's late April.

"My name."

I shake my head. I'm an ass. "I'm sorry, June. You're new and I was in a hurry. That was rude. Can you please get the horrible woman from Chicago on the phone for me? Also, don't tell her about my schedule ever. We're going to keep her waiting."

"Um. You mean Ms. Miller?"

"Yes. I do. I'm running downstairs for a bagel. You want one?"

"You want me to call her and you're leaving the building?" Her brow is furrowed.

I toss my sweater back on and waltz past her. "And I'm getting a bagel for myself and what is it you like to eat, June?" I'm growing impatient with intern number three. Usually, they get on board a little quicker with this game.

"I like croissants."

"There you go. Croissants are for closers. Be back in twenty. Call her in five."

BETTE

OH MY GOD. IT'S LIKE HE KNOWS THE EXACT BUTTONS TO PUSH. I won't react to him, but I can swear like a sailor to myself. He makes me mad. I've decided to work from home for the rest of the day. I transfer his call to my cell and take off, while still on hold. I know he thinks I'm going to hang up but I think he'll be annoyed if I'm still on the line. So, I stay.

He's not on social and if I google him, there's only a Halloween picture where he's wearing Hulk makeup, and some corporate group shot that's too grainy to see him clearly. He's tall and insanely ripped. I may have developed a slight Hulk fetish ever since I found that picture.

It's quite a fucking feat in this day and age to be hidden. If you google me, there's a million Elizabeth Millers. And Bette always returns Midler. I feel secure in my hiding place.

The intern apologizes every thirty seconds. It's like she has a timer. After the fourth time, I clocked her and told her it's fine. And then, thirty-nine seconds later, she was back.

I have one earbud in and my phone is in the pocket of my trench coat. I love this coat so much. It was Kris's. Her mother gave it to me. She had a bit of an Audrey Hepburn obsession. Her short pixie cut was one of the ways she honored her. She and I found this coat in San Francisco. My father thought I was at some library thing learning about poetry. Kris snuck me out and we spent the day thrifting. I pull it around me. It's a little big; she was six feet tall and gorgeous. She was the best friend and the universe didn't see fit to let me keep her. You'd think after the Danny debacle, I'd get to keep her, but nope. Cancer had other plans. This was her *Breakfast at Tiffany's* coat. I'm always thrilled when we make it to shoulder seasons so I can wear it. It's like she's with me.

I'm sitting on the El, almost to my stop, when he finally comes on the line.

"Bette Miller." His voice almost purrs my name. I don't like what my vagina just did. It did that surge of excitement, clenching thing. Nope. Down girl, this one's not anything. He's pandering and I'm not sure what he's up to.

"I was worried your ego had actually swallowed you."

He tosses back, "Funny. How are you?"

"Since an hour ago, fine. I had a quick bout with the flu, but I've recovered nicely. Is there something I can do for you?'

"I was thinking about our skirmishes," he says slowly.

I put all my stuff into my bag and stand by the door, waiting for my stop.

"Battles?" I say.

"War."

"Go on," I answer. The Sedgwick stop is announced, and I hold on, waiting for the lurch.

"Where are you?"

"Wieners Circle. Did you want to place an order?" I

answer with the first thing that came to mind. I'm nowhere near the place but how could he know that.

"Where are you, seriously?" He seems genuine, but I can't let down my guard. Despite the slight flush in my cheeks as his voice becomes more comfortable and vulnerable than snarky.

"When have we ever been serious?" I say, avoiding the subject. I regroup. "Point taken. I'm on my way home. I work better on my couch sometimes."

"I have the same thing, but it has to be at my dining room table. Or this café down the block from my house or..." His voice drifts off, as if he's going to say something else and thought better of it.

"Or what?" I ask.

"Nothing. Just those two places." He doesn't want to share. Why would he? This is the most civilized we've ever been. His voice is smooth and rough at the same time like a really peaty Scotch. He's a study of opposites, dangerous and completely safe because he's far away from me.

I say, laying down my gauntlet, "I write in cafés, too." I'm walking and talking to the man, and realize we're revealing actual things about ourselves. I can't have that. I let the silence go on and it's more comfortable than I'm comfortable with.

I break our moment. "Anyway. Why did you call?"

"The truce you started to mention is a good idea."

"Agreed."

"You're fucking kidding me. Bette Miller agrees with Hayden Corelli. We should timestamp this," he kind of yells.

I say with a smile in my voice, "Do we need to draw up papers or something? File it with the authorities?"

"Nah, we can handshake it." He sighs.

"I'll write it up anyway."

"Fair enough. Truce. Shall we set the rules?" he asks.

I'm two blocks from my apartment and my phone dings. My mom is calling. I send her to voice mail. Normally I wouldn't, but this call is so odd and intriguing. My mind often conjures an image of Hayden Corelli. Sadly, his eyes are always Danny's. But his body is bigger and so are parts of him I'd never ask about. His BDE, big dick energy, is overwhelming most of the time. I just hope I'm serving BPE right back.

"Are you flirting with me, or do you really mean to call a truce?" I ask honestly.

He responds, "If I was flirting with you, you'd already be panting."

And we've taken another turn. Not sure I know what to do with this, so I volley back, "Is that so?"

"What would I be doing if you were flirting with me?" he says.

"Which I'm not," I stress.

"Of course." His voice drops almost an octave. "Wouldn't dream it possible."

I open my door and toss my things on the kitchen island. I don't know what game he's playing, but I'm intrigued. I'm going in. Hopefully it will scare him off and I don't have to think about him for a while.

"Well, if I were flirting, which we've established I'm not, you'd already be stroking your dick, dreaming of what I could do to it." I do NOT know where that came from. Holy shit. What am I doing? I'm on a path now. I should stop this path. I take my coat off and turn in a tight circle. I keep shaking out my hair, as if that will take it back. That was not what I intended to say.

He growls a little. "Solid, Miller. That's some solid dirty

talk. Do you need me to send some back or are you all set?" I'm flustered is what I am. I'm baffled. I need to get this back on track.

"Rules of engagement," I say, trying to get back to the truce.

"So, now we're engaged?" His voice is low and throaty, and now, in a shocking turn of events, I'm wet. How the fuck did that happen? I hate this man and now I'm picturing fantasy Hulk servicing me on his knees. Shit.

"I've already made that joke. Just as I suspected none of your work is original."

"I can think of lots of original things I'd like to say to you."

And this pops out of my mouth: "Or do to me."

I slam my palm to my forehead. BETTE. Stop flirting. There's a pause.

I say, trying to get away from whatever the hell I was doing, "Rule one. No sabotage."

He clears his throat. "No pranks. No calls."

I don't know what he means by the call thing. I kick off my shoes. I love a good shoe but some days I wish I was a flip-flop girl.

"No calls between us?" I say and my voice is little lower than I'd hoped.

He comes back, purring again like a damn jungle cat, "I didn't mean that. For the first time in our twisted relationship, I'm enjoying something about you, and it all centers on this call."

Suddenly, I'm thinking of his date, and I hate Leslie/Lee. Chicken Paul was right, I spend so much time obsessing about his next move, and making sure I'm perfect and on point at work, in email, on Zoom calls, and the phone. Shit. We might as well date each other with the amount of time spent in each other's business. I need to put the Hulk to rest.

"Bette?"

"Here. Sorry," I say quickly.

"Where did you go?"

I say, "Someplace darker than expected. I'm back to me now and putting this all behind me."

He says, "Behind you? That's an interesting thought."

Oh, Christ. Do I masturbate or call HR?

"Sadly, not sure you could take that. It's a pretty powerful place to be." Stop my insanity. I slap my hand over my mouth. I want to win this conversation and have him leave the call first. I want him to want me. That's wrong. Nope. Stop. Maybe I'll gain an edge if he wants me. However, I'm a little lust addled by my sworn enemy. Shit, did he just gain an edge?

He says in a low rumble that could probably remove my thong without trying, "Fuck. We have got to get off the phone."

My voice is sweeter. "And why is that? You still in public?"

"Not for long." He's gruff and urgent.

"Enjoy your date," I coo at him.

"She'll certainly enjoy it." And now I'm incensed. Did I wind him up to go fuck Leslie/Lee? And then he says, "But I'm pretty sure I won't enjoy it quite as much as I did this call. Have a good night, Bette Miller. Perhaps our next call we get down to the order of the day."

I gasp out, "No. It's a whole new world order, now."

"Fuck, yeah it is."

I hang up before I say anything else with no filter.

Why am I so obsessed with the person behind this stupid deep and calming voice. It wraps around sentences that are full of snark and makes them sound sultry. One minute I'm worked up about how much I hate him, and the next I'm just worked up. I'm hot and the thought of him touching my skin or taking me from behind has me diving for my vibrator. He's definitely not an order chicken kind of guy.

HAYDEN

My cock and I have a good relationship, built on mutual admiration, respect, and sick, dirty thoughts. We've always been cool. But the last twenty-four hours I've hate-stroked to that woman six times. It's like I'm sixteen again. She's Benjamin Buttoned my cock.

I didn't sleep with Lee with the terrible name and fabulous body. Instead, I bolted back to my place to evoke my fantasies of that fucking woman mixed with the one who is always the star of my deepest sexual moments. The one who ruined me and dashed all traces of my heart. I don't date. I hook up because there's no way for me to connect to women deeper than that. Literally, my heart's not in it because I gave it away ages ago. And then that fucking Bette stirred me in a way I didn't think was possible.

I loathe Bette Miller, but she fucks like a goddess in my mind. My shaft is starting to rouse again, thinking about it. It will weep in a minute. But while it gets its groove back, I've research to do.

Google Images search brings up Bette Midler once again. And a slew of women across this country, not one I'd like to fuck. She has to be hot. Today in my mind, her hair had honey highlights.

Her ad awards are listed, but the pictures are always of Sophie, her partner. There's a picture of her at the AdAge Midwest banquet at a table in the back. Here's what I know —she once wore a green dress. Her face is turned to the side and she's sitting next to a man. Her hair is up and it could be red, or dark or dirty. That's all I have to go on.

There's no record of her in Chicago public schools and no amount of social media research returns a damn thing. She comes up on those research sites and I think she's an organ donor and lives on Wells Street in Chicago. There's twenty-seven other Bette Millers in Chicago. But I swear I heard the word Sedgwick over the loudspeaker when we were on the phone the other day. And I looked up the El train and Sedgwick is a stop near a Wells Street.

I flip out a yoga mat and hold a pose that's supposed to clear my mind. I breathe in and out, filling my soul and toes with a cleansing breath. And then an image of her flickers through my mind.

I fall to the mat and reach for my phone to try and scrub it from my thoughts.

HAYDEN: You owe Leslie an apology.

BETTE: We text now?

HAYDEN: We do. On company issued phones only. Watch yourself.

BETTE: Give me her number. What does she need?

HAYDEN: Probably a vibrator.

BETTE: HA HA. Couldn't get it done?

HAYDEN: Didn't even try.

I have to walk away. My dick is hard even with this contact. Fuck it. I rip off my shorts and my cock springs out. I hear the phone ding as I walk to the bedroom. I ignore it. I stroke myself and there goes my dick, pre-cum easing my tight fist up and down. This is going to be fast. I grab lube and the sound of another text popping off gets me going even faster. My blood is molten hot for this fantasy. I pull harder and faster, fucking my hand. I can't even lie down. I imagine her from behind. Shit, that's it. When she said that the other day it became the only thing I could fixate on. I need her ass to be perfect and because she's a fantasy I know exactly the one to picture. I groan as I fist faster. I'm thrusting into myself and my balls draw up hard. The burn in my abs begs for release. I'm so crazy with lust and my desire to come, I throw my head back and let it go. Only after I'm done do I realize I have to wash my comforter now. I'm catching my breath as another text comes in and my dick stirs like it's Pavlov's cock.

HAYDEN

It's been a relatively quiet couple of days. The truce is so boring, I'm pulling my hair out. It's Saturday and I'm not good with weekends if I don't have plans. I lace up my shoes, tuck a sketch pad into my bag, and head out to Boston's Museum of Fine Arts.

I walk in and Shelia and Madge are behind the desk. "Oh, look who's here?" Shelia says. "It's mister too important to visit his friends."

I laugh.

"Where ya been, gorgeous?" Madge yells and her cohort snort laughs.

"Quit busting my balls. I've been searching for women as perfect as you two. Came up empty, so now I'm back."

"Alright. Keep it in your pants. Love to your mother," Madge quips, they used to play bridge together.

They giggle and nod at me as I stroll right through. I wave to the other folks behind the desk and shake the guard's hand as I set off for the antiquity rooms. I want to find some peace after the disturbing and confusing phone call and text exchange that set off this week's Chicago-based StrokeFest. Even now, in my sacred space, my dick is getting hard thinking about her hating me. I fucking dream of her submitting to me, finally, with a defiant look and her legs opening wide. I have a problem. I want to call and see if she'll fight with me.

I shake my head and find a bench and stare at an ancient drawings that have fascinated me since I was a kid. This particular one is on a Sumarian water jug. I love that the mundane was decorated and celebrated.

I flip open my pad and the sound of pencil scratching on the thick paper instantly soothes all my frayed nerves. I have to draw dog food later, but for now, I let my pencil massage the paper in sensual curved lines of the vase.

Strangely, today was different.

I was totally focused on my nemesis, Bette, when I let loose all over my house. She's simply a current fantasy. In the future, my thoughts will drift back to the one girl who split me open and took my heart.

Several hours later, I close my pad and do a quick Downward Dog in front of the antiquities. Then I wave to the staff. Some of them have known me since I was seven and discovered a different way to communicate. All the bungled up shit in my head could come out in a drawing instead of me having to fucking talk. I hate talking about my feelings. Mostly because I have to admit I have them.

I talked about hopes and dreams once. I chatted about my "emotional inner life" as they call it. I told her everything I'd ever thought I'd be and how I felt when other people didn't see it the same way. I blathered on about what I wanted most in this life and what I found beautiful. I admitted flaws and traps from my own life. And when she stopped taking my calls, texts, and emails, well, that was the last time I did that shit.

I pull my bag's strap over my head and head out into the sun as spring is turning over to summer. I need to focus on our Arco pitch.

I'm drawing it, then doing a watercolor of a pastoral farm scene to bring back an old-time values feel. I haven't painted with watercolors in forever. The Arco people want to evoke warm family dog images. I'm sure she and her demon sidekick have a better idea than painting a farm. Shit.

DAX: Hey man. Where's the goods? I want to render it and ship it the hell off.

HAYDEN: Give me like an hour.

DAX: Where are you?

HAYDEN: Why?

DAX: I'm at your house.

HAYDEN: BMOFA

DAX: You ok?

HAYDEN: I am now. Let's burn the witches to the ground.

DAX: No problem. BTW–head witch in charge sent an email making sure I knew you have a prank truce. But, dude, we uploaded her resume to BeANanny.com last week.

HAYDEN: I'll tell her. You pull her resume.

DAX: K-but she already has like six interviews set up. I feel bad for the people who need a quality nanny.

HAYDEN: She's not it. And they'll back off once they hear from her character references.

I scrub my hand through my hair. My head is all over the place with the past and present. My phone rings and I don't recognize the number. Perhaps it's the minx from the City of Big Shoulders calling from someone else's phone.

"Aren't you supposed to be being brilliant or some shit?"

"Hello, Brother Hayden." *What is this?* "I'm calling because you expressed a keen interest in the Church of Scientology. We'd love to have you come in for a reading and talk."

I'm going to kill her.

BETTE

I FOUGHT A WOMAN FOR THE LAST CAN OF TRADER JOE'S TOMATO sauce. It's the only one I like and I'm making spaghetti tonight for Three-Date Tate. He's mildly amusing. He might be in trouble when it comes to getting serviced tonight, though. I'm a little sore after servicing myself four times in the middle of the night to the thought of that asshole's voice. He wasn't gentle, either. I shake my head and grab some fresh parm.

I have high hopes for Three-Date Tate. Although things have been rather tame, I'm hoping he surprises me. I'm fourth in line and the woman in front must feed dozens of linebackers. My phone vibrates in my pocket and I can't get it out easily in these jeans. I'm in my smidge-too-tight jeans, so I have to wiggle and work my hand into my back pocket. Fuck. I accidently make a call. I hear someone pick up, but I can't get to it.

I'm hopping around with my head turned back towards my ass and yelling, "Hold on. Hold on. I'm coming. I'm coming." People are looking at me and I glare at them. "Not like that." I finally get my phone out of my pocket. Sadly, it flips out of my hand and skids across the floor. I'm afraid it might be Three-Date Tate texting to confirm and now I've called him. I'm going to sound more eager than I am.

I crawl across the floor and when I'm an arm's length from the phone, I say it one more time. "Hold on. Oh, my god, I'm coming. Right now."

I get my ear to the phone and the voice fills me with ice-cold seething, like a burning sensation.

"I'm good but I'm not that good." He sounds like he's purring.

"Shit. Hayden. What?" I grabbed my work phone instead of the other one. Three-date Tate is probably out of his mind with worry because I haven't answered his confirmation texts.

"You called me," Hayden says.

"No. My ass did."

"What else can your ass do?" I bet he's smirking.

Trying to keep it flirty and not sounding like he's been a frequent thought lately, I say, "Tease you into submission. It's that good. Now, why did you text me?"

He groans and my body lights up. *Remember, you hate him. Hate him so fucking much.*

"It was a preemptive apology. And I'm curious how many more Mormon calls I'm going to have to field. They're starting to wear me down," he says.

I laugh, moving forward in line, leaning on my grocery cart. "Sorry, I removed you from the lists, but sometimes I can't stop it. But what were you saying? Go on." I wish I knew what he looked like.

He says, "Before we called the truce, I did something."

"WHAT?" Everyone jumps around me as I yell.

"Calm down there, loud woman."

I look around and shrug at everyone still staring at me.

He continues, "About three weeks ago Dax and I set up a profile for you on BeANanny.com."

"That explains the random calls asking for references and telling me how impressed they are with my early childhood skills."

He laughs. Again, my blood freezes, then boils. I push my cart up a little more. Someone behind me yells about beer. And then a staff member rings that captain's bell they have over at the little manager booth off to the side.

"Dax is taking it down now. No more au pair or nanny inquiries. I'm serious about the truce. As long as you stop signing me up for different religious affiliations. The Scientology guy would not take no for an answer."

The noise behind me intensifies as a little kid wails.

I laugh. "Oh no, the Jehovah's Witness people might be calling, too. But no more. I promise. And I'll call and cancel all the movers."

"What movers?" he says harshly, but it comes out like he's exaggerating to make me laugh.

"This might be one of my better pranks. You know when you fill out the moving form to get an online quote?"

"That's fucking brilliant. They never stop. Fuck. I'm going to have to change my number."

"Six moving companies will be calling to give you a quote. But I know who I called. I'll have my assistant stop them." I lean on the cart and slowly move it forward. I'm shifting my weight back and forth. A kid behind me screeches loudly.

His voice goes a bit distant. "Do you have a kid?"

I'm a bit offended. "Does that matter?"

"No, not at all, it was simply surprising, that's all. I know how hard this job is and I know you're single—" He was concerned I was a single mother. Interesting. Wonder if he comes from a single-parent home.

I interrupt, "You know I'm single, do ya?" I say with a leading tone.

"I have friends in IT as well."

I laugh very hard. "Fine. No. No kids." I surrender to the moment.

"Where are you?" he asks.

"You're always asking me that question. Do you always call from the same place or should I start inquiring about your whereabouts?"

What the hell is this? I'm baffled by all the calls and flirting. It's odd to free up the plotting and revenge part of my brain, but strange to use it this way.

I say, "Trader Joe's, buying ingredients to cook Italian food." I need to bring this back to colleagues. This tiny bit of trust might bite me in the ass.

"And you're cooking Italian food? Do you know what you're doing? You do know my last name, right?"

"Yes, Mr. Corelli. Didn't know I needed to have Italian blood to cook the food of your people for my date."

There's a pause and he clears his throat. I can feel the chill through the phone. Then he finally breaks the silence.

"Does he have all of his shots?" And there's the asshole I know and loathe. Not sure where my fucking brain was turning.

"Yes, and has been apprised of my vicious and vindictive nature." My tone shifts back to work-enemy mode.

His voice is clipped. "Good. I don't have the time to warn the decent good-hearted men of Chicago of your true nature. Gotta go. I'll take the nanny thing down. Have a good date, Harpy."

"Ciao, Asshole." I end the call before he can.

Fucker. God, no one makes me this angry this quickly. Why act like a dick? He contacted me. Asshole.

"Ma'am, do you want to check out?"

I shake my head loose from my anger. Well, almost.

"Ma'am? I'm freaking twenty-eight. Save your ma'ams for when I'm older."

"Fine. Can we get going, miss?"

Dick. Nah. Not in the mood for this. I take a bottle of wine out of the cart and toss a twenty at the kid. "Keep the change. And enjoy putting it all back, junior."

I'm unhinged. I just shut down that innocent kid. That's not who I am. I smash out a text to him and start the car. Three-Date Tate is getting takeout and real lucky tonight.

BETTE: Asshole.

He answers instantly.

JERKFACE: You already said that. Did you need something?

BETTE: ACKKKKKKKKKKKKKKKK. I cannot wait to bury you and your smug assface.

JERKFACE: Smug face or assface?

BETTE: Leave me alone.

JERKFACE: Then stop texting me.

I toss my phone in the back of the car. I scream as I'm pulling out. There's no one on this earth more confusing than Hayden Corelli.

Harsh sunlight is streaming through my window. I'm a little sore from yesterday. I roll away from the light and towards the rest of my bed. I look over and smile at the pillow across from me. It's empty. Shutting down Three-Date Tate was the right thing to do. His kiss was drab. Can a kiss be colorless? Well Three-Date Tate's was. I'm pretty sure his kiss will color someone else's world, but it's not mine. I'm going to skip my workout today, stay in bed, and not think about work or him.

BETTE

"YO! I NEED YOU HERE. THIS SHIT ISN'T GOING TO SELL ITSELF. WORDS. I need words from you."

I look up from our well-loved cherry-covered couch as Sophie's waving her arms at me. She's holding up two fantastic pieces of dog food art. We went with a cutting edge, modern sense. To update the ideas behind a one-hundred-year-old company. It's as good today as it was for a farm dog in the depression. The company has innovated and the food is now organic and woke. Can dog food be woke?

Sophie looks haggard.

I ask, "Did you stay up all night and do these?"

"No, these took a couple of hours. I stayed up all night doing some dude named Chad." I roll my eyes. "Come on. Chad's a cute name. And his dick was def the cutest I've seen in a while. How was Three-Date Tate's dick?"

I shrug and get up. I write the word "Arf" on a giant sticky note and slap it on the artwork I like better.

"None of that is helpful to me," Sophie says, then climbs

onto her chair and squats, pulling her arms around her knees.

"Fine. I sent him home after he scoffed at me for ordering food instead of cooking for him. So sadly, he'll forever be Three-Date Tate. Never making it to four."

I have an idea. I grab one of those jumbo Sharpie markers and slash it down the middle of her mock-up. I stand there, pleased with what I've done. She's horrified, but she won't be in a second.

"What the fuck are you doing?"

"Stay with me. What if we did, like, a split screen thing, using your modern idea, but putting half of it in black-and-white. Put 1922 on one side and 2022 on the other. Then identical dogs. Each just saying 'Arf.'" Sophie starts sketching. "And then we tag it. If it was good enough for Scruffy's great-great-great-great-grandfather, it's good enough for Scruffy."

"Scruffy?"

I shrug. "It's a working dog name. But concept-wise, what do you think?"

She's drawn half a turn of the century farmhouse and half a modern modular house mashed together, but divided down the center of her paper. She sketched it that quickly.

I say, "ARF." I raise my eyebrows and she throws her arms in the air and we dance.

We sit back down and Sophie says, "So you had an expiration date."

"What?"

"It's the date when they hit that point and you let the almost relationship expire."

I nod. She's clever, but I don't want to talk about my string of tepid husband-material dud dates. Dudes who will most definitely fertilize a lawn in the future. Or own a lot of wrenches and know what to do with them, even if they can't find a clit.

I turn it on her, "Says the woman who is an all-you-can-eat buffet."

"Yes, but you know after the asshole I was married, this is my reward for divorcing. This pilates body was meant to fuck twenty- and thirty-year-olds well into my eighties."

She grabs our coffee mugs, and I flump down in my chair. Then she crosses the room and puts a hand on my shoulder.

"You can't stay hung up on a thing that happened to you ages ago. No man or woman is ever worth this much brain space."

"He is. I mean, was. I've told you it all before. Blah, blah, blah. Danny is my unhealthy standard and until I get that deep-in-my-soul ache and flutter, they'll all be Three-date Tates."

"That doesn't even sound like a hopeful romantic."

"I have this job and I'm going to get the better job. I get to crush my rival." Whoa. Did my adrenaline just surge at the thought of Hayden? No. That's a terrible idea. I cannot crush *on* my rival. I will not allow myself to be sexually attracted to a voice. It's just another way of not actually dating anyone. Masturbate to him, ok, sure. It's great fodder, but like him, hell no.

I put two fingers to the pulse in my throat and make sure my heart rate is normal. I flip my wrist to see my Apple Watch telling me that it is, indeed, racing. I'll harness this reaction and redirect it towards loathing.

Sophie is standing with one hand on her hip, mugs in the other, wearing a quizzical look. "What the fuck was that all about?" Then mimes me calming down and checking my watch.

I clap and hold my hands together, then point at her. "Game time focus."

"Then why are you flushed?"

I feel my overheated cheeks betraying my purpose. I might need to take the morning off to retreat to my bedroom with batteries and work this out of my system.

"It's nothing but pure rage."

"Good. Funnel it."

The art looks killer and my words are flowing. This pitch is going to shut down all other "rounds." There's no way they don't give us the job immediately. It's been a couple of days of sheer focus and freedom from the Boston mafioso. Three-Date Tate was useful for something, he scared off Hayden. That is a good thing. Clear minds all around.

The truce was the best idea. And in a weird, warped way, I trust him. It's an alliance and an honor thing. I'm more relaxed at work and I have a shit-ton of extra time because I'm not scheming. I'm a little bored but nothing a new hobby can't fix. Perhaps, I'll knit.

I'm staring at the door when our Admin director, the one that handles everything but the creative stuff, Chet, fills the doorframe. He always talks as if we're all in a 1940's newsroom. He even wears a vest most days. I imagine if they'd let him, he'd chomp on a stub of a cigar and call us all "Scoop." He smooths his vest, then tugs it into place, as if it will cover his hips or middle-aged beer belly if he pulls hard enough.

"What's up, Chet?"

He points at me, and his face is a bit red and hard. "Miller. Your keister. Conference Room. NOW." He jerks his chin. I'd take offense if it was anyone else. But he refers to everyone the same way. He's an equal opportunity keister labeler. And his tone of voice never shifts.

I could be in trouble or getting praised, it all sounds the same from him. It took me two years not to take things personally, triggered by my upbringing. I used to take everything personally and didn't want to disappoint him. I was raised to never question, but now I know differently.

A picture of Kris and me in front of the house where I grew up catches my eye. My parents moved to a town an hour away when I went to college. I'm pretty sure it was out of spite and to put me far from Kris, who my father thought was a bad influence. But after she died, I stepped up my life. Pushing back on all the boundaries she taught me to challenge.

Right before my dad passed away, I let loose, raging against the narrow gilded cage he tried to keep me in. I called him a gaslighting bully. Then he scolded me for an hour. He disapproved of every decision I made on my own: career, college, love life, friend group, even exercising at a gym. His philosophy was only the lazy needed to pay to sweat around other people. He never stopped trying to control me, either behind the scenes or by shame. I'm sure I sent him to his final beyond pissed off.

After his hospital bed lecture, I kissed him on the forehead and walked out the door, grateful I'd become my own person. And I've never regretted a second since.

People stare as I follow Chet. I shrug as I pass, but everyone is pale faced and one girl has her hand over her mouth. WTF. These people work for me. I don't like to be kept in the dark. This shit stops as soon as I'm done with whatever Chet needs.

He stands by the conference room but won't open it, just gestures to the window to the left of the door. He only crosses his arms that way when he's about to ream us for something. I can't imagine what I've done. He double smooths his vest. That can't be good.

HAYDEN

I SPENT THE MORNING WORKING ON THE MOCK-UP OF OUR KILLER concept. Matching the old to the new. I painted all night. It got that woman out of my head. Honestly, the thing that pissed me off the most was the idea of her making Italian food. I know she fucked it up. I could've helped if she'd asked.

I stretch out on the carpet and let the lull of our detente roll over me. I'm a touch hollow, though. I've felt the lack of Bette over the past week. Might have to fire up an intern competition. I breathe in and out. Then my peace is broken by four things simultaneously and I sit straight up.

Monica bolts into my office.

Dax follow Monica.

My cellphone rings.

My office phone rings.

Monica and Dax talk over each other.

"What the hell did you do?" she squawks.

"Don't answer that." Dax warns as he attempts to show me something on his phone.

I jump up and grab my cell. I glance down and my cock stirs when I see it's my little Chicago Harpy.

Dax gets insistent, "DON'T answer any of those!"

Monica is huffing, and I answer my phone, blowing off his warning and waving him off.

"Well—"

I'm interrupted, and not by her warm, sexy voice. "You. I loathe you. You fucking lying piece of shit. I fell for it. I truly thought we were at a place where I could at least trust the alliance, if not you. And you're shit. I'm so disappointed in you. I'm pissed at myself for trusting you. You played me. You destroyed my team's confidence in me. Among a thousand other things. I'm fucking stunned by your charming deception. You really want to destroy my career. You lied."

"Slow down. I've never lied to you." And that's pretty shocking for me with women.

"Truce over. You can hang yourself with your project for all I care. Don't speak to me. Go through my assistant. I don't want to hear you or from you. You're an unscrupulous piece of garbage."

It's like I stepped off a plane in Iceland without a coat. I have chills running everywhere and my stomach turns. She hates me for real. Like, not just competition ribbing hate, but soul crushingly despises me, and I don't know why. I don't understand anything coming out her mouth. I've never heard her this truthfully angry. Dax shoves his phone in my face and I see the bill of sale. Then he pulls up a text that reads: *Done.*

My head falls to my chest as I sit on the edge of my desk. She's still yelling at me—the words are running together as my brain focuses on my colossal fuck-up. Monica is scowling. I cover my phone to whisper to Dax.

"Fix it. I'll pay anything. Get a crew there NOW." He nods and disappears to take care of it.

She slows down and I interrupt her, "Bette. Please. Listen."

"Nope." And she hangs up. My posture slumps as Monica glares at me.

"Mon, I forgot. I swear."

"You forgot what? Business ethics? Humanity?"

"I thought the BeANanny.com was the last thing going. Shit. I custom-ordered 15,000 ping pong balls months ago. We prepaid a dude to break in, dump them, and crawl out through the ceiling tiles. It's an impressive and expensive prank." I try to get her to see this was an act of genius. She scowls at me. "I get it. But it's ping pong balls. Seriously, it was six months ago. I was totally down with the truce. I swear on my honor."

"Swear on something else." She pops a hip.

"I swear on your honor. Dax and I forgot."

"Don't put the blame anywhere but squarely on your shoulders. He may go along with your asshole behavior, but he's not the asshole." I rush over, putting a hand on her shoulder, and she bristles.

"I promise, I forgot but it's just ping pong balls. I did it to annoy her, but it's different now." I'm uncomfortable in my skin. It's like it's too small for my body.

She turns to me. "It sure as shit is. She's sitting in HR getting reprimanded and possibly fired for 15,000 ping pong balls that say 'I Love Dicks.' With her name on the other side. Chet freaked out and now Eva and Rinaldi are getting into it. Sophie's being questioned."

"Why?"

"They think she pranked Chet. And HR is calling it a gay slur." Oh my fucking God. This went so sideways.

I run my hands over my face and into my hair. "Why am I not being hauled to HR?"

Monica stares at me for way too long. I'm flicking my fingers at my side like I'm getting ready for a gun fight.

"Because she's not you."

It takes a moment for it all to sink in. Dax gives me a thumbs-up that the cleanup crew has been taken care of. It hits me as Monica slams my door. Bette didn't tell them it was me. She took the rap. She didn't give me up. This is a fucking mess.

Why not throw me under the bus? I tossed her under for the eggplant thing. I pace the room. I might need to fly to Chicago and apologize. No. That's stupid. I've never seen the woman. What, am I going to stalk the twenty-seven Chicago Bette Millers? I could go to the office and wait for her.

She's a better person than I am. I have to be better.

I whip open my door. "Monica!"

She doesn't even stand up from her cubicle. "What? This bettah be good and it bettah be contrition." Everyone's looking at me.

"Everyone, back to work. Prank gone wrong, that's all!" I lean over Monica's desk and she still won't look at me. "Are they in New York?"

"Zurich."

"Get me on a call with them first."

"Tell me you're doing more. You need to do all the fucking things right." She never swears at me. I'm a bit nauseous.

"I will. And I'm sure if I forget some of them, you'll remind me."

She flips me off.

I walk away and pray whatever bullshit I come up with

appeases all. It certainly wasn't meant as a gay slur, just a Bette slur. We've never been caught before. Even the printer thing never got any major attention. She didn't even get dinged for it, really. Just a quick wrist slap.

The ping pong balls were retaliation for her two full days of hourly singing telegrams. She even sent one to a restaurant while I was on a date. Dax runs in with a company-wide apology memo explaining our badly timed and ill-conceived joke. It states we'll take all the blame.

"Change it to only me and add a copy of the bill of sale with my name on it. I'm fucking serious. Don't screw yourself over with my shit." He shakes his head. "I'm not fucking around. You're my boy and we don't do each other like this. My idea all the way. I can take the fall."

He shakes his head no, "I'm along for the ride." I smack his shoulder and nod.

Back in my office, I slip on my shoes, hitch my bag on my shoulder and nod to Dax. He'll send it out. We have a rhythm—sometimes even entire conversations in a nod.

I truly dislike the pinched-ass woman who runs our HR office. I breathe in and exhale loudly, and as I'm about to knock on her door she says, "Of course, Hayden Corelli is involved in the scandal that's rocking our company." Never fuck anyone in your office. It never goes well.

I'm afraid to talk to her. But if Bette gets fired because of this, I'll be disappointed. I want her gone, but not like this. And then something warm and wonderful thrums through my core. Do I want her gone?

BETTE

JERKFACE: I'm so sorry. I forgot. If you don't believe me —Dax is the responsible forthright one. And he forgot too. Please forgive me. I can't stand you being in trouble. Hate me for my work and my devastating good looks, but don't hate me for a prank gone wrong.

JERKFACE: We're taking full responsibility. You will be exonerated. Exalted even. Especially when they fire my ass for this dumbass prank. I'm truly sorry.

Asshole pulled off some kind of charming sorcery, like the hot blond long haired Henry Cavill in that show that's like a Twilight/Superman spin off or something. I don't remember but the point is he's Teflon.

He saved both our asses. I didn't give him up, but it says a lot that he confessed. I wanted to protect him and live up to our truce, even if he couldn't. But in an odd way, he did. Within an hour of my ass being scolded, the ping pong balls were cleaned up. I might have kept one.

BETTE: I hate you because the prank was so good. But sadly, whatever trust we had is gone. Your pretty words mean nothing. Now, I get to bury you without remorse. Thanks for that.

We're a week post the PPB incident and we've turned in our work. It's a blind selection from Arco Dog Food and Eva and Rinaldi. We all hate not being in the room. But our work needs to speak for itself. We'll know by the end of the day. I've been flipping a pen cap on and off for about twenty minutes. We literally have no work. Nothing to button up or brainstorm. Sophie throws a pillow at my face.

"I'm going to kill you if you flip that fucking cap one more time."

I throw the pen across the room. She dodges it.

I say, "It's the only thing keeping me sane."

"The pitch is awesome."

I stand and put my purse on my shoulder. There's no reason we should be here. "Let's get drunk."

"Cool, I'm going to pee, then we'll go." Sophie always informs me of her bodily functions. No clue why.

I was flipping the pen to stop myself from texting him. We've not exchanged messages since his apology. The next round of this insane competition, we fly to New York and he can't dodge me with Hulk makeup. I know Sophie and I will go on. Maybe I'm so anxious because I want him to go, also. I don't want to get this job out of pity from the fucking PPB incident. I want to face him head on.

It's as if he's reading my mind.

JERKFACE: I'll show you mine if you show me yours.

I grin at his double entendre.

BETTE: On the count of three.

JERKFACE: One.

BETTE: Two.

JERKFACE: Three.

I push enter to give him access to a folder on our cloud. And he does the same.

It's stunning. They hired an artist to paint a watercolor. Theirs is more pastoral, but we basically pitched the same fucking concept. Ours had a more modern edge to it and we didn't commission outside work, but it's good.

JERKFACE: You've got to be kidding me?

BETTE: I know! Insane. Yours looks really good. Not as good as ours but good.

JERKFACE: I disagree. Ours is the better version. But 'ARF' is inspired.

BETTE: Well, I guess if they hate our collective concepts, we're all out.

JERKFACE: Or we're all in. And then New York.

BETTE: And then New York.

BETTE

I'M SITTING OFF TO THE SIDE AT A BAR IN CLINTON, ALSO KNOWN as Hell's Kitchen. I'm humoring Sophie by going out because she flew here for moral support. I'd rather be back at my hotel. Four teams moved on: Vancouver, LA, Chicago, and of course, Boston. I can't wait to meet him, then crush him. But there's also the part of me that wants to see him. I'm curious about the person that's opened me up a bit. I still hate him, but I wouldn't miss this meeting for anything in the world.

Sophie is sucking face with some shaggy-haired blond man. Kinda hot watching them. I can't imagine what it's like being them. He seems familiar, but it might be because she has a type. Oh. She just made a big move and climbed on top of him.

I need to climb on top of a man. It's been so damn long my vagina would probably creak if I spread my legs. I start thinking about Hayden a bit. What if he's not the Hulk? Hideous? Or finds me hideous? Or I've imagined all this heat?

Sophie waves to me and drags the man behind her out

the door. The voyeurism portion of her evening is complete. I wave and play with my ruby drink stirrer.

I have a killer outfit for tomorrow—chic and it hugs all my curves. I might be on the shorter side, but I'm proud of my hourglass figure and my shoes. They're Chanel, and I slept with them on a pillow next to me last night.

I really need to get laid. Or a hobby.

My mind wanders, searching for that ball of confidence I'll need. Like a specter in the dark, there's a spicy, citrusy, musky smell behind me. My brain is conjuring figures from shadows deep in my recollections. If I close my eyes, I can picture the boy the scent should belong to. First, I get warm all over, then that familiar twang of lonely that always follows his memory washes over me. I'm left with the feeling that I was foolish to believe he loved me. Or that love could honestly conquer all.

I sigh and stare at the rest of the bar. There's a bunch of girls dancing. Kris used to force me to go out there. She taught me not to care what other people thought so much. I should be a dancer again.

Nah, it's too late to be a dancer. I try to shake off the imagined scent. My sense memory is working overtime tonight. I stir my drink more violently, waiting to escape his grip.

That smell is unhinging me.

I slam my drink. I turn around and a pair of blue-grey eyes are about to bore a hole right through me. They're older, but they're his. The boy that belongs to the citrus smell. His cropped dark hair has grown out. His body filled out, broader and more powerful. He seems taller somehow. He's flicking his thumbs out of his clenched fists. And my heart aches. He's across the room, and I'm afraid my mind is playing tricks on me.

He's so unfamiliar, but his eyes belong to me. My body is a symphony of nerve endings trying to communicate, but it's all a mass of loud noises inside my head and soul. He's staring at me, and I hope I don't have something stuck to my face. Does he recognize me?

Perhaps the one who ghosted me is, indeed, a ghost. He can't be real. I'm overwhelmed with all the emotions in the entire damn world and my knees buckle at the weight of carrying them. I can barely breathe. Like, super shallow, I'm-going-to-hyperventilate breathing. Hopefully, he has a paper bag or something to make sure I don't pass the fuck out from the sight of the man who disappeared and left a hole inside me that's never been filled.

I have to know if he's real. I jerk my body to the side and his eyes follow. Then I jump back to my original place and his eyes move with me. He's real. His lips curl up in the corners, like in the reaches of my memory and I return the smile. I've never loved anything like I loved those eyes and the boy attached to them. I walk towards him as if there's anywhere else in the world I could possibly go.

I touch his shirt to make sure I'm not absolutely lock-me-up insane. And I shudder a bit from the brief contact, but I have my proof of life. When I look up again, there's nothing but his gaze and our history caught between us.

He steps toward me and invades my space. I should scream and run or smash his face in. I should yell all the things and ask all the questions that have no answers.

He picks up my hand and rubs his thumb over my left ring finger as if to ask if I belong to anyone. How could I when I've never stopped being his? I shake my head slightly to indicate there's no one else.

His hands slide around my waist and mine go around his neck—as if we just did this yesterday. He drifts a light knuckle down my cheek and traces my jaw. My breath and nerves steady with his touch. Then he traces my lips. Ten years and an unspoken lifetime sit between us, but in this space and time right now, in this second, we're us again. I've never been more terrified or elated. I exhale slowly but don't break eye contact.

He puts his forehead to mine.

We're touching for the first time since we left Paris. Since he said, *I can't wait to see you.* Since he told me he loved me. He was hidden from my world for a decade, and it's as if someone just lifted a veil and revealed he'd been here the whole time.

"Lizzie." A name from history. It's barely a whisper, but I can still hear it.

I breathe out, "Danny." And then his cotton-candy-colored lips are lightly pressed against mine. All my scattered pieces are like a series of camera flashes suddenly making sense in a timeline I never thought would be repaired. He kisses me, then buries his face in my neck. I find myself on his shoulder, clutching him closer. Tears fill my eyes as I exhale all the sorrow I carry like a good-looking tote bag. You know, the kind that goes with everything, so you use it constantly. That's my sorrow. It just goes with everything, always has except what is happening right here. Finally, I get to set it down for a moment.

He whispers as he tangles in my hair, "Come with me." I grab my clutch. I back up and look at him.

I whisper back, "Yes. My answer to you has always been yes." And the boy who showed me everything I thought love was supposed to be, leads me out of the bar—neither of us explaining or saying a word to each other. I simply float after him onto the noisy streets of Manhattan.

His large hand is soft and warm like I know his heart to

be. Damn. This is the heartbreak of all heartbreaks and the love of all loves. I didn't realize I wasn't fully breathing until he kissed me. And now I'm lightheaded with all the air filling my lungs and body. Just outside, with the humidity reminding me what time of year it is, he pushes me against the wall.

Our voices are low. His fingers caress my jaw and he's staring at me. "You can't be real. This can't be my Lizzie."

"I am. I always have been." I'm completely unguarded. I'm vulnerable and open, and I don't care if he knows I've pined.

He exhales and I continue quietly, "I couldn't find you. You broke me. And all my pain is just gone, disappeared as you touch me."

His lips are on mine before I can finish. There's a need and a hunger that's familiar, but different. It's full of melancholy and lust instead of youthful fervor. That feeling when you're young—that nothing has a deadline or could possibly have an ending—is gone from this kiss. We know things can end.

He's rasping at me, "Lizzie. You disappeared from me. You broke me. And now, I should ignore how good it feels to hold you so you can't break me again."

I'm kissing his neck, then pull back. "What?"

We both look at each other. I don't know how to process this.

I say, "You left me."

"Never."

I'm not comprehending information correctly. I'm scrambled and excited. He's forceful as his lips claim mine. His matured and skilled tongue is different and much sexier than high school Danny's. My tongue battles his for dominance, almost to prove we're both here, and this is happening.

He moans in my ear, "Christ, Lizzie. I want all of you. I want all of you again. Is that something I can have?" I pull him to my lips and chase his tongue in his mouth.

He speaks on my lips, "Who do I have to fight to claim you again?" Tears fill my eyes. "Shh. Ne pleure pas mon doux pétard." He calls me his sweet firecracker and I feel any last shred of self-control or doubt rip from my heart. I may get burnt to a crisp again, but I welcome the heat.

I exhale my soul to him. "You. I belong to you."

His lips are firm and insistent. His tongue is wild inside my mouth and I want it in other places. I feel his desire trapped between our bodies and I want it. But I also want all of him. The musk of this man is teasing and tempting me. He pulls me closer. I have to stop this before I'm carried away and don't get my answers.

'I'm so confused,' says my head but my heart compels me to hold him tight. My head shifts back in charge to try and think through this rationally. I've got to walk away from him right now.

I have to prioritize me. I can't miss the meeting, not because of Hayden, but because of the job. I threw my world away for Danny once and it was a disaster. The scramble to set things right and the climb out of the plans we made almost destroyed me. I have to get this job for me. But I think I get to have this man, too. This fucking man who was fated to me long ago and for some reason is here, in front of me.

He kisses my neck and makes his way to my ear. I moan and gasp at how skillful he's become.

His teeth capture my ear and he whispers, "I don't think either of us has the entire story. But I have to go. I hate this, but I have to fucking go. I don't want to leave you tonight but I have no choice. Because if I stay, then I'm not sure I'll ever walk away."

"I know." Thank God he has to go. Perhaps together we can find the strength to stop from fucking on the sidewalk.

"Say you'll be with me tomorrow. That you won't disappear or run. We talk, we reacquaint, without our bodies that seem to remember what to do. I need to know why and what happened to you. I want to tell you everything that's happened to me since the last moment you told me you loved me. I want you, Lizzie. I can't have either of those things tonight. Tomorrow. But I have to go now. Trust me when I tell you it's important."

I smile. I put my hands on his face. "Danny. My Danny. Yes. Yes. Meet me tomorrow and then I'm all yours."

"Fucking perfect." He reaches for my purse and opens my clutch. He pulls out my work phone and I give him my real phone. He puts his name and number in my contacts, then texts me. "Please say you won't ghost me."

I say, "You can't leave me. Please tell me you'll meet me. First, we talk."

He nods. "As long as the talking is quick." His lips curl up and I laugh. I touch his face. He says, "It's too much. This is too much. Trust me. I'll be there. I'm trusting you." I know what he means. I can't have Danny floating around in my head as I prep to conquer.

"I have to go for tonight, before I can't," I say.

I break away from him, but he pulls me back and we spend the next ten minutes kissing, as if we're in some kind of competition. My body and mind are so light. Brain buzzing. Where has he been? I've never been able to find him. Not anywhere.

I've searched for Danny Danson, artist, maybe a million

times. I searched every gallery in the Northeast. I searched the NFL records for my former high school football star. It was too painful to follow his football career in college, but I've seen some highlights when I search for him. There was an injury and Danny disappeared. He was gone, no address and the only Christopher Daniel Dansons I found were a car salesman in Iowa and a criminal in upstate New York, but that's a Chris Danson.

My Danny was supposed to be there at my door. He was supposed to be on that plane all those years ago.

Then I disappeared into a life without him and without explanation. The pain was always with me, sometimes so crippling, I'd do reckless things. I did all the things my father forbid. I slept with strangers. I took random pills offered to me. I'd drink until I was surrounded by friends of friends because my actual friends couldn't be around me. I wanted to be numb, but the pain was always waiting for me when I woke. And then I began to move on and simply carried it with me.

I numbed it all until Kris pulled me out of it and reminded me who I was. There'd be no Bette without the pain of Danny and the strength of Kris. She helped me reinvent. Then she died and now I've been strong for both of us in this life. It's her voice telling me to leave Danny tonight, so I can make sure to claim something for myself. Don't be someone's accessory.

I've cried very little since that time—like I used up all the tears I'm allotted for a lifetime on him. I still ache for him from time to time, but now it's just the sorrow I live with. What if I've built him up? What if he's not the perfect man who lives rent free in my head? My questions quiet with his touch. He's the piece I've been missing. The one I glossed over and pretended I didn't need.

When I got married, it was Danny I dreamed of. I thought if I forced myself to belong to someone else, I could escape the heartache. Dumbest three months of my life. But it was something my father opposed, so I made it a priority. After a year of being numb from heartache, I woke up and realized how many strings in my life my father was pulling. My entire schedule at school and the professors themselves were all under his control. I changed majors, got new advisers, and slipped away from his grasp as quickly as possible. My ex-husband took on a key role, as if that was the moment of demarcation between Lizzie and Bette. My wedding was when I truly became Bette Miller, leaving Lizzie Fox to wallow in the past, weak, broken and subservient.

Two weeks before I got married, Kris and I went on a rampage of searching for Danny. As if she knew I needed to put it all to rest. Kris reached out to everyone from that trip. Unfortunately, no one had any clue, and Tony was the only one who blew us off. My father refused to call me Bette, and it was gratifying to defy him and redefine myself.

Danny never responded to me, so I moved on. Eventually, that sharp pain in my soul dulled. And then it was something I always carried with me, like my phones. Don't leave home without your heartache. How could it all disappear? I'm willing to give in instantly to his touch after a decade of pain, longing, and confusion.

He hauls me back to him tightly. He's in my ear again, so I don't miss a word he has to say. "Lizzie. Fucking Lizzie right here in front of my face." I stand back and smile. He rushes back to me and says, "And I get to have you tomorrow." We've only spoken in whispers and hushed tones as if we're afraid of scaring away this reality.

"Tomorrow," I mutter to him.

He kisses me once more quickly and jogs away from me. I feel exhilarated and really fucking confused.

DANNY: Tomorrow, my Lizzie. We figure out what happened. And then we let it go. Tomorrow you're mine.

LIZZIE: I already am. But tomorrow I get to hold you.

DANNY: This time I'll request you don't let me go.

LIZZIE: Same.

DANNY: 1 pm meet me at La Grande Boucherie in midtown.

LIZZIE: French. How fitting.

DANNY: I think so.

LIZZIE: I can't believe this is real.

DANNY: Me neither, but let's just go with it. Perhaps we're both dreaming.

LIZZIE: Or hallucinating.

DANNY: Best fucking drug ever.

HAYDEN

I NEED THIS MEETING TO BE QUICK. I HAVE A LUNCH TO ATTEND, questions to be answered, and a woman to bed. Good fucking night that kiss was hot. She's the woman version of the girl I've dreamed of every fucking day since she stopped taking my calls. Since emails and texting halted and she broke my heart. I never should have left her last night. I didn't sleep, crazed by lust and the desire to know why my soulmate walked away.

I want this fucking job. I thought I'd be battle ready. I wanted to see what Bette looks like and see if that thing I felt for her the last couple of weeks translates in person. But mostly, I want this meeting over so I can get back to Lizzie. My mind is reeling. Dumbass move to leave her last night. I think I was in shock.

She shattered me, then disappeared off the planet. I mourned her like she was dead, and it didn't work. I still fucking thought about her all the time. Everything was perfect, then I was told not to get on that plane or speak to her again. Then Lizzie Fox disappeared completely.

I checked obituaries and social media for years. Never a

mention of Liz or Lizzie Fox or Elizabeth Fox. Or Elizabeth Marjorie Fox. News of her father popped up for papers he'd published, but never a mention of her or even a picture.

I got the nerve up to call her father at work my senior year of college, after I ripped up my shoulder and any hope of the NFL was crushed. It had been three and half years since we spoke, and I still measured every girl to her. I wanted someone in my corner who didn't give a shit about football, or what I could do with it, but cared about me. I thought that was Lizzie.

He told me she was engaged to someone else. That's the moment I let hope die and turned towards a different life.

Then, there she was, in my arms and on my lips, as if not a moment had been missed. No ring on her finger, no resistance in my arms, and I walked away last night, trying to make sense of it all. Today she doesn't leave my sight until I get answers to why and what and how I can still feel so intensely about her.

I don't know where she lives or if she ever got married, but I do know a piece of me came back to life last night. That fucking kiss.

I need to calm down so I can nail this meeting. I take out my keys and stroke the Eiffel Tower key chain Lizzie bought at the flea market all those years ago. It's my talisman and perhaps it brought her back into my life. Today I get my dream job, bury my rival, and claim my love.

* * *

The dynamic duo of advertising gods—Eva and Rinaldi enter with a flourish. They're the ones who insisted upon creating this Thunderdome of a circus to vie for the top position. I'm anxious for Bette to arrive. I've been captivated by her but I'm captured by Lizzie. However, I still want to put a face with the fantasies in my head.

"Hayden." I give a quick back-pat hug to Eva. My head is solidly back in this game and away from Lizzie's lips.

"Eva, Rinaldi, you look as well as ever." They walk behind the desk, moving in tandem. Eva sits in the office chair while her husband/partner/lover—we don't really know what they are to each other—slings himself on the desk with one leg on the ground. They're both wearing slightly oversized white suits, as if they're a Talking Heads tribute band. They have homes in Aspen, Zurich, Belgium, and Paris. Ah, Paris. No. Focus, Hayden. Lizzie later. Crush Bette now. Rinaldi nods towards me.

Eva speaks and she's trilling her R's. "Hayden Corelli. Darling. Boy Genius. The hope of our future. The not-quite chosen one. Scamp. Rake. Prankster." She holds out the last "r" in that one.

"Again, I'm so sorry for the ping pong ball misunderstanding."

Rinaldi says, "Hardly a misunderstanding. A full-on assault and we secretly loved it. Your victim should be here any moment."

"She's hardly a victim." I defend her. I don't want her to fail because of fucking ping pong balls. But every moment she's late is a moment away from Lizzie. I'm on the edge of my seat waiting for the big reveal. I'm wearing a suit that matches my eyes and a tie that matches Lizzie's chartreuse ones. It's what I wear when I want to dominate.

I cross my legs. "Can we skip all of this and tell me my start date? You know that difficult woman from the Midwest can't possibly keep up with what Dax and I have been doing."

Sophie can stay but Bette goes. I need her gone. Damn, that sounded like Michelle Michelle.

I thrive on competition. I've always been grace under

pressure. When I was signal calling, it was the thing the announcers remarked on. On the field or in this fucking room, I'm completely in charge.

“Hayden, not yet, tut-tut.” They waggle a finger at me. “Next round, we're switching creative teams. You must be able to work with anyone and do it quickly. Dax might retain his place, but today, because your campaigns were so similar, it gave us a deliciously wicked idea.” Eva climbs on the desk and kneels. She leans forward and it's both disturbing and intriguing.

“You will create a 360 campaign for Boast soap in a month. Pressure." They both wave spirit fingers in front of their faces. And Rinaldi whispers loudly, mirroring Eva, "Pressure."

I lean forward. "You want a lightning-fast turnaround on a pitch with someone I've never worked with before and don't know."

"You know her!" Eva smiles like she's deranged, throwing her arms in the air as Rinaldi steeples his fingers.

My heart sinks as the two of them grin and say nothing. Fuck no, this can't be happening.

I put my hand up. “Don't say her name. this won't work. Don't do this to me, it's cruel and unusual punishment. Please don't say her name.”

"Bette Miller," Eva yells, jumping off the desk and striking a dramatic pose. Rinaldi mirrors her pose and they point to the empty chair next to me.

The door opens as her name is spoken aloud, like they summoned the beast.

"I'm here. I'm here." Her voice shoots right to my balls. This can't be happening. She's balancing too many things and drops her keys.

I pick them up and my world flips completely upside

down. There's no justice in karma. I'm speechless and unmoored as I retrieve her keys with a worn pink Eiffel Tower key chain to match my own.

She's spinning around looking for them and it's charming and everything I don't want it to be. Then she sees me as I hand them back to her, our eyes as wide as possible as we realize what's happening.

Her voice is snapping into my brain as pieces come together in our fucked-up puzzle. How did we not notice for years? And if it had flickered recognition, what would I have said? *Hey, are you Lizzie Fox?* Did she know it was me? Her reaction and kiss last night says otherwise, but neither of us recognized each other's voices. It's wild and fucked-up what the mind can do.

Rinaldi stands and gestures to each one of us in turn. "Good. Good. Hayden Corelli, please formally meet Bette Miller."

Her voice sounds as dry and cracked as my throat feels. "Danny."

My response slips out, soft and scared. "Lizzie."

Part Three
Troisième Partie
Still the Present

BETTE

It falls out of my mouth. "Oh, my fucking God."

I've never hated and loved someone with equal intensity at once. This is a lie and the cruelest prank of all. He must have known, we can't both be clueless idiots.

Eva and Rinaldi come over and give me a hug. Danny, Danny Danson. Danny Danson is Hayden Corelli. Hayden is Danny. How? Who the hell is Danny? How did Hayden replace him? Is he a doppelgänger? No one will ever believe us because this is absurd. But what happened to him? And does he know how intensely I hate Hayden? Or how much Danny wrecked me? Or how much I loved sparing with Hayden? That I'm still in love with a version of Danny. That I compare all other almost relationships with the way I remember feeling about him. Shit. I hope he can't read all of that on my face.

There's a burning in my brain and fluttering in my body I'm not sure I can stop. It's possible I'm in A-fib. I glance at my Apple Watch, relieved my heartrate is rapid, but not in a danger zone. I look back up at his eyes and halt a rush of tears from flowing down my cheeks. I blink them away, but I know he sees them.

He nods at me and his lip twitches. It's definitely the guy from last night, the boy from Paris, and the man from all those flirty texts and calls in the last month. The man I loathe for his pranks and love for his belief in me a decade ago are the same damn person.

Eva says, "Bette, are you alright?"

It snaps my focus away from his face and say, "Excuse me for a moment?"

Hayden leans forward as I rush to leave without an answer because I must get my shit together. I instantly dial as I hustle down the hallway. I pull my shirt into place as I pass people, as if the only thing wrong in my life is a wardrobe malfunction.

Sophie picks up immediately. "Is the job ours?"

"Soph. Keep me together."

I speed walk and try to pass it off as casual. Then I sneak into a dark office, close the door, and slink to the floor.

"I'm freaking out."

"Did you get it? Is Hayden hideous?" I breathe in and out. "Are you hyperventilating? Dax said he's not bad-looking."

"Dax?"

"That's the dude I fucked last night. We were way past go when we revealed our names. After a brief moment of laughing, we got down to business. I'm with him now, let me gloat while you breathe."

I tuck a stray hair behind my ear and pinch my leg. It hurts, so I know I'm not in some kind of fugue dream state.

"There's not enough oxygen in the world. Hayden is Danny." There's silence. "High school Danny." I grit my teeth and say forcefully, "Danny."

"Danny with the ridiculous last name that no one believes is real?"

I fling my arms around, as if she's in the room. "YES! He must have changed his name. I don't fucking know."

"And you never recognized the only love of your life, the reason you've had pathetic sex with a string of insanely boring men, was on the other end of the phone? You know you sound like an absolute moron, right? He didn't recognize you, either? Or did he?"

He wouldn't play me like that—or maybe he would? He did break up with me in the dumbest, cruelest fashion. I'm hanging on by a thread, but I defend myself.

I say, "Would you recognize the voice of someone you haven't spoken to in ten years and only knew for three months?"

"Point taken. Not even sure I'd recognize my ex-husband's voice and it's only been two since we last spoke. You never suspected?"

"How? All he did was cut me down and prank me, and Danny only ever propped me up."

"You never told me about the insanely short timeline on this little tale, by the by."

"Whatever. It was love. It was important and I've never felt like that again. That's all beside the point because he's in an office down the hall, and I hate him. We hate him, right?"

I hear her scream across the room, "Dax, did you know Hayden used to have the name Danny? He's texting. Gee, I wonder with whom?" She puts me on speaker and I hear his response.

Dax says, "Holy fuck. She's Lizzie. Bette is Lizzie. Are you fucking with us?" He knows about me. "Babe, did you know Bette was Lizzie?" She's "babe" already? Interesting.

Sophie tells him, "Yeah. You deal with him. I'll deal with her." She takes me off speaker.

"Ask him where the name Hayden came from." I pause and wait.

"No go. That puts me more in the middle, ask him yourself." Sophie yells to Dax, "I know... It's really her... Fucked-up... It's like a wacked-out plot twist no one will buy."

I yell at her, "EXACTLY. But it's real."

Sophie laughs and says to Dax, "She just said the same fucking thing! Ha!" She comes back to me. "Bone him."

"I most certainly will not." But I kind of want to.

Sophie says, "He's as messed up as you right now. Dax is on a group text with Hayden. And some dude named Tony says hi, and that you should rise to the occasion, brave knight. Whatever the fuck that means."

Knight? Then it dawns on me. "HOLY FUCKING SHIT. Dax Ladd is Tony's brother?"

I hear Sophie ask, "Is Tony... oh... got it."

"Yes. Hold on." She shuffles and I hear her repeat exactly what Dax is saying, "And he witnessed this epic love story the two of you tell, and says it was storybook perfect until you broke his heart." Sophie's tone shifts. "Wait."

"Seriously, hold up," I yell.

I hear her challenge Dax, "She didn't break up with him. I've heard this story enough to know he was the dick." They start fighting.

"SOPH!" I need to get back to the office. And now, more than fear or rage, I have an intense curiosity. How did this all happen?

"Woman, this is fucked-up and we're smack in the middle. And I want Dax to smack my ass again. Try to keep the collateral damage to a minimum. I have no advice. No one on the planet would have advice in this situation. Do your best."

"Super helpful. Thanks." I hang up.

I pull at a carpet fiber until it's a long loose string. I have no idea whose office this is. I have no idea what time and place I'm in. Perhaps we're in, like, a space bubble, in that blue phone booth that's has to go 88 miles per hour to send us back into orbit.

Lizzie is done falling apart, it's time for Bette to figure things out. I'll go back in there with all the BPE I know I can muster. I fix my lipstick, straighten my skirt and check my hair, then glide into the room like I own it. Hayden, I mean Danny, puts his phone back in his jacket pocket.

I say, "Sorry, I must have swallowed a whole bunch of bullshit last night and it wasn't sitting well."

Rinaldi winces and puts his fingers up in a cross. "No sickies in here."

I grin. "I'm not sick, just disappointed. I promise."

Rinaldi pulls out a scarlet silk mask from his pants pocket and places it over his mouth. Eva pats him on the back and says, "It's reveal time!"

I'll say it is.

I have extreme emotions and a touch of nausea to contend with right now. My ears are pounding with my own heartbeat. My nose is filled with his maddening citrus musk, and I want to kill him for being both these people. How dare he fucking hide from me for the last five years of corporate bullshit and two years of constant Zoom meetings? If he'd shown his fucking face, we could have avoided all of this. Imagine if I'd shown mine and he didn't show his.

Rinaldi says, "Bette? Can you hear us?" He snaps loudly and I come back to my body.

I turn to Danny, I mean Hayden, and put out my hand. He shakes it and that fucking electric touch—I hope it's torturing him as well. His eyebrows raise and we hold hands longer than we should.

"Nice to put a face with a name," I say and the mutha-fucker scoffs at me. I hate him so much for being the love of my life and I strain to push down my desire.

"Likewise. Elizabeth, is it?" he says.

"Formally, yes." I pull my lips into a tight grin.

"And Miller?" he asks, as if that makes any sense to anyone in the room but us.

"My married name." He goes pale and I don't want to tell him it was a thirteen-week lark six years ago. Fuck him.

But Eva ruins my fun. "Married?!"

Hayden says under his breath, "I was unaware you actually went through with it."

I grit out a fake grin and take a seat. How did he know I was engaged?

"Annulled long ago. Two kids trying to outrun heart-break." I stare at him and all the anger and rejection build to a fine point. All the frustration and heartache that disappeared last night in his arms is right here in this room. I feel the tension coming off him in waves. He's cracking his knuckles and making fists.

This asshole ditched me a decade ago and he's spent the last two years making my life a living fucking hell. Before that, in my first three working at the company, he was a minor annoyance, but there's no world in which Hayden Corelli is my Danny.

He grins at me and flashes his eyebrows. I turn towards our bosses.

"Am I here to claim my job?" I pat Hayden's arm and unfortunately, his bicep is fucking ripped. "There, there,

Hayden, there will be other jobs." I pull on my Bette mask and try to resume who I am. How our relationship should be or how I know—OH MY FUCKING GOD. HOW DO I DO THIS?

Rinaldi starts talking to Eva and the two of them chatter and barely paying attention to us.

I whisper out of the side of my mouth, "How did this happen?"

He leans forward, as if he's tying his shoes. He turns his heads slightly and whispers his reply, "I don't know. How the fuck are you here? And why are you so goddamn beautiful?"

I lose all my breath. And damn, how does he look so good? His suit matches his eyes. I look forward, then glance down at his chest and my mouth falls open. His tie is the color of my eyes. His lips pull into a slight smile, then looks straight ahead as he whispers, "Yes. It's my Lizzie tie."

Eva clears her throat and we both snap to attention again.

Hayden crosses his legs and I hear him breathe in slowly. He used to do that to calm himself down. I don't know if it's from anger or if he gets excited from being insulted.

"You have a month to create an original pitch for Boast deodorant soap. They're doing a rebrand and want your best ideas. You're going to be a fab team."

My head whips to Eva and Rinaldi. He pulls his mask down so they can grimace in tandem. I'm sure it's a grin but the fillers are strong with these two.

"You and Hayden vs the Vancouver and SF offices, who we teamed together as well. All of the regular partners will be compensated, but aren't participating at this level. The leaders of the winning campaign will be in solo consideration for the VP Creative Director job here at the New York office."

Of course, I have to spend time with the one person who controls all of my emotions. I can't let him get ahold of me again, so I muster iron will in an attempt to, hopefully, straighten my spine and allow resolve to replace remorse. I'm in control of me but he's going need to smell different.

"Let our assistant know which city you're working from and they'll make the arrangements."

Wait, what?

He replies, "Sounds good. We'll be in Boston."

"The hell we will," I say. He does not get home-court advantage. Fuck that. "We'll go to Chicago."

Rinaldi speaks as they glide to the door. "Good. We'll put you here on neutral ground in Manhattan for the next month. You can stay in your suite. Ta!"

"What suite?" Hayden is quick to jump on it. He's on his feet, as nimble as he's always been, and turns to them.

Eva says, "You two didn't realize you have an adjoining suite? Open the doors. Bask in the competition! Let my games begin."

Because the coincidences never stop with us. It's like fate isn't just pushing us, but punishing us. It's squishing all this convoluted shit into our narratives.

I look up to the ceiling and question my guardian angel. Kristin, did you do this? How long have you known? A pencil randomly falls from the desk and rolls to my feet. I scoff at the ceiling, *fuck you, Kris.*

Rinaldi leaps into the air, does a pirouette, then says, "There's even a kitchen and a balcony! Exeunt, my darling baby!" Eva shuffles out of the room like her clothes are binding her legs together and giggling. If they didn't pay so well, not sure I'd endure all of this.

The door closes and I immediately leap up to land against the wall furthest from him. The ground is breaking all around us and we're each clinging to facts we know and problems we understand. I can see it in his eyes as they slide back to Danny's slate blue.

"How does this happen?" I reiterate what I've already said, "How does THIS happen?"

He smiles. "Hey, Michelle Michelle. Stop repeating yourself." He shakes his head. We stay suspended in a vat of chaos.

I say softly, "Who the hell is Hayden?"

His shoulders slump and his voice drops to match mine. "You got married." Then he says more forcefully, "To someone who wasn't me. Like, right after you dumped my ass and disappeared. Where the fuck did Lizzie go?"

"She died the day you left her sitting alone in a hotel room in a prom dress crying until dawn."

"Can you blame me after what you did? Without even fucking talking to me."

I spit back at him, "What the fuck are you talking about? You changed your name to hide from me?"

"I changed my last name because of things that happened in my life, not you, you daft woman."

"Showing off your vocabulary. Stay in your lane, graphics."

My life is inside out that he's not dead and wasn't hiding. I had dental work the day of our first video meeting, and my face was swollen and puffy, so I used an avatar. He did too. We kept doing it, neither of us ever showing our face. But his voice. Why didn't I recognize it? To be honest, it's not like hearing it now even feels like Danny, it's too angry.

"You kept the name of a man you didn't love? And who the fuck is Bette?" He shakes his head.

Tears flood my eyes and I'm pissed off. I want to be a fucking iron tiger right now and I'm going to be a marshmallow bunny instead.

I sputter out, "I needed to be someone different. Lizzie had so much pain, so I rebranded her and shoved it all down. I took his last name and Kris came up with Bette. Lizzie Fox's heartbreak was too much to live with, but Bette Miller had a clean slate. She gave me the excuse to find a way past the debilitating agony and low self-esteem."

The anger wanes for a moment and a flicker of Danny surfaces. My soul and my arms want to reach out to him, but my head and the shattered pieces of my heart want to scratch out his slate-blue stare.

"I don't think we're working with all the information. But my job matters, so we need to focus on this campaign. Let's do this, then I can be out of your life again, just like you always wanted." His voice is loud and harsh.

What is he fucking talking about? I flatten my tone of voice. "This is my job. I'm the more poised of the two of us."

I see him amping up to take me down and I can't do this anymore. He can win, I don't have any more fight in me today. He can have all the last words so I can take a minute and process.

"Says the woman who's falling apart in a business meeting." I flinch. "Sorry. I don't know what I'm saying. Shit. Lizzie, sorry, I don't—" He puts his head in his hands.

I turn towards the door to hide the building tears I refuse to shed. My voice is weaker than I'd like as I reach the door. "I have to go."

His voice is teeming with fury. "No, you don't. The only

thing on your agenda today was to meet me. Stay right here so we can talk about all of this, Lizzie."

He can't see me, but the fucking tears are now on my cheeks. I have to get out of here and work through this.

My voice is shards woven loosely together. I can barely get my words out without breaking into a sob. "I'm Bette. Not Lizzie anymore. And I can't be near you, please let me go." I turn towards him with the purpose of letting him know I've cracked. His face falls. He knows he's overstepped and walks towards me. I quickly leave, closing the door behind me, and run towards the elevator. I duck into the copy room to the left of the reception desk as I hear him calling after me.

His voice is booming. "Lizzie. Bette, I don't care what your name is. Stop."

He looks at reception and asks, "Did you see Bette Miller run out here?" She shrugs. She saw my tear-stained face. He tries again. "Beautiful, striking woman, light-green eyes, chic brown hair with a reddish tint? Wearing a cream pencil skirt and blouse? Green necklace that dipped just below her neckline?" It's killing me that he called me beautiful. And he's memorized my outfit.

"No, sir."

Atta girl. Chicks before dicks.

He mutters something in frustration and he's gone. I hear the elevator ding and the reception girl says, "It's all clear, you can go."

"Thank you. It's me, not him." I don't want them to think he did something to me. "I must be hormonal. Seriously, he's a good guy. The best I've ever known." And the worst.

She smiles and nods.

HAYDEN

She doesn't get to slip into nothingness again while I seethe with anger. I'm the one who gets to be pissed and hurt. How is it that Bette and Lizzie have dominated my thoughts for five fucking years? Ever since she started at the company, they've been a seesaw of thoughts, and they're the same freaking person. Such a twisted mindfuck.

I've hated her, wanted her, been challenged by all her pranks, and taunts. Bette's the only woman in all these years to spark me in any way since Lizzie. My heartache occupying the rest of the news cycle when Bette wasn't. Jesus, I even let my mind wander to what it would be like beyond all the anger.

I stalk back to the hotel. The city's whizzing by me, but it's a different city now. Last night I was planning to walk to all the romantic postcard places with Lizzie. I thought if we walked in a city together we might rediscover love.

But on the plane ride here, I had thoughts of walking these streets with Bette as well. Maybe not the Hallmark places I'd take Lizzie, but I was going to suggest we go to the Guggenheim and dinner. I wanted to know her because there was always something more about her. Turns out, she's the one who decimated my heart. Fuck her and her untouchable gorgeous face with her Bette business outfit on Lizzie's curves. Her fiery red lips that belong to sassy Bette, but the smile is pure Lizzie. I want to fuck her, kill her, hold her, and ruin her. I hurry through the revolving doors and punch the elevator button. I throw open the connecting door to the mystery suite and it's stunning and huge. It's a shared living room and kitchen with a dining table and a terrace, for Christ's sake. But I slam my communal door hard, so she feels the shudder.

I shout, "Honey, I'm home. Where's my fucking slippers?" I stand in the middle of the room to taunt her into facing me. Lizzie will hide, but Bette will rally to fight me. Bring on Bette, so we can get to the bottom of Lizzie and Danny.

I cross my arms and shout, "Shouldn't you have the Boast account all buttoned up so I can take credit for your work?" That should be enough to pull Bette into the arena so the battle can begin.

The adjoining door to her room flies open and shakes the bad Southwestern artwork on the wall. I stand ready to do battle with this woman who has governed my thoughts and world for way too long.

Her face is streaked with dried tears. She's cleaned her eye makeup and her hair is down and wild. She takes my breath away, but I rein it in. Just need to tell my dick that. He's working on his own timeline here.

She shrieks, "Who do you think you are ordering me around?"

I toss out, "Tonight, are we Bette and Hayden? Or Danny and Lizzie?"

"Fuck you." She turns to leave and her curvy ass taunts me.

I widen my stance. I'm sure to her it looks like a power pose, but it's to give my dick a little breathing room so he calms the hell down. "Bette. Good to see you." She whips her head around and stares at me.

Her voice is strong and sure. "Why did you stand me up?"

"Ok. Hello, Lizzie! Jesus. What do you want from me?"

I circle the room and pull my hair all the way to the ends. Stand her up? She's got to be fucking kidding, I'm seeing red. She's still wearing that cream fucking pencil skirt. Her ass is mocking me with its perfection and that's illegal in a fair fight. She has the edge and it's up to me to make sure she doesn't know that.

I breathe in and out while staring at her as her chest rises and falls quickly. She's twisting her thumbs then she puts her hands on her haughty and deliciously curvy hips.

I say in a tone that will worm its way into her brain, "Got it. So, we're fighting as Hayden and Bette over Lizzie and Danny issues. Cool. Now that I know who to be, go ahead. Any more lies you want to spill all over these proceedings?"

She says, "Why didn't you ever tell me it was you? That's the lowest fucking prank. Fuck the ping pong balls that almost cost me my career, but this shit—this long con of yours is deplorable."

I laugh at her. Really? "Long con? What am I, a grifter?"

"Yes," she says arrogantly and it's almost too sexy.

"I'll add it to my resume." I'm so fucking frustrated, confused, and insanely pissed off.

"Go right ahead, you'll need it soon," she says. I'm pure aggression and I want to win, but I also want to collapse in a heap and have her take care of me. How fucked-up is that?

I plant myself in front of her again and she steps back. "Whiplash, darling. Let's fight over one thing at a time. I didn't know it was you. In a rational state of mind, you can't possibly believe I was able to keep that secret for almost five years. You're delusional. Choose one thing to fight about."

"Prom."

"Done." Jesus, she's so hot and powerful. I think of my Lizzie finding her voice and evolving into ballbuster Bette and I want her more. She keeps biting her bottom lip. I'd like to do that. She crosses her arms and glares at me, as if daring me not to find her the most attractive woman on the planet.

I step to her and we're almost chest to chest. I'll bet she put her sky-high heels on to distract me and even out our heights a bit. She's shifty and smart. Lizzie wasn't shifty. What the hell happened to her? She wants to talk about it. Fine. I've never told anyone this entire story. I was saving it to spit in her face someday. Welcome to someday.

I put my hands on her hips because I can't resist touching her for one more second. She flinches the tiniest moment, then relaxes into me. "Sit your perfect ass down."

Her eyebrows raise.

"That's sexual harassment."

"I'm not your boss. I'm your ex-boyfriend. Your ass is perfect. Deal with it." She huffs, breaks our connection and my arms drop to my side. As she turns, I see a slight smile. I say, "Now. Sit the fuck down so I can tell you my story."

"No. I'll stand." So obstinate. Maddening.

"Fine. After I got your breakup call, I spent the night sitting on my suitcases on Tony and Dax's back patio. I used all my money on a useless plane ticket and the cab to the airport. Tony and Dax came to get me and took me to their house on the Cape for the weekend. Not the fucking dream weekend I'd planned."

Her eyebrows knit together and she exhales. "What call? Why are you lying to me now? It's time to put it all out there and you choose to be a dishonest dick."

I want to shake this woman. "All truth. Call Dax. Thank God I had them to pull me through. I've never been more humiliated and devastated than that weekend." I back away from her because my voice is betraying my confidence.

"Same," she bites out.

I yell, "Yo. Crazytown. Why the fuck would you be embarrassed? You did the dumping."

She slams her finger into my chest. "YOU DID THE DUMPING. Hell, you ditched me on prom night." Tears spring to her eyes.

I put my hand on her shoulder and she shrugs me off. Fair enough. But it pisses me off further.

I'm setting this record straight. "I did nothing of the kind. I fucking pined for you and nursed my dazed heart for years. I closed the wound the best I could, but trust me, every fucking day since you disappeared from my life feels like a slow bleed of pain and regret. Just a trickle these days, but it's always fucking there."

I can tell she's trying to process, but I can't stop now.

I move into her eyeline and say, "You changed your email. Blocked my calls. Got a new number. You moved with no forwarding address. You, not me, did all the damage." I point at her chest. "You didn't even have the decency to call me yourself. You hid behind your father. I guess he's the one who really broke my heart."

"What the hell are you talking about?" She looks confused.

How could she not remember? I wonder if this is how she ended her marriage, too. A call from dad.

I cross the room to the kitchen slamming cabinets doors open and shut. She can't even take responsibility ten years later. She turns and she's angrier than before. I need to shift away from this. But not before I say my piece.

I put my palms on the kitchen counter and lean over so we're face-to-face.

My voice is swift and harsh. "I would've followed you to the ends of the earth. I would've quit football if you told me to. I would've buried my life as I buried myself in you. Don't get it twisted, you fucked me over, in more ways than I can even explain to you. But you don't deserve to know those things. You have to fucking earn them."

She spits out, "Like you've earned your place in the company?"

I stand up straight and throw my arms in the air. "Bette, how lovely of you to join the party. What the fuck do *you* want?"

"The only reason you're here is your charm. Everyone loves Hayden Corelli. He's hilarious. He's so charming and talented they wouldn't fire you over the prank that almost ruined my career. Yet, the two women in Chicago have to work twice as hard to get as fucking far as the charming Hayden Corelli and his fabu sidekick, the dashing Dax Ladd. What do you have to say about that, Hayden Corelli?"

"Stop saying my name like that." I know she has a point, but this company isn't like that. She's looking for something more to fight about or to shift her guilt. But the flush in her cheeks has my engine revving in the red and I'm not sure I can be around her.

"Hayden Corelli," she says with a sassy tone and sway of her hips.

"Stop it with your teasing." I spit out. I start flicking my thumbs and yoga breathing. I can't take this.

"And you're stealing my job. I don't care how gorgeous you are." I flick my eyebrows up. I have my opening. New plan, I'll fuck some sense into her. I'll fuck her so hard she has no choice but to tell the truth.

I smirk at her. "You think I'm gorgeous?"

We've solved nothing, but now her cheeks are pink and she's biting her lip again. My dick is so hard and hidden behind this counter. It sprung to life the moment she licked her lips entering the room. She's breathing irregularly and my pulse is snapping.

She retakes her super hero pose. and stares at me, but the Lizzie blush remains despite Bette's bluster. And now my cock is taking all the blood and sense from my head. I've never wanted anything more than the woman standing in front of me.

She says, "What of it?" So sexy in her defiance.

I smirk. "Nothing. Just always nice to hear someone as attractive as you give me a compliment."

"Shut up. I'm not attractive."

"That's Lizzie talking. Bette knows she's stunning." I round the kitchen counter like I'm stalking prey. I don't care if she notices my cock. My hormones have gone from nuclear to feral. I walk towards her and she doesn't move. She shakes her head quickly, trying to get a hair out of her lip gloss. I want that red coral color on my cock.

"You can say that all you want, doesn't make it true. You're sexy and perfect." I reach her and she crosses a straight arm over herself. But when she looks at me, her eyes are hooded, her pupils dark. That shade of green I've only seen in my dreams for a decade, and I know her desire matches mine.

Her smell is all the good in the world condensed into one fucking scent and it's killing me. She's roses and lilacs as well as good cognac, freshly cut grass, and cinnamon. Because cinnamon is the absolute best thing in the world. I step closer.

She hisses, "We're not discussing me. We're discussing you."

"And how gorgeous I am?" I purr.

She shakes her head and more hair gets caught in her lip gloss. "You're an asshole."

"So you've told me."

"But you are." I step closer. Our breathing is ragged and wanton. The air is thick around us. I'm not sure I'll survive sex with her, and I know I won't survive if I don't fuck her. I wait for a signal. She bends her knees in a broken doll pose and fuck me if I'm not gone.

"I hate you," she says.

"Cool. I have an idea. Let's hate fuck. Because I have to get rid of this rock-hard cock somehow. And burying it inside of your hot fury sounds like the perfect antidote. You're the living embodiment of every fantasy I've had in the last decade. Is that what you want? A hate fuck, little firecracker?" I step closer to her. Her eyes flare as I call her my nickname from Paris.

There's a long pause and our chests are expanding and constricting. We're staring at each other and she flicks her hot-pink painted index finger from her lips. "Ask for it, Lizzie. You have to want it. Do you?"

Her lips are parted and I want in. All parts of me inside of her. She licks her nail and flicks it out her mouth. And then she exhales and it's almost a moan. Her voice is low and throaty. "Yes."

And with that our rubber band snaps and all our tension bites us in the ass. My mouth is on her in a nanosecond. The kiss is hard and unyielding but her lips are open and welcome me home. She nips at my tongue and I moan at the slight pain. Fuck me, she's so hot. All I can think of is fucking her so very hard.

The kiss is wild and I dig into her hair to pull her as close as possible. Her tits smash against my chest and her arms go to my shoulders. She digs her nails into the top of my back. She moans as I tangle my tongue aggressively with hers. It's as if we're bantering with our tongues, trying to gain dominance or best the other one. I'll kiss her even harder if that's what it takes to shut her up. Her hands are moving up and down my biceps and she scrapes her nails under my lapels and pushes my jacket down my arms. I release her head and shake it off onto the floor. I take her face into my palms and pull her back into an engaged kiss. I'm frantic and frenzied. Sloppy and wild, our tongues press into each other's mouths, desperate to be deeper.

She unbuttons my top button. I pull back from her and rip my shirt off, popping buttons all over the room. She moans at the sight of my adult chest. I work hard for it, always have. Her fingers drift over my abs and I know she's mentally counting them. I don't have fucking time for this. She can admire me later.

I spin her around and she gasps. I reach down to her tight pencil skirt's slit and yank the fabric apart. She moans. As do I, when I see the sweet black lace string framing the ass that should have a monument to it. I rip open the zipper of her skirt and it falls to the ground. She turns around as she pulls her shirt. I lunge for it and she puts a finger up.

"Hold up, Hulk. I like this blouse." I'm too far gone to laugh at her joke. She sees my face, shrugs, and rips the blouse herself. I reach around her and undo her bra. I'm desperate for all of her. I don't know if I'll ever get this chance again. I rake her to me and take her erect pink nipple into my mouth, tasting and groaning at the familiar and all-new erotic feeling. She unbuckles my belt and my pants slide down. I step out of them but my mouth never leaves her body.

She throws her head back and rubs my insanely hard cock through my grey boxer briefs, and I might come on her just from that. I move to her neck and suck. I bite down ever so lightly because I can't stop myself. She gasps and digs her nails into my shoulders.

"More," she says breathlessly.

I lift my head before I kiss her wet parted mouth again. We're desperate for each other. She reaches for me and I pull away, teasing her.

"We're fucking hot as adults. This is fucking hot. You're fucking hot. Who taught you to be this hot?" I say.

She bites her lip and stares at me. "You did."

Her mouth curls in a sly little smile that's got me in a time warp. I know that 'fuck me' smile. Suddenly, I'm struck by how many people have likely seen it since me and I want to rip their fucking heads off.

BETTE

It's like I turned on a green light with that statement and I want him to fuck me savagely. He opened me up to accepting all of myself and he didn't stick around to see the fruits of his labor. He can't make love to me like Danny. I need Hayden to fuck Bette, hard. I need to release a shit-ton of anger.

I can't deal with any emotion except hate and revenge. I want to show him everything he's missed for a decade. I don't care about anything except being wanted and wanton. I've never felt this kind of heat, even when we were together as kids. Turns out Hayden is scorching. I stroke the soft skin that doesn't yield to my touch since his abs and chest are so taught. Not bulked up like I remember but cut and smooth. I flick one of his nipples and his head comes up from my neck. His face is so close to mine and our hands don't stop.

"Seriously hot. I hate how hot you are. How I want you more than I've ever wanted anyone or anything. I jerked off to you, Bette. So many fucking times. Each fantasy dirtier than the last." My mouth falls open and he fills it while his hand travels south. But not before twisting one of my nipples as he swallows my moan.

He slides through my pussy as our tongues swirl and teeth scrape as we attempt to get closer. He mumbles on top of my mouth, “Well, you’re rather wet for me. Did Bette masturbate to the thought of Hayden, too, or is this all because I sucked on your tits?”

“Tits.” I won’t admit Hayden fantasies.

“Liar.” He bites my bottom lip, pulling it out as I gasp. He lets it go as he swipes up to my clit and circles it. Then his long finger finds its way inside of me while his palm massages that fabulous bundle of nerves. I can barely contain myself as I wiggle and without warning, he thrusts a second finger inside and pumps hard. I happily ride his hand, always hitting that one spot no one else has ever found.

“Come.”

“What?” I gasp.

“I want to see you come. I want to see it now.”

“I can’t,” is all I say. I don’t want him to know he’s the only man to ever make me come. I only come by myself when I mimic my memories.

He pulls out and I pout just a little. Despite my lack of male-induced orgasms over the years, it doesn’t mean I want him to stop trying.

“That’s not fair,” I say.

He steps back and I’m standing there exposed and needy. He removes his briefs and now we’re both naked and staring at each other. His large, beautiful, dripping and ready cock juts out. I reach for it and he holds my wrist before I can wrap around him. Then he twists me around, his cock digging into my back.

He’s on my ear as his hands snake down the front of me.

He's moving slowly like he's mapping my body. He murmurs and his stubble against my cheek makes me almost lose my mind.

"What do you mean you can't?" He thrusts his fingers back into me and I arch into him.

He plays with me and I enjoy it like it's a really good carnival ride without safety restraints. He pulls out and spins me around again. His lips are on mine, telling me that he's in charge, and for the first time since Paris, I give up control.

"Tell me why," he rasps. He leans down and sucks on my nipple, and I shiver as I begin to build. "Tell me why or I stop."

It explodes out of my mouth, "Not since you. No one since you."

He growls and now he's relentless in his pursuit of my orgasm. I close my eyes. I'm so full of his long fingers as they search for a perfect spot. He's pulling them all the way out and back in. I rasp out, "Christ. Make me come."

"Look at me." I open my eyes and he's so close. "Come while I watch you. I don't want to miss a flutter of your eyelashes or a tick of your mouth. Come now, my badass goddess. Let me remind you how good it can be when you let go. Come all over my hand before I turn you around and fill you with my cock. Do you get me, Bette? Come. Submit to me, don't think."

He gets more aggressive and he palms my breast, tweaking and pulling my sensitive nipple in rhythm with his other hand. My breathing gets faster and my vision clouds at the edges, there's starbursts as I snap. It washes over me again and again. The largest, most perfect orgasm slams into me and I don't think I'll survive this much pleasure.

I almost fall to my knees, but he catches me with his long and perfect arm. He doesn't stop his motions, only slows them as I contract around him. His breath catches as I attempt to catch mine.

"Hayden," I whisper.

"Fuck. That was poetry. That was art. But I still have some anger issues to work out."

"Same. Think you can handle me?" I want more. I didn't know I could still come that hard. I don't know what the hell I'm saying, I don't want more. Except, I do. Because in that moment of pure ecstasy, all of the pain, anger, and hate ebbed away. I want to chase that again.

"Buckle up." Without hesitating, he lifts me and wraps my legs around him. His cock is pressed between us, and I move up and down on it, sliding with my own wetness. He groans. He puts me down in front of the counter and cages me. His kiss is fierce and punishing. He reaches across me to his wallet on the counter and retrieves a condom.

He pulls back to roll it on his deliciously long dick. Before he puts it on, he strokes himself while I watch. Dirty delight dances across his face. He reaches over and gathers my wetness, smearing it on his dick.

"You always did like to watch. Come here." He smiles. I laugh and do as I'm told. I come to him and stroke his long beautiful cock. He rolls the condom on after a few more rough tugs and I'm on fire. My core is burning hot and I have to have him.

"Jesus, I hate you, cocky mutha—" My mouth is filled with his strong tongue trying to dominate me. I give as good as I can get as I try and climb him. But he won't lift me. He takes a half step back and takes my hand. Then he twirls me around and slams both palms to the counter, spreads my legs wide, and I'm trapped under him. I try and lift my hands but his lips are nipping and kissing my ear.

"Now, where is it you think you're heading? Let go, I got you. You once said I wouldn't be able to handle you from behind." He smacks a cheek and I gasp. Then he's rubbing the spot and soothing me all over. I'm on fire, with every nerve ending begging for more.

Somehow, in the depth of my soul, or my aching pussy, I trust him. I stop struggling and arch into him. "Good girl. Now don't move. Keep them right there. I need to fuck you so hard you forget anyone who's been here since me. Do you understand?"

He pushes his dick into my backside a bit. Not enough to penetrate, but just enough to feel fucking good and dirty. I turn my head to his and we attack each other's mouths. He pulls on my neck and puts his thumb on my jaw to direct my face closer to his. I don't move my hands. It's like they're glued to the counter. He drifts a palm over them. "Very good girl."

He lets go of my ass. I gasp as he notches himself up. He grabs my hips roughly and thrusts forward, filling me completely in one quick motion. I'm so full. It's brutal and delicious. Then he swiftly pulls out and bucks into me again. It takes my breath away and my head drops to the counter while I wait to acclimate. But he doesn't wait. He pushes on. In and out, grunting and moaning.

"So fucking tight. How are you so fucking tight like you were the first time? Jesus, this is too much. The way you hold my cock. You take possession of it like it's yours. Fucking epic."

I say, "Keep fucking me like this. So fucking good. How are you as good as my memory?"

He's grunting. "How are you talking? Apparently, I'm

not going hard enough, I want you at a loss for words." And he doubles his speed, stealing not only my voice but my breath.

"Yes. Yes. Right there. Fuck, my pussy loves your cock." He growls and slaps my ass again. I moan loudly. Then his hips are pistoning in and out of me, and I'm slamming my ass against his abs as I move against him. He's so deep.

I feel torn in half as my orgasm begins to spiral. He wraps his hands in my hair and pulls my head up. I've always dreamed someone would do this but never imagined it would be him, of all people. We were sweet in our exploration of each other's bodies a decade ago. But this is divine. I'm so wet and he's finding my most divine place inside of me.

"Come. Now. I can't hold on. Come now!" And my girly parts respond as if he's been in charge of my pussy this whole time.

He smacks my ass again and I moan loudly. "Fuck. Your ass is so goddamn fucking perfect. Lizzie, Bette. Whoever. You. Are. Christ, I love your ass. I've never wanted to come on something so badly."

"You love Christ's ass," I moan.

"Yours. Your ass. Your tight pussy. Fuck. I need to pull out and come on your ass."

"No." He reaches around me and pinches my clit. "Oh God. No."

"Leave your clit alone?"

"No. Do that again. Don't come on my ass."

"Fine. Fuck. You're killing me. I'm going to lose it now. My balls are so tight. I need to fill you. Come. Come. Come now for me."

And then he reaches around again and with his chant, I'm so close. I can feel the fingerprints on my hips. He's gripping so tight and pumping so hard and fast now. My chest is flattened on the counter; he's fucked me into the counter. It hits me like a tsunami of pleasure and I scream the name of the man fucking me, not the boy I was in love with. He smacks my ass and jerks deep inside me as I convulse and pulse around him. It's so long. I think I might die from pleasure. Fuck. He keeps moving but slows his pace as we start to land from our orgasms. I've never come that hard. Ever. Even when I think of him. Even with him before. I never let go like that.

He leans down onto my back and kisses my neck. Then he curls his arms around me as he slides out. And I know I've never felt so empty in my entire life as when he's no longer inside of me.

We finally regulate our breathing and he says, "Why?"

"Why what? Why did I break up with you through my dad? Which I never did." And we're right back in it.

"No. Why can't I come on your ass?"

I buck him off me, straighten up, and smile wickedly. "Because I knew you wanted it so badly."

"Spite?"

"Yes." I grin.

"You're saying that someday if you're less mad at me, I can jizz all over your peachy goodness?" He rounds the counter and finds the garbage can under the sink and deposits the condom.

I say, "First off, that's disgusting. Flush that. Don't make the poor hourly wage workers pick up your semen."

"Why are they picking it up? I tied it off. They won't even know it's there. You're changing the subject. And BT Dubs, that was the hardest I've come in years. You're incredible. Are you less mad at me now? Can I come on your ass yet?"

I put on his shirt and he stays behind the counter and we're facing each other semi-concealed.

I try to tease an answer out of him. "I don't think I'm ever going to be less angry at you if you keep lying. My dad wasn't a great guy, but what you're telling me is a bit much. So no. You'll never get a crack at my crack. You'll never get to batter my boobs or any other part of me again. Despite the fact that I do like that—and everything you did—I'll never speak to you again."

I can see his eyes pop open. Then he looks at me sideways and says, "You like that? You're killing me." He groans and smacks the cabinets.

I raise my brows at him and place my hands back on the counter where he demanded I keep them during sex. "I've evolved since I was eighteen. There's lots of filthy fucking things I like."

He pulls through his hair and steps closer to the counter. "It just doesn't seem fair that I get to know these things and not do them."

I say, "Don't lie and we'll see what the day brings us."

He groans loudly and I walk to the fridge to grab a bottle of water. I turn and see he's staring at me.

"It is good, isn't it?" I say, waggling my ass at him. He nods. "Water?" He nods again and I give him a bottle. "Now, tell the truth so we can move on. Why the fuck did you hurt me like that?"

He pauses and his lighthearted demeanor is replaced with consternation. I don't care for it. How dare he get indignant?

"Cool. Let's not move forward. I'll write the pitch. I'll art direct. I'll grab the job that you were never going to get anyway."

My skin prickles. I forgot about the job for a moment.

"We talk business and you stay the hell away from me until you're willing to admit you ruined my life. And this time, it's my turn to ruin yours. I'll start with nabbing the job that's mine." I turn away from him and flash him my ass.

"Last look?" he yells at me.

I say, "Something to use next time you masturbate while thinking of me."

He snaps back at me, "You know you DJ'd the hell out yourself while thinking of me. And I mean Hayden me, not Danny me. You like it a bit wicked. Like recognizes like."

"DJ'd?" I turn back and he flattens his palm and pretends to scratch a record... I roll my eyes. "And for the record, I loved Danny very much. Hayden can burn in hell."

He throws his hands in the air and yells, "You are the most maddening, ridiculous, tempting, useless, gorgeous, insane woman who has ever existed. THEY'RE BOTH ME. BeLizzie, I do NOT know what to do with or about you."

"Well, don't call me that name and how about not talking to me for a couple of days. Sounds like a good fucking start to our business partnership, you asshole. Just leave me alone, Danny. I can't with all of this."

"FINE! But when you're sore tomorrow, remember I'm the one who fucked you hard. Hayden, not sweet Danny!" His voice rumbles through the room and I shudder a tiny bit. I slam the door, locking the adjoining room behind me.

He yells through the closed door, "You locked it? Come on. Afraid I'm going to come in there in the middle of the night and argue with you some more? I'm fucking done. I won't call you the word that keeps floating through my mind, but each moment with you it's getting harder not to."

I fling the door open, and he's startled and still naked. How is he this gorgeous and comfortable in his body? He's so muscular, it's like looking directly into a lightbulb, so painfully beautiful. His dick isn't even shriveled and flaccid. It's still full and goddammed gorgeous. Then he smirks because he catches me ogling his pretty cock.

I glare and say, "I'll say the word. Fuck off, you little bitch." I slam the door again and hear him growl.

"MADDENING!!! You're Looney Toons, woman."

I yell back, hoping to get the last word, "Badeep, Badeep, Badeep—That's ALL Folks!"

BETTE

THE FIRE-ENGINE RED CAFÉ TABLE IS A LITTLE WOBBLY ON THE sidewalk today. I'm tucked into my now normal space at Buvette. I come here most days to work. There are two tiny tables with a wooden bench tucked against the front windows of the French bistro down in the West Village. I like to sit outside and stare at people going by, and the waitstaff is used to me scribbling in my oversized notebook. I'm here to get away from him. Ironically, I feel at home surrounded by French food and the language. I love this place, it makes me feel like an adult, the way Paris did.

It's been five days since our sex fight. We haven't spoken or "unpacked" any of it, as he likes to say in meetings. Mostly, I've tried to work far away from him. I can't break first, but I wish he would. I'm lost. I don't know who to be without the pranks, work, Sophie at my side, and decade old pain to hide behind. It's fresh again, not buried deep so I can ignore it sometimes. It's right at the surface and I don't know the way through it. The really messed up part is I miss Hayden. I miss the playful, sexy, intelligent part of him. But when I banished Danny, I banished him, too.

Work has always been the thing to redeem my life. To make the noise of lonely fade into the background a bit. I'll turn up the volume on work so I can get rid of him forever. He can go back to Boston and I can pretend anything north of Manhattan doesn't exist. Sorry, Vermont, but you've got to go.

I blow some breath out as the lush trees jostle in the temperate breeze. I stare straight ahead at the brownstones and stoops lined with families and people laughing. They're joyous and I hope they're not pretending for my sake—putting on a show to prove to me that carefree can exist on the other side of whatever the fuck I'm feeling. I catch myself rubbing my thumb across my lip the way he did.

I don't regret my actions. I made the first move by vaulting at him and assaulting him with my tongue, but he sure as fuck finished it by bending me over the counter. I've had hot sex, unfortunately, always finishing myself off, but fucking Hayden was death row sex. I don't want a last meal or rites, have sex with him one more time. I'm squirming in my seat thinking about it. I don't want to talk to him, work with him, or sort things out, but sex—um, yes please.

High school sex is very different than adult hate sex. I'm surprised we didn't combust.

We have three weeks to sort this out. The job, not each other. There's no sorting that. I called and texted on prom night and the next day, but everything bounced. I was a shell, and my father was thrilled to step in and take over again. He got me into Berkeley last minute. I was a zombie. I don't even remember picking my classes. It wasn't until the end of sophomore year when I was sitting through yet another Melville/Hawthorne literature class, holding a transfer transcript to Stanford, that I woke up to the life my father designed. I dropped the class, my advisors and my major. Then I joined a sorority. He tried to pull me out of Berkeley. That was the day I stopped doing anything he said. That's when I started advertising classes and sleeping around. I wanted to write. And it was the fastest way I could think of to get away from California.

I never understood his pathological need to control my mom and me. It was so complicated, so detailed. There was so much to engineer and then the upkeep, if he did break us up. My father was a fucker, but I hope he didn't do this. There's a chance he did this. Fuck, did he do this?

I pull my focus back to the market research I'm reading through. We need to come up with a pitch that will decide who gets this fucking job. And us working together to best each other makes no kind of sense.

I haven't done much at this café but eat eggs or almond croissants this week. I sip wine and pine for Paris. And now he's ruined Paris all over again for me. He can keep it.

I turn my head to catch more sunlight on my face. I'll take my Buvette and try to... fuck me. He's here. I saw him when I glanced back through the front window that I'm leaning against.

He's been here for at least an hour because you can't get in the door without seeing me. He's at a little table off the bar. Ok. I'm going to peek at him. I slink down and turn to look through the window into the restaurant. There's a person seated in the solo window seat inside, and I peer through their legs. I'm grateful it's a woman in jeans, not a skirt, or some dude who could catch me checking his package. This can NOT get worse.

It got worse. He's laughing free and easy with a brunette. He's on a date and I'm the creatively blocked girl drinking wine alone. At a table designed for one. I have extra bread and a bottle perched on my tiny singlet table and he's warming up a chick to take her back to our fucking hotel suite. OH MY GOD. He's going to sully our home with this tawdry and cheap affair.

I slam my wine and shrink down on my little bench so he doesn't see me. I've gone completely insane. My palms are sweaty and my heart is racing. I want to walk away and leave a wad of cash on the table, but I don't have money. Who carries paper money? I have to get the attention of the waitstaff, pay, and sneak away before he sees me.

I don't think I'm ready to talk to him again and certainly not meet his new fiancée. You only laugh that free and easy with a seasoned lover. Five days and they're free and easy. They're too happy for them not to be engaged. He's completely moved on. I saw his genuine laugh. He picked up a woman since we had sex. Only explanation.

A panic bolt zings down my stomach. What if he got married in the last five days?

She's not drinking wine. She probably conceived on their wedding night at another hotel. Then he covered up his perfect wedding, returning to our hotel suite that night to keep the charade going so we could work together civilly. I heard him come in late last night. Ok, I was listening to see when he came home. Home. It's a fucking hotel.

I'm spiraling, and now I'm losing feeling in my left arm because I crouched down on it to hide from the glow of their newlywed bliss. I'm going to die alone. Do I get them a gift?

I'm waving at the staff while squatting in front of my tiny bench. I start flapping both arms and it's not working. I slide out, hopefully clearing the window. I start whispering to the staff as they pass me on the sidewalk, trying desperately to get the attention of a striped-apron server. I wildly wave like I'm a carwash dancing blow-up man. But my gesticulations aren't garnering the attention I need.

Without moving my head, I quickly side-eye inside and he's staring at me. I jerk my head back towards the street as if that will undo everything. I attempt to grab my bag and run. I'll throw my credit card at Annie, the server, and come back for it later. My bag knocks the wobbly little red café table and now everyone is watching. I laugh like I meant for the table to make that loud scraping sound and crash on the sidewalk. The table falls and there's nothing I can do but bask in the humiliation as my glass shatters and a baguette rolls down the block.

Hayden bolts from the café and sets the table back up.

"You ok?"

These are the eyes I dream about from long ago, wide and open.

I nod. He takes my hand and my body reacts as if something has shifted in this moment. As if nothing else matters but his touch. He nods to the staff and gestures inside. The men and women all nod and swoon as he gives them that million-watt smile. Then he turns it on me and my innards become goo. I'm a gooey lunatic with no sense of where my horizon is. I can't seem to get my equilibrium.

My father made me a sensible girl, but what I've discovered over the years is that I'm ridiculous mess. I'm good at hiding it, usually, but not today.

He grins and rubs his thumb over the back of my hand, and I exhale. I didn't realize I'd been holding my breath. He tightens his grip and pulls me inside. I reluctantly go, mostly because I don't want to stop holding his hand.

"Why are you being nice to me?"

He winks. "We can't let the West Coast team win. We

need a nice day. And I like to keep you guessing. Trust me." I follow as my stomach attempts to return to its normal place and stop flipping.

He stops again and turns towards me. "Because we need to lay down our swords for a moment. Can you be in this with me? You can go back to hating me later today. But can you be here with me, please?"

He looks so much like my Danny. I want this so badly, but I'm terrified to trust him and helpless to stop myself.

"Yes. I can play nice."

"I remember." He smirks and my fucking resolve is toast. I'm a puddle of lust and confusing emotions for him. I bite my lip and then lick the spot where I bit it.

Just as he turns forward, he says, "I saw that. If you want to not hate me later, you can do that again. Or you know, there's always..." I smack his back. He was going to say "hate fucking." I laugh and push him forward.

He guides me to the table where his stunning shampoo-commercial-worthy brunette 'wife' is seated. I tug at my scattered locks, but she's show ready. I'm usually more put together than this.

"Claire, this is Li... This is Bette." Of course, she's freaking stunning. Of course, his new wife is otherworldly beautiful. She puts her hand out. I lean up to whisper in Hayden's ear, "I'm not having a three-way with you."

His eyebrows shoot up and down quickly.

He leans down to my ear and my body is on fire with the tickle of his stubble on my cheek. He whispers back, "But it's French. I thought you loved all things French."

I glare at him.

He coos in my ear and I'm having a hard time remembering I don't want to sleep with him, whether there's another woman there or not. "Relax."

Then he says loudly as he turns towards her, “This is my sister-in-law.”

I relax into a full-body smile. Thank God it’s not his new imaginary dating/engaged/married/about to be a father with woman.

She greets me and the world is a little lighter around her. I shake hello. I say, “Hockey brother or baseball?”

He grins widely and I realize I’ve revealed I know a lot more than I’ve let him believe. He now knows I’ve followed his brothers’ careers. One to the NHL and the other is currently playing AAA ball in Reno with the Aces waiting to be called up to the Diamondbacks bench.

Her face lights up as she says, “Hockey. We play the Islanders tonight and I remembered this one was in town. Do you know Robbie?”

I shake my head and his hand appears on my lower back. We both pause for a second to relish the feel of it. He guides me to sit.

“No. I’ve only heard stories and followed his success. He has quite the career with the Flyers.” Hayden pinches my leg and I try not to react. Now he knows I looked for him.

“He does, but he’s winding down. He’s a bit old to be losing teeth. Or a bit young.” We all laugh. Then she gestures to him. “I love how Hayden is still talking about his big brother’s career. Have you known Hayden long?”

She’s fishing and I don’t know what to say.

“I mean are you... you know? I don’t think I’ve ever met —” Hayden cuts her off.

“Bette and I used to date.”

She squeals a bit and claps like a seal.

She sips her water. “Hay, I was under the impression you didn’t date. Well, except for that one tragic time.” She sweeps the back of her hand to her forehead in an overly dramatic way.

We both freeze, then he leans towards me, faces her, and speaks. "Would you say it was tragic?"

I grin, answering him, but looking at Claire. And suddenly we're in a different place again. We're not Hayden and Bette and we're not Lizzie and Danny. No one's hurt, our minds and bodies are just remembering we were friends.

"Hmm. I mean, not *Romeo and Juliet* tragic, neither of us went running for a dram of poison or anything. Well, there was that one time you almost dropped me off a roof. But on a scale of happy to tragic, I'd say a bit devastating."

He nods sharply and laughs a bit. "I'd agree."

Claire slams her hands to the table. "NO! Mother Mary and Joseph. That's a wicked-ass thing to say to me. Is this Lizzie? Are you the fabled Lizzie who disappeared from the earth and none of us believed you existed, except for the thousands of pictures he'd stare at, well past the breakup? And the drawings. Uck, with the drawings. So many, I should have recognized you from them."

He looks down and growls a bit. I did that, too.

I grin. "Yes. I used to be Lizzie."

Claire sits back and looks like the Cheshire Cat as she bites into a pastry. She says, "And I thought Bette was your mortal enemy at work?"

I raise Hayden's glass to her. "I'm her, too." Then I sip his wine.

He takes his glass back, sips, and says, "And I used to be Danny."

HAYDEN

Claire says, "Danny? They called you that on the field sometimes."

I bite some bread. "Prep school/football nickname."

Bette turns to me. "What are you saying to me? Danny was a nickname?"

I look at her, totally confused. "Why are you surprised? Dan was a team nickname for my last name and you're the only one who called me Danny."

"Daniel is your middle name. What are you even saying to me?"

"They called me Danny Boy because there was another Chris on the team, so they changed my name."

Her jaw is wide open and she keeps shaking her head.

Claire and I bust up laughing. "You thought my name was Dan Danson?" I can't help but laugh harder. She smacks my arm. "And you were in love with me, right? You were in love with Daniel Danson. You wanted to be Mrs. Dan Danson?"

"No! I mean, yes. Ugh. Stop it. I thought it was Christopher Daniel Danson."

Claire and I laugh hysterically that this great love of my life didn't even really know my name. She slowly starts to giggle and then a full-on Lizzie-worthy guffaw erupts from her. One of my favorite sounds in the world. Would only be better if I could make her snort laugh.

When we all settle down, Claire says, "Christopher. It's been a long time since I heard the 'C' word. Clearly the two of you need to talk. And Bette? What happened to Lizzie?"

I still can't believe she's sitting next to me.

She says, "What hasn't happened to Lizzie?" We all laugh and she continues, "I got married, divorced, and used a different derivative of Elizabeth."

Claire fist-bumps her forehead. "You were both looking for different people this whole time?"

I let that settle over the table and we ignore the weight of it as I pass a chocolate croissant to Bette. She shoves half of it in her mouth. Again, I stare at her, but this time because the image of her lips wrapping around that long pastry is a bit more than my eager dick can handle. He's about to punch through my jeans if she keeps moaning like that. She sees me staring and heat flashes in her eyes.

"This is really good." She pats the powdered sugar from her shirt and drops the pastry. "But I'm going to go. You two catch up. Nice to meet you, Claire. And, Danny, I guess it's nice to meet you, too." We laugh, but we're only starting to unravel what happened to us. And even if I can't stand her on the other end of this conversation I need to know what the hell happened.

BeLizzie stands up.

"Nope. Sit your ass down Bette/Lizzie. Elizabeth Marjorie Fox Miller. BeLizzie, if you will. Claire, you can go. I'll see you tonight."

BeLizzie flumps back down as I pull her arm. Then stands again. I cock an eyebrow in warning.

"I'm going to the bathroom. I'll come back, but only for five minutes." She skips off and I watch her ass.

When I look back to Claire, she has her arms crossed over her chest. "Oh, my brother. This is the most fucked-up situation ever. You're in it. You still love her."

"I don't know her." It's true. I love Lizzie. Hate Bette and who the fuck knows where my head's at right now. Other than the need to be with her again. This wave of possession won't lift. It keeps crashing into me and knocking me over with all the thoughts. I want to explore all the places on her body and in her life that have filled out.

Claire who is waiting for a better answer. "I'm not in love with her."

"Bullshit. You've been annoyed by her for five years and full-on fighting with her for the last two. And were hopelessly in love with her a decade ago. And what about those flirty texts you were having a couple of weeks ago?"

I lift my wine and speak over the top before taking a sip. "You know too much."

"I know just enough, and I'm an expert at this and Danson men."

"I'm not one of them." My voice is harsher than I intend.

"His name doesn't make you him."

"It doesn't fucking help."

"Fair enough. Just figure this out. It's all tied and connected. There's happy on the other side of all this murky water. I know it. Clear it up, asshole."

Bette comes back to the table and I shoo Claire away. "Be gone before someone drops a house on you, too." Bette looks confused as Claire laughs at me and sticks out her tongue.

Lizzie tries to grab her bag. "I have a ton of work. I'm only staying another minute or so. Claire, it was lovely to meet you, but you don't have to go."

The two women shake hands and Claire places an extra hand on top.

"I can't tell you how good it was to meet you. You're a myth, a legend, and I'll be delighted to inform the rest of the family you're not a delusion."

Bette looks embarrassed and her head bows to stare at her feet. I want to reach over and pick up her chin. She says, "It's lovely to meet you as well."

Claire throws her crossbody purse on, then looks directly at her. "Look, I don't know what's going on, but perhaps you could give him back the thing you still have that he gave you. His mom would love it if he could finally move on."

I groan. Claire can't help herself, but I need her to shut up.

She and my brother were middle school sweethearts, so she's always been in my life. She knows me better than almost anyone else. She was the person who encouraged me to draw.

Lizzie cocks her head to the side and says, "What do I have?"

"His heart."

I choke a bit and my bitch-ass sister-in-law walks away with a mic-drop gesture.

I glare as Claire hustles out of the restaurant. The waitress with the cool decorative eyeliner, Annie, comes over. She's curvy and gorgeous, and if my entire being weren't wrapped up in Lizzie, In another reality I'd invite her to join me after her shift. But I have to figure this out with Lizzie or Bette. One of them has to know how we move forward.

God, I want to kiss her again. That taste a week ago was a terrible cock tease. Then this week's furious schedule of painting the tile in the bathroom as I released all my anger and anxiety over her being a room away and I can't touch her. I can't hold her or listen to her. And I can't ask her what the fuck happened.

I won't let myself be held by our unexplained past any longer. I stare at her and she's squirming in her chair. Everything needs to be laid out on this table. I can't stand it another second. What the fuck happened?

"Spill it, BeLizzie."

She rolls her eyes at my stupid new nickname for her. "Spill what, Daniel Dan Danny Danson?" She bites her lip and hooks her thumbs together.

I lean back and another bottle of wine appears. I glare at the door and Claire proceeds to make an "O" with her fingers and slam her other index finger through the hole. She's finger fucking herself. I casually shoo her away again, but she turns around and pretends to make out with herself, wrapping her arms around her back and moving up and down. She's laughing when she turns around, and as BeLizzie looks down, I flip Claire off. She smiles, kisses her middle finger and returns the gesture. Then points with the middle digit towards Lizzie and starts thrusting. I look away and she cackles as she leaves, catcalling as she disappears. She and my brother love to give me shit and this is a whole lot of ammunition.

Maybe if Bette doesn't pick a fight, we can get some closure. Then maybe I'll take her to the hockey game tonight. I don't know how the fuck to handle this, but friendship seems like a path forward. I've locked that pain away for so damn long. As I let it surface, looking at her face, it feels fresh. I keep waiting for it to not hurt. Answers. I need fucking answers.

She won't say anything.

I try another tactic. "You follow my brothers' careers?"

Her voice is strong, laced with sweetness. That's who she's always been. "I couldn't find you."

My heart cracks wide open. "I couldn't find you, either. What the fuck happened? I know you became this Bette married person."

She waits a beat and her voice is low. "I married him to get over you."

"Christ. I changed my whole life—"

She interrupts me, "And name."

"And name, to get over you."

We both sit back and pour more Sancerre. We sip and she's somehow more beautiful than my memories. And I can wax pretty damn nostalgic if I let myself. Almost everything looks better, feels better, and is prettier in my rearview mirror. Almost everything.

She breathes out. "Danny."

"Lizzie."

"I don't know what to do."

I lean forward across the table. "Me neither." Her face mirrors my smile. "I simultaneously want you, want to bury you, fuck you, best you, hold you, and forget you."

She sips her wine. "Good luck with that. I'm unforgettable."

I rib her right back, "You're telling me, you let a single day pass without thinking of me?"

I hope to hell she thought of me. It would be like we were in this together and I wasn't the only one hung up on the pain. Or the intense FOMO.

"Oh, how I wish I could have left your arrogant ass in the dust without ever knowing it was you."

I say as earnestly as possible, "You don't actually mean that, do you?"

Her mouth pulls into a straight line and she shakes her head no. She shifts in her chair and her eyes start to dance in the Parisian-like light of this café.

"I wish we were in Paris."

She looks quizzically at me. "You know, I can't go back there. I tried once. I had a panic attack in Gare du Nord station. After puking on the platform, I turned around and went back to the safety of England through the Chunnel as fast as I could."

My mind is reeling. That's surprising. It's the one place on this earth I feel connected to myself and my heart. And to her.

I change the subject away from our direct heartache. "You followed my brother, but did you know..." I drift off. I don't know if she knows about my shoulder and why I didn't enter the draft. Very few know the real reason, but the world does have something to hang the story on. Did she at least know that story?

Lizzie takes an earnest tone and stares at the ceiling before speaking. "Not sure what I'm hiding. It's not like I've been living a full-on, balls-to-the-wall life. It's been a half-life since you."

My heart seizes as she speaks. The air is too thick and heavy around us. It's weighing us both down. She gazes at me as she unfolds a piece of her missing decade.

She leans forward and offers more of her missing puzzle. "I watched game replays to see if you were behind the bench at your brothers' games. You were only there once."

"I'm usually up in the suite."

"Ok. But I did. I knew. I watched your game replays on YouTube or ESPN or wherever there was college football until it was too painful. Until you kissed a cheerleader on the jumbo cam."

I ball my hands into fists. The first of my run of perfectly lovely women I wouldn't commit to.

"You got married, so don't step to me with that bullshit."

"Let's try to keep this civil. I was jealous then, not now. It was the last time I watched. I'd scan stats or game summaries to make sure you were doing well. It was the only way. It was painful to watch you be fine after ditching me."

"Correction, woman. You ditched me. And I was far from fine. I've never been fine, just reinvented."

My voice is rougher and more vulnerable, but not angry. There's no malice in our conversation, only frustration and ignorance. I want to be enlightened why those fucking twelve weeks have painted the blueprint of my life.

She swallows what I assume is a baseball-sized lump in her throat. In a hurried tone she says, "Then you got injured. I reached out to your coach after a couple of months to try and find you, but he said you vanished."

The sound of the busy bistro masks a bit of our conversation, and I'm grateful for the distraction of forks clinking on small plates and glasses sliding across their wood tables. The bar bottles are jingling and a loud joyous gaffaw bursts from a man two tables down as he backslaps a red-faced laughing man. I'd paint all this noise if I could, but it would probably come out with her fucking face again.

I look at her and say, "Where were you? After my injury and a couple months of rehab, I flew out there. You vanished from your home, and your school. I emailed and called your dad at work."

"Oh my God."

"I know. I was quite the idiot thinking if I could just see you, things would fall into place."

"They might have. Nothing's ever felt totally right."

I say, "The last time I tried to find you, your dad replied with your wedding invitation. When I read his obituary I reread the part, 'survived by his only daughter, Elizabeth' repeatedly." She shifts to a seat next to me. I turn to her. "It was the first piece of information on you in eight years I could find."

She takes my hand and squeezes but says nothing then puts down some cash.

"We've already paid."

She says, "Then let's walk. Let's get lost in a sea of people who don't give a shit about us."

A swatch of sun catches the red that threads through her chestnut hair, and I'm transported back to that day and night. The one I thought was the start of my forever. Also, as she walks away, I'm desperate to get my hands on her again. But we should probably sort through our shit first then we can go back to hating each other, and I can bend her over another table. I adjust myself and follow behind.

Out on the street her skirt is ruffled by a light breeze. It's warm and sunny but I pull my sunglasses out to shield myself from the world. Then I roll my sleeves up because we have work to do.

I fall into step with her and we walk about a block, saying nothing, and turn up onto Bleecker. The shops are spilling with sales and chalkboard easel signs onto the sidewalk.

"Why didn't you ever play again? Where did you go?"

Well, let's just dive in.

"I rehabbed and was on the mend from the rotator cuff surgery. Range of motion prognosis was good. I worked my ass off for every millimeter. All the painful seconds were worth it in my mind to get to the NFL Combine and show them what I could do. I lived for the draft. I didn't date, I fucked, but no dating. My studies went to shit. I was obsessed with getting drafted and proving myself. I wanted the world to know I wasn't a liability, but an asset. The only thing I knew for sure was the draft was pushed a year. I'd have to play my extra season. Since I was redshirted as a freshman."

"I don't know what that means."

I instinctively pull her towards me. I forgot how removed she is from sports. I squeeze her and let her go, and we keep walking on the shady side of the street.

"I rode the bench my freshman year, trained with the team. They saved me for my sophomore year while their star quarterback finished out his senior year and I could play as a fifth-year senior."

"Oh. That's smart. Do that. That would work. Wait. Why didn't you do that?"

"My dream of going number one was probably dashed, but I could go second round. Or if I could work my ass off and have a stellar season, then I might crawl back to the first round and be a starting QB instead of a backup. I could be a franchise signal-caller somewhere. That was the plan. I wanted a career and was ok not being the star."

She touches my arm and we slow down a bit. "That was the year Robbie went first round in the NHL, right? He waited a year after college."

"Yes. He moved home to train and be close to our ma, so our brother could go off to college in Florida."

How was she always so close and yet invisible?

I exhale and push my sunglasses tighter on my face. I breathe in and out slowly. Only six people know this complete story. My family, Claire, and Dax. Not even Tony knows everything that happened. He knows I changed my name, but he doesn't quite know the whole story. She takes my hand and it's reassuring, but I look straight ahead. This missing piece of my decade is a little tough to take.

We walk hand in hand. Our undulating and natural grip falling into a comfortable rhythm. People walk around us like we're an inseparable couple.

"It's ok. You can tell me."

"My dad's eyes were different that night. Like all pupil and no color. Really terrifying. You know he smacked us around for the littlest reasons, but he always saved his savage for her. We tried not to leave her alone. That's why Robbie went late to the draft and deferred college earlier. We wanted Law to get out of there. But when I got injured, Robbie took his shot because I could stay home.

"Did you all carry this burden?"

"Just Robbie and I." Her arms snake around my waist for a squeeze, then she backs away again.

I continue, "I got home late from PT and he was wailing on her. I should have left on time, but I wanted to get in another round of reps. I instantly got between his fists and my mom. He was pure rage and venom. He targeted my arm and yanked hard. My shoulder separated again under the force of my father's anger. And please don't tell me it's not my fault for being late that night. I'll never get over that, so don't try."

She gasps, but her grip on mine remains sure and true. In my peripheral, I see her wipe a quick tear. She says nothing but squeezes my hand tighter.

"That set him off even more when I hauled off and hit him. He had a sick grin as he called me an unlovable, lazy piece of shit. He grabbed my shoulder again and undid any hope and all the good that surgery and PT had fixed."

She pulls my arm to her but never once makes me look at her. "Oh. God. Hayden. I'm so sorry."

I'm so grateful she called me Hayden.

We bypass the Bleecker Playground and head towards a bench in Abingdon Square. The bench is surrounded by beauty and flowers and shaded by a nice tree. There's laughter and kids screaming. People living good lives all around. I sit her down and she never lets go of me. Thank fucking God.

I turn to her and plant my sunglasses on my head. I want her to see my face. Maybe we can actually move beyond all this pain if we face all of our shit. We'll get to our why and how in a minute, but for now, I desperately need for my Lizzie to listen to this story and help me rid myself of all this bullshit. But I'm drowning in this shit, I need a second to reset and not be so heavy.

I smile at her, "Tell me something, anything. I'm so weighed down by this story."

She lowers her sunglasses and raises her eyebrows, and I chuckle.

"Surely you realize you just hit me with a cliffhanger. Come on, out with it. I'm not going anywhere. You have the whole lousy day to tell me lousy things."

She knew I needed a second of levity. We sit for a moment in the sun, and I breathe in and out centering myself for the rest of this.

She squeezes my thigh and her tone shifts again, "You don't have to tell me any more if you don't want to. But I'm here." I nod and stare straight ahead for a moment and let the noise of the city lift me away from the situation in my head.

I can't look at her, but I need to get this out, "I got up when he kicked her. I rammed him into the kitchen sink and slammed my head into his nose. Blood went everywhere, but he didn't even blink, he just dug his thumb into my shoulder until I was on the ground. Then he stomped on my forearms and hand. Breaking everything he could to not only stop my future in football, but to make sure I couldn't hold a pencil or a paintbrush. All the while yelling, 'You don't get to dream. You get to fucking suffer like I did. Robbie is special. He's my ticket out of this shithole with shit kids and that needy bitch.'"

I outstretch my crooked knuckles in her hand, and she sees that they didn't heal right. She rubs the tiny scars where surgery put them back together with pins and plates.

She rubs my back. She's almost sitting in my lap and I'm tempted to put her there. I want to make the pain go away by burying myself in her. But with each sentence and each touch, I do feel it all dissipating somehow.

"He went for her again. She was bleeding and passed out. He was going to kill her. I don't know how, but I got up and bashed him with a chair over and over." I pause and look over the park as I collect myself a little bit. I've relived that scene a million times.

"AND. Please do not stop telling this story."

I grin at her. "You know it's not fiction. It's not a Hallmark special."

Her voice is soft. "Please tell me your mom is ok. Even if we don't ever see each other past these couple of weeks. Tell me I get to meet the kick-ass boy-mom who raised sweet, kind champions."

I put my arm on the back of the bench and slide to the end to get a better look at her.

"I called the police. He's still in jail and only Law has gone to see him." She grins and I touch her cheek lightly with my knuckle. She closes her eyes and it looks like she's savoring my touch. I fucking need that to be true. I pull us out of the moment and finish this part of my story.

"We moved to Philly as soon as Ma and I got out of the hospital. My aunt and uncle helped us get out. Robbie bought a condo with his signing bonus and provided for us while Mom and I recovered. We never looked back. I've never wanted to be associated with Christopher Danson again."

She pulls her legs up onto the bench and rests her chin on her knees. "OH! The name change. He's the criminal upstate!"

I chuckle and nod. She must have googled Christopher Danson a few times.

"My middle name, despite what you thought, is Hayden. Corelli is my mom's maiden name."

BETTE

TEARS SLIDE DOWN MY FACE AS HE RECOUNTS WHAT HE'S LOST AND gained. It hurts.

"Why aren't you more upset right now? I'm a fucking mess."

He grins but doesn't quite laugh. "A shit-ton of therapy, and the fact that he'll rot in jail. It turns out, he stole quite a bit of money over the years from people who didn't appreciate it. He never really had a job. He let us believe he was a pillar of blue-collar stamina and integrity. He bitched how his hard work paid for our equipment and sports club fees. He stole it all. Prep school was a scam. I found out I was on a handshake deal and a partial scholarship. He never paid them, but I did last year."

He threads his fingers in and out of mine. It's not sexual but easy. It's like we left Hayden and Bette behind so Lizzie and Danny could catch up. We don't say anything else as he pulls me to standing.

We're strolling down Bleecker and our hands are still intertwined. Like this is something we do all the time, strolling down a lively city block, like we did in Paris. Like we've continued to do it for the last ten years.

I break our silence. "This is nice. I don't want to ruin it. But I need to know more."

Hayden's rich dark hair falls in his face. It's not as poofy as he's had it. I like it less than perfect. "Firecracker, there's not much else to tell you. You kind of know it all. The specifics are: I recuperated when we all moved. I changed my name and got a Graphic Design degree from Temple and lived at the condo with Ma and Law. He came back to help us recuperate before we forced him bak to FSU for the spring season."

I roll my head back and snap it forward. "That's why I couldn't find you at BC. That's how you disappeared."

"And you? There's no record of a Lizzie Fox from Stanford."

"I became Bette at Berkeley. I gave up Stanford, remember?" I raise my eyebrow at him.

He hits his head. "Ahh, yes, you certainly did, for me."

"For us," I correct him. "And no worries, I still don't regret Stanford at all." I blurt out, "Why did you stand me up?"

The pain tugs at me. He lets go of me and turns me towards him. He gently pushes me up against a wall and places his hands on my shoulders. Ok, then. He waits until he has my full attention.

"Don't get mad again, but crazy, fucking beautiful, nutty-bonkers woman, you told me never to contact you again. But more importantly and poignantly, your father told me you didn't love me. You didn't know how to break up with me, so he did it for you. He threatened me with legal action because he claimed you said I was stalking you.

There was a restraining order pending and phone records would be checked. Tony's father confirmed all of it for me."

Holy shit. That's detailed. But it doesn't sit right with me. "And you believed him?"

"I was eighteen and essentially alone. Clearly, I couldn't go to my parents but your dad did file for a temporary restraining order and your signature was on it."

My jaw drops. My whole being goes cold. He did do it. It was his way of getting me back under his thumb. So fucking evil and sick; he can't have gone to this depth lightly. This is pathological.

"I didn't sign that, my dad must have done it. I would never say any of that."

He inhales in a sharp breath and I try to look away. He pulls my face back to his. He places his forehead to mine and we stand there, letting the pieces fall. Neither of us speaks for minutes.

I start, "That night when my dad and I fought about prom, I told him there wasn't anything he could take away from me. That I was old enough to make my own decisions. I was wrong. There was one thing he could take, so he did."

Tears well up and I can't stop them, so I just let them fall. He looks concerned and I hold up one finger as I try to collect myself.

He asks, "Can I hold you while you say whatever it is you're going to tell me?"

I shake my head no. I've had a lifetime of being angry at my dad. This is my undoing. Eighteen years of resentment, but in the end, doing as I was told. I lived up to his mold for me, until Danny let me know that what I had to say and think mattered.

Hayden's anger will be fresh and raw. I want to give him

that so maybe we can get through this. But holding me will only muddy the issue.

I gasp as I try and control the crying. "He showed up at the hotel I booked us for prom. He gave me a printout of your email. You wrote there was no place for me in your life. That your athletic career had to take the front seat. And that you didn't know how to tell me you didn't want me in Boston. You couldn't shake me off because I was clinging to something that wasn't there. And my father was kind and gentle as he delivered the message. He was there as I crumpled to the floor when my world fell away."

He's walking around, alternating clenching his fists and running his hands through his hair.

He grabs my hand roughly and pulls me into the closest bar. He sits and snaps at the bartender, "Bourbon. Neat." He looks at me and I nod. "Two."

The bartender places them down. He shoots his and I take mine. He takes it out of my hand and I start to speak. He places his finger over my lips and shoots mine as well.

I smile and put up two fingers to the bartender, and he fills the glasses again.

Hayden turns to me. He speaks through clenched teeth. "Is there more?"

I turn towards him and nod.

He slams the drink. "You know I didn't send that. You fucking know that, right? Jesus. How the fuck could we be that stupid?"

"He was a genius puppet master. I found out later he'd cancelled my phone contract, which is why none of my calls or texts went through, and neither did yours."

His eyes are so full of hurt and anger.

Hayden pulls me off my barstool and into his arms.

He mutters into my neck, "I never ever did, felt, or said

such things. I was told you wouldn't want to waste your time with a Southie like me."

I'm stumbling over my words. "I didn't do that. That doesn't even sound like me."

He pulls back but his arms settle around my waist. "'Athletic career.' You thought I wrote 'athletic career?'"

I smile as tears well up again. "I lost it that night."

"No. Really? You never lose anything."

I blurt out, "Except you."

It's barely out of my mouth when his lips are on mine. I lean into him. It's a sad and sweet kiss that reinforces we were played for idiots. Neither one of us ever broke up with the other. He pulls out his phone and orders a car. I slam cash on the bar and we run out of the bar. I stop and his mouth is on my neck as I lean back.

He growls, "How do I get revenge on a dead man?"

"Be with me."

"Christ, I need to get to our hotel."

He mashes his face to mine. Our needy lips and tongues trying to outrun our lost time and prove to my dead father we were meant to be together. Fate saw it, even if he didn't. I believe more in fate than I ever did in my dad.

A car pulls up and we get in it before he kisses me again.

I look at him and say, "I didn't talk to my father for the last three years of his life. Does that help?"

"Regrets?" His anger is still simmering, but it's also an honest question. He's checking in with me.

"No regrets. Only issues to work through."

He winks at me. "I've got a guy if you need him."

I tried therapy, but I got too angry at everything in the world and didn't like being angry all the time.

"Perhaps anger management might be a better route for me. But there's something more I need to tell you." We both laugh but it's forced. I turn my body all the way to his, and he sits up a little straighter.

I stumble over my words. "Uh. You're..."

He squeezes my knee. "Find your words, then tell me, Lizzie. I'm not going anywhere."

I exhale and almost cry again. I'm a sappy, saucy puddle of confusion right now. I look out the front window for a moment and find it. The thing he gave me so long ago.

"You're the reason why. You telling me to be brave and be bold and go after things I want and love. You're the reason I write advertising copy in Chicago."

"And you're the reason I found a way to be into the 'arts.' You told me talent can be used in many ways and that it's ok to be good at two things. How did we get here?"

I take his hand before he can make a fist and flick his thumbs in and out again.

"Thank God for whatever mystic force brought us together."

"Eva and Rinaldi?"

I grin, then touch his face. "I don't know how much longer I could have gone on as half a person. Thank you for reminding me I'm Lizzie, too."

He pulls me close and holds me, as if I could fall out of this cab and slide back through time. "I don't know what this all means, but I know I'm not a whole person without you, either."

He kisses my forehead and I feel something wet hit my arm. I look up at him.

"You can't leave me again," he says. "I won't know what to do. Are you planning to leave me?"

I shake my head.

"Well, I do have lunch plans tomorrow with Sophie, so

I'll be gone a couple of hours, but for the larger part, no. What about work?"

"Not now. Later."

"And shouldn't you be heading to your brother's game?"

He kisses me slowly. His lips feathering over mine. He hovers, making me want it even more. I break the spell by nipping at his bottom lip. And then the kiss becomes feral. His tongue slides against mine and I shiver everywhere, as if a sudden chill came over my body, but it's him. It's the excitement of him kissing the hell out of me and the words we shared. Did he mean it? Does he want to keep me? Because I sure as hell want to keep him. His hands move up my legs and tuck under my sunny yellow skirt, and I gasp. His fingers gently feather over my skin and goosebumps erupt everywhere.

He takes my earlobe between his teeth and tugs. "Tonight, I need to be with you properly. Not hate fuck you but find my way into this divine pussy that I dream of all the damn time. I need to make my fantasies, realities. I want to hold you and taste you. Then I'm going to tell you how much I've missed you."

"That sounds good. But if we never actually broke up, you should know, I've cheated on you a lot."

He nips at my neck and says, "Can't decide if I should punish you for that or enjoy the results of all that practice."

I stare up at him and realize—in his eyes is the only place I've ever truly felt safe.

"How about both?"

HAYDEN

I WAKE WITH HER ARMS DRAPED OVER MY CHEST AND HER HAIR everywhere. Her mouth is open and there's a touch of drool. And it's so wrong that the sight of her drool is turning me on.

I thought kitchen hate sex was the hottest sex. Turns out, it's Bette/Lizzie sex. That's the hottest sex.

We're healing all the hateful things we've said to ourselves over the years and letting go of all the pain. We know each other so well, despite the time lapse, that nothing is off limits. And that makes sex blistering. My dick and I are so happy I skip out of bed and pad to the kitchen.

I have no clue what today will bring, other than a mostly naked morning. We need to figure out how to be with each other again. Because being without her isn't an option. Seriously, who gets a second shot at their soulmate?

I should've married her the moment we hit US soil in New York ten years ago. Sure, we would have been the only married people in our graduating classes, but he couldn't have pulled us apart that easily. I mess with the tiny coffee packets for the machine in the kitchen. They're not the cups or anything workable. I end up ripping the tiny little filter bag and grounds go everywhere.

I miss my coffee pot at home. Wow, home, that's going to be a thing. One of us will have a new job here and the other is supposed to go home.

I'm wiping up the mess and my mind wanders. What if we were meant to be pulled apart and her dad was just fate? I wouldn't have been there the night my mom almost died if I was with Lizzie. Perhaps we weren't supposed to be together until now.

I wouldn't have gone to the house. I might be an orphaned football star about to retire on top. But would we have survived it? If my mother had died, there's no way I wouldn't spend my life blaming myself and resenting that I wasn't there.

And if I was a football star, what would she have done? If Lizzie was happy in my shadow—maybe brave Bette would have stayed hidden and who can say that would have been better? I probably would draw occasionally, but not like I do now. Painting and drawing were my only way through the pain of losing her and football. We'd be different versions of us. I wouldn't have my studio, which is, other than inside of Lizzie, my favorite place in the world. And I can't say those versions of us would have been better.

The grounds are sticking to me and I'm trying to rinse them off, but they're stuck. I slip into her hotel room and jump in the shower for a second. I soap up quickly and remember we need to get more condoms. Last night was a four-time epic marathon. I adjust my dick as he begins to reminisce.

I want to be intimate with her again. Not just sex, but know her noises and routines. I'm an impatient guy so I might need her to write them down so I can study them like a playbook. I toss my shorts back on, run a towel over my head and resume trying to find sustenance.

I open our fridge as if there's food in there. Just my ever-present Greek yogurt. I wonder if she can cook. I started doing it when Mom's arms wouldn't heal, and the physical therapist thought it would be good rehab. I can dice like a mutha. I want to dice for her. Maybe I'll go get omelet stuff. Then I remember I'd have to leave her and I'm not doing that right now.

She wants to call her mom today and see if we can unravel this further. Sophie and Dax came to town so I'll grab some Dax time later. I don't think we're in a double date kind of place, so we'll each retreat to our original partners.

I call down and order eggs—hers runny and mine over hard. Sourdough toast, bacon, and sausage—links, not patties. I don't need to ask her. Those are some of the billion details, I memorize and buried about her. I order her some English breakfast tea with extra lemon and honey. And a pot of coffee. She may like coffee now, that I'm not sure of. I know she liked a white hot chocolate in the afternoon, but who knows her Starbucks order these days? Christ, I want to order it without asking her. Is that the definition of intimacy? I hang up the phone and her voice bellows from the other room.

"Why? Why am I naked and alone?"

I run and jump on the bed. She props herself up on her elbows. The sheet falls precariously low.

She grins. "And why do you have shorts on? And you showered without me?"

I sit back on my heels as she gathers the sheets around her. "Last one without you. I promise."

She points at me, then flips her hand over and curls her finger to me.

I shake my head slightly and stare at her. "You're miraculous. You're no longer that scared, timid girl, huh?" She bites the inside of her cheek. "You're exactly who I saw that first night, you just didn't know it yet."

"Aren't you fucking clever?" She chides me and I laugh at her. "I wasn't timid. I was a rule follower," she says.

"No, you were always a rule bender."

"And you're a rule breaker."

I lie down on top of her and brace my arms on either side of her head. "Yes." I kiss her gently and drop my lip below hers and suck. "My cock instantly wants you. He's always been a slave for your pussy."

"Oh God. I adore adult Hayden's version of dirty talk."

"I've had some practice. Now, are you going to lower that sheet so I can lick that tasty clit of yours or am I going to have to rip it off?"

She pauses and her eyes dance with light and dark. She rasps, "Rip it off."

Fuck, she gets better and better.

I lean back and snap it off her. She's splayed before me and I remove my shorts while she watches. Then I stroke myself as she reaches for me. Her nipples are peaked from the sudden exposure. She tugs at my arms to join her. I lie down again and kiss her. It's all different now.

She stops. "I don't know how to get out of this bed."

"Neither do I, but let's keep doing this until we figure it all out."

"Done."

I flip her over and she's straddling me now. "Ride me," I command. She slides a condom on my incredibly hard cock then sinks down. When she finally looks up at my face she sees that we've both been watching where we're joined. It's hot and vulnerable.

"Come here."

She leans over me and kisses me softly and I lift her ass up then slam her down again. We both groan. She moves her hips and I help her go faster.

"JESUS. We are so good at fucking." She screams and I laugh until she swivels her pelvis and then all thoughts are gone from my mind as I stalk another epic orgasm.

BETTE

SOPHIE BLURTS OUT, "YOU KNOW WE STOPPED FUCKING TO SEE you."

"I appreciate the sacrifice." It's nuts to me she's shacked up in Boston with Dax. They came to town to check in with work and us.

Her long purple nail flicks a piece of chicken off her plate towards the street. Then she rearranges her salad, so the proportions are even. She always does this with salads. She sees the world differently aesthetically.

"Soph." She's avoiding talking and I don't know why.

"Bette. Are you still Bette?" She sips her midday cocktail and points to me.

"Of course, I am. Are you pissed I'm with him?"

"Are you with him? This is a big fucking fat deal. I said fuck him not move in with him. A couple of conversations and you're together?"

I talk through a big bit of food. "And fucking. We did that, too. And I came. A lot."

She rolls her eyes. "As happy as I am you finally orgasmed with someone else in the room, are you still going to wrestle the job away from him or just wrestle with him?"

"Both." I scoot my chair back a touch and wipe the condensation off my glass of iced tea. It's warm today, but Sophie is coming in hot.

She leans forward and moves her sunglasses to the top of her head. "You've worked too hard. We've invested too much into bringing those assholes down for you to blow it because he blew you."

"You're dating one of those assholes, too."

"Fucking is different than dating. You think you're dating him now? You're all twisted up in his nostalgia-cock."

I'm offended.

I say, "And you haven't left Dax's side. Why aren't you back in Chicago?"

"Touché."

"Don't speak French to me."

She smiles and then her mouth is drawn into a very serious expression.

"Here's English. Get the job, then fuck him some more. Get your head in this. Don't give it all up for some asshole like I did." Her divorce story thrums in my brain.

"Not an asshole." I find it odd I'm saying this since I've called him Assface for two years.

Soph points at me with her fork. "He used to be. Has he even shared his pitch with you?"

I haven't shared my idea yet, either.

I get defensive. "We've agreed to go after the job."

"You have to get over him. Treat this like closure." I look at her strangely. I turn to the side, trying not to roll my eyes. "Don't with that bullshit. Just because his cock is magic doesn't mean the rest of it is solved."

"He didn't ghost and neither did I. But look who's talking? You've spread your legs enough, but still haven't found that."

She sits back and crosses her arms. "Until now," she says.

"What's wrong with wanting to be happy with the person I set out in this life to be happy with? Ok, there was some fighting and a decade apart, but what if we could figure this out?"

"And what if he's using this to his advantage?"

"He's not."

"How do you know?"

"I know." I look at her as she drains her drink. "Wait. Back up a sec. Did you say Dax was your happy?"

She beams as I say his name. She nods.

"Sophie!" I grab her. I've never known her to invest in anyone for more than a night. "Really? He's your happy?"

"Yes. Trust me, I'm as fucking stunned as you are. But it's like we've always been together. Neither of us are anxious or nervous, we're instantly settled. And believe me, no one is more fucking shocked than me and my vagina."

I raise my glass and my eyebrows. "I think the male population between the ages of twenty-five and sixty are in mourning a bit."

She fills her mouth with salad and says, "Eighteen to seventy-five."

"What the fuck?"

"I'm not ageist."

I laugh and she winks at me.

"Dax has to be, like, ten to fifteen years younger than you."

"Thirteen." I choke a little on some ice. "He's also not an ageist."

I sit back. I can't believe this is all shaking out like this. "And you really think I should be careful? I mean, you're smitten with his best friend. You clearly trust his judgement—"

"I do trust his judgement, in all things vagina and Sophie. And his work. Hell, I do trust him. I think your dad fucked you up and over so much more than you're coming to terms with."

I shift and recross my legs to swing them out onto the sidewalk. I stare at my shitty pedicure left over from when I was just coming out to New York. He wanted me, even with chipped OPI Lincoln Park After Dark peeling off my toes.

"I went to the Boston office with Dax one day. Do you know he has targets all over the place with your name on them for Nerf gun practice? They have a notebook with pranks and things to do to us, and they've only done half."

I laugh. Of course, they do. I sit back in my seat and watch the traffic for a moment. I love the hustle of a city. The noise fills all the empty spots or lulls in my life. Will he do that now?

I turn back towards her and offer up, "We have the chalkboard of ideas."

She gestures with her fork. "True, but I'm wary of a guy who was so invested in taking you down now being so invested in you."

"You know I can handle this, and you know how important this is to me."

"Dax filled in his side. It's quite a thing you two need to come to terms with. I want you to be careful. Don't lose yourself and your dream job in a man who pre-purchased those ping pong balls six months ago."

"I'll be mindful. But I'm also falling hard and fast for the memories of him and the Hayden I know. All those pranks and passion for hating me has kind of flipped, and now it's playful and perfect. He's more caring and attentive than any man I've ever been with. Since I've been sitting here, he's texted several times. Once with a work idea and once to remind me I need toothpaste."

"Horse breath? Won't kiss you?"

"No! I'm out of toothpaste and he noticed."

"Fine. Fine."

"How do you know Dax isn't playing you?" I throw it back to her.

"That's the difference between you and me. If he's playing me, I'll get even, then I'll get over it. But you, you never even got over being ghosted by a boy you knew for twelve weeks. You spent a decade being sad, lonely, and disconnected. But also brilliant, vibrant, and amazing, don't forget that part. The point is, I'll be fine if Dax and I don't work out. I don't think you'll recover a second time. Be cautious until the job is settled. Just trying to have your back."

I flip her off.

Her laugh fills the patio. "Fair enough. Let's get day drunk." She gestures to a random waiter. "We need like thirty Aperol Spritzes. Or maybe one round, then straight shots of Don Julio." He shakes his head no and turns back to his table.

I roll my eyes as she stands up.

"Never fucking mind, you twat. I'll get them." She takes off into the restaurant.

HAYDEN: Can you get some condoms when you get toothpaste? PLEASE. I seem to have used all my stash.

BETTE: I have some in my room.

HAYDEN: No. I will not fuck you with condoms meant for another man.

BETTE: They weren't for another man.

HAYDEN: When did you purchase them?

BETTE: They're fine. I got them like a month ago.

HAYDEN: Did you think you were going to see me?

BETTE: Of course not.

HAYDEN: Then they were for another man.

BETTE: By that logic, I used another women's condoms. You'll get over it.

HAYDEN: You're a stronger person than I am. Please get me unsullied condoms.

BETTE: Let's get blood tests? I have an IUD.

HAYDEN: Hmm. That's an awfully big step after only being together for a week.

BETTE: Ten years and one week.

HAYDEN: I'm not sure this has staying power enough to go bareback.

BETTE: HA HA

HAYDEN: Shit. Now my dick is hard even thinking about it.

I laugh as Sophie places an Aperol Spritz in front of me and a bottle of tequila in front of her.

"What? It'll save the waiter a trip. Now he only has to bring glasses, ice, and limes. Also. They don't carry Don Julio."

"Where did you go?"

"The bar next door. I'll pay a corkage fee, but I'm not drinking shitty tequila."

HAYDEN: Hello?! Hard dick situation here. Any response?

BETTE: Sorry. I think we might need to get those tests tomorrow. I'll take care of the dick tonight.

HAYDEN: Why not now? Dax is hunting down Sophie as we speak. We're almost done here.

BETTE: {INSERT PICTURE OF SOPHIE WITH AN EVIL GRIN AND THE BOTTLE OF TEQUILA}

BETTE: I think we're just getting started.

HAYDEN: Aw shit. Looks like there's a double date about to happen. Where are you?

BETTE: Sophie's texting Dax.

HAYDEN: Thank God. It's been like four hours of missing you. And now I'll get to see if drunk Bette is anything like puking drunk Lizzie.

BETTE: Nah. Bette's a seasoned salty pro.

HAYDEN: We'll see.

HAYDEN

We're stumbling a bit. Sophie's insane and the opposite of Dax. She lives her entire life out loud. She holds nothing back. Dax is a quiet, pretty closed-off person. He loves an economy of language, but Sophie almost never stops talking. And he's crazy for her. I can see it. He doesn't even want to be an inch from her. I think she's in her late thirties or early forties and Dax is thirty. But somehow, they don't seem like a boy toy situation. Sophie's expression when she looks at him seems genuine.

My arm is around Lizzie and it's so perfect. It's almost everything I've ever wanted. How is it that I get that? After the fucked-up life I've had and the fucked-up life she's had. How is it that we get to be happy now?

We've been walking for a block or two saying nothing. She breaks our introspective moments.

"I like you."

I laugh at her, then pull her closer and kiss the top of her head. "You do? That's a mighty nice thing to say."

She pulls away and slides her palm against mine and

we keep walking. "I mean, I loved Danny." I grin. "Hated Hayden." She shakes her head quickly as if she's shuddering from how much she hated me. "But I like you. Whoever you are."

"I'll take it." I lean over and kiss her lightly and we walk on into the night. "And, for the record, I like you, too."

I'm so buzzed from the tequila and her skin. I kiss down her back and kneel behind her, holding her ass as the water cascades over us. I kiss it and she squeals.

"I'm still not less mad, just so you know."

I squeeze it and stand back up. I kiss her neck from behind.

She moans and turns in my arms. "I'm so sleepy."

We finish rinsing off and her tits are so shiny and pretty. I lean down and lave my tongue over her wet nipples, and she laughs.

I look up at her. "What's so funny?"

Her eyes are glazed over and she has the dopiest grin on her face.

"My nipples like your tongue. They're less mad at you." Her eyebrows raise.

I'm not getting her meaning. "But the rest of you is still mad?"

She stamps her foot and her tits shake a bit. I watch as if I'm going to be tested on it later.

"Do that again," I say, and she does. "Your jiggly perfect boobs are dancing a little bit. I like it."

Then she kisses me. It's sloppy and our tongues are everywhere. No finesse or skill. Just blobby drunk tongues smooshed into each other's mouths. She pulls back.

"Doritos."

"We don't have any. And you just ate Mexican food."

She stumbles a bit as I'm holding her. I'm not sober, but my girl is drunk. Is she my girl?

"Are you my girl?" I ask, honestly wanting to know the answer.

She looks up at me. "Really?" She pops a hip. Her mascara is streaking down her face and she's laughing manically as she tries to be serious. I turn the water off and grab towels. I dry her off and it's difficult not to lick her. I wrap the towel around her and one around myself. She stumbles towards my bed. I throw her over my shoulder and turn back to the bathroom vanity. I need one of those wipes she uses to remove her makeup. She's shrieking and laughing as I nibble on her ass.

"My ass is still mad at you. Still mad AT you."

"Ok, Michelle Michelle."

"Fuck you. Fuck YOU. You should get fucked." She laughs hysterically at her mildly funny joke. And I squeeze her tighter to me before placing her on the counter and finding what I'm looking for.

She turns and sees herself. "AH! I'm a horror show."

I move her hair out of her face. I gently rub the wipe around her eyes and down her cheeks, collecting the black flakes and smears as I go. When I'm done, I look into her eyes and she's smiling with her whole body. I can see it. She's on the same wavelength and it's nice not to be alone.

I tuck her hair back and rub my knuckles over her cheek. There aren't real words for this kind of beauty. All I can think about is painting her. I can't possibly express to her what I'm feeling, but I think I might be able to put it down on paper with pencil or acrylics.

I kiss her softly and she sinks into the kiss. I pull back

and get her hairbrush, then I pick her back up and place her on the edge of the bed. I get behind her, straddling her and pull my towel between us. Honestly, the towel wrapped around my waist and a thin shred of self-control are the only things keeping us from a good ole sloppy alcohol-infused fucking.

I brush her hair out and she closes her eyes and hums a bit. I run the brush through my own hair and she leans back on me. I think she's almost asleep. I guide her down and cover her up. I flick the lights off, then let my towel drop and crawl in beside her. For the longest time I lie on my back with my arms behind my head. I listen to her as she slips into sleepy breathing. It's a soundtrack I'd like to hear forever. I don't know what we're doing. I don't know if we can make this work. I certainly don't know what to do about getting the job over her. There are so many moving pieces, I'm not sure we're stable enough to keep them all intact.

She rolls onto my chest and I surround her, tugging her closer to my heart. As if that's even possible with how far in it she is already. Her hand is playing with my smattering of chest hair.

She whispers, "I am."

I whisper back, "You are what, little firecracker?"

"Your girl."

And bam, my chest explodes. Busted apart, for all the world to see, by that little firecracker in my arms. And now I realize what she meant by her boobs are less mad at me. Perhaps I remind her of that drunken rambling in the morning. Missed opportunity.

I'm not sure how we're dressed and actively working, but something clicked. I'm sketching soap and she's coming up with taglines. She's not afraid to fail and put it all out there. She walks around pitching one line after another. It's impressive and dizzying.

But she knows it's how you're successful in this business; you fail a lot. For every great pitch, there are a hundred in the garbage. You can't get married to an idea until the client does. Every aspect of a campaign can change until it's out in the world. Nothing is precious and she gets that. It's fascinating to watch, considering the eighteen-year-old I knew was terrified of getting a B in school. The idea of failing was beyond her. I'm proud of her in a strange way. She slides back on to a chaise lounge opposite mine.

We're sitting on our balcony and the sun is getting a bit sweltering. I step inside and leave the slider open. I pick up the phone and order a club sandwich, a Cobb salad, and two iced teas.

She yells into the room, "How did you know I wanted a club sandwich?"

I lean on the open sliding door. "Guess I'm having a Cobb salad, then."

"No. If the club was for you, we can split it." I kiss the top of her head as if this is the most normal thing in the world. As if we didn't miss years together.

I say, "Fair."

Her smile is bright. The sun is lighting up the highlights in her hair. And her eyes, damn, those peridot green eyes of hers are sparkling and adoring.

There's a question in the back of my head. I know we're only two weeks into this, but it pops out. "Could you love me again?"

She draws in a quick, sharp gasp.

"No lube? Just right in there asking tough questions without warm-up. That's not like you. You're more considerate than that." She laughs.

"Also, quick aside, are you less angry at me now?"

"You still want to come on my ass?" She draws her legs up to sit lotus position.

I grin and nod wildly. "Very much."

She shrugs. "We'll see."

"Cool. Circling back to loving me."

She scoots against the back rest of the chair, and I take the other one, mirroring her position. She's wearing these little black and pink polka dot pajama shorts that make her stems look long. They drive me fucking wild. I cross my arms and wait for her to answer.

She asks, "Is that where we're heading?"

A breeze kicks up and my papers start to scatter. She moves to grab them and I bend down to retrieve the ones that have fallen. I sit on the ground and lean against the side of the building. She's still collecting the papers. She's avoiding my question. It might kill me if we don't move forward. If she doesn't see us beyond whoever gets this fucking job. If we don't define who we are to each other before the client meeting, we'll never make it past that. The clock is ticking. I know all about her work life from the last five years, but I don't know almost anything personal. I need to work on that. Of course, I'll have to open up more about shit. I'm not used to doing that.

She sees me sitting and drops down on her butt. Her legs are out in front of her and I pull them onto my lap.

"Seems too good to be true," she says.

"We're owed this." I run my hand up her leg.

"I guess we are."

I say, "But I get it. I'm a bit jumpy. What happens on the other side of this month? How do we handle one of us being unemployed?"

She doesn't hesitate. "We face it together."

BETTE

I SET UP OUR LAPTOPS BACK-TO-BACK FOR THE WEEKLY DIRECTORS check-in meeting. He runs his hand over his face, then his stubble. I know what he's thinking and I pull his hands off his face. "Don't even think about it. The stubble stays."

He pulls me to him. "Someone likes a little sandpaper action?"

"Well, today it's soft, and um, there are certain parts of me that like the scratch a bit. Shave later."

He winks at me. "I'm Italian, it will come back."

"You're also Irish and it doesn't come back fast enough for me." He grins. The black hair that frames his luscious mouth makes me very, very happy. And turned on.

He settles across from me. "How the fuck do we do this without telling each other our pitches?"

"I don't know. Rinaldi put the call together." I grab a pen and start flipping the cap.

He leans over both computers. "Fine. You have your call while I suck an orgasm out of you." He raises his eyes. He can't get enough, but I'm insatiable, too.

I say, "We'll have to use our avatars." I raise my eyebrows at him. Then I laugh. He's insane.

He grins. "I will. I fucking dare you to go live while I eat you out."

I shake my head. "Intriguing offer."

He says, "Let's go, the meeting started."

I join the call. "Hey, everyone! Good to see you."

"It's so good to see you. It IS good to see you. To see you."

Hayden snickers at Michelle Michelle's greeting.

Rinaldi says, "Ladies and gentlemen, it's time to discuss budgets." I mute and groan. Hayden waves to everyone and flips on his avatar. He's muted. I look over at him and he's missing. And then I feel him. I don't look down because I'm on camera, but I double-check that I'm muted. Rinaldi is drowning us in numbers, and his hands are on me. I glance down and he's grinning wildly. He pushes my skirt up. It's not tight so it's easy access for him. I'm not wearing anything else. His fingers immediately find me and trace my clit. I'm trying not to make any moves, but I'm so turned on.

I unmute to answer a question. My voice stumbles as he flicks my clit with his finger and a bolt of lightning hits me in all the right places.

"That's the number I want as well." I sound like I'm in pain.

"That's fair to us, too. Sorry about earlier when I was a bit late," says Vancouver Bob.

Rinaldi says, "Hayden, you want to weigh in here?" I thrust at him and he puts his headset to his lips.

"I'm on board with it all. I trust Bette." And then he thrusts a finger inside me. He twists his microphone away from his mouth and hits mute. Then his fingers spread me open as he licks me straight up the center. I bite the inside of my cheek. There's no way I can come with everyone watching me. I have to get out of this.

"Oh," I say too loudly as he nips at my clit and circles while pumping fingers into me.

Michelle Michelle says, "Oh, what? Bette?" Shit. I didn't mute.

Oh, he just pinched my clit again and isn't letting go. My insides are on fire.

My voice is gravely and stilted. His fingers are curling inside me and I can't take much more of this. I paste on a pained-looking smile and try to keep my eyes open.

"Oh, we should do the thing you were talking about."

And then Hayden speaks, his fingers pinching my clit and another moving inside of me. I'm going to come while he's talking.

His voice is a touch desperate sounding as well. "I agree with Bette's point about Michelle's numbers. They are impressive. There's a lot of cash to be made in California. You just have to massage it right."

He lets go of my clit and I gasp. And then he pets it. Pleasure purrs through every part of me, and I struggle to maintain.

Hayden continues talking while working me. "I think if we tweak the market and work it hard, we can get it to come to us. Coming might be the most important thing we can get the tech giants to do."

Everyone laughs. It's becoming too much. I slam my hand on my computer and hide my camera. I mute and look down at him. He puts a finger over his lips. The chatter is going on but I slump down, offering more of myself. He sucks my swollen clit, then fucks me with his tongue for a moment. Then he clicks his microphone back on, and I'm a writhing wet mess of need and want.

"And I can personally say I'm looking forward to the culmination of these ministrations we've been dicking around with for the last couple of minutes. I mean years."

And then it's on. I unmute. "Well said, Hayden. Sorry, something's going on with my computer and I can't get my camera to work. But I'm here." I want to play his game. I breathe out. "Things are coming together nicely for us here in New York. We should be on the other side of all the buildup soon and the release will be nice."

I mute and look down at him. He withdraws from me and I think I'm going to die. Then he pops up on his side of the table. My eyes are wide as he pretends to pay attention. He's left me dying to come.

I stand and walk over to him. I straddle him and unzip his pants. His cock is hard. It's always hard for me. Especially if he's got me this wet. I palm his tip and he groans. I slide down between his knees and take him fully into my mouth as he slams his fist into his thigh and then flicks his microphone on.

"Bette. what do you think of a video presentation versus a physical presentation?" My head pops off his cock and I stare at him. He offers me his microphone.

I do care about this issue. "I personally only like video if we're pitching video spots or social. A physical pitch is much stronger and provides us with more freedom to stretch concepts. If you show them a video, then that's how it's going to play out. Less open-ended and you're trapped in one idea."

I'm staring at his face and his jaw drops. I let the tiny microphone on his wire headphones go. And then he's pulling me up onto his lap and his lips are on mine. His tongue assaulting and exploring every inch of my mouth. We're carnal as they drone on over what I said. I can't get close enough to him. He backs up and mouths to me:

Get on my cock.

I don't hesitate, standing, then holding his hard-as-hell cock and sinking down onto it. As soon as I'm fully seated, I let out a loud groan. His eyebrows raise, and I'm overwhelmed by the feeling of him without a condom, which we've both realized just happened. It's so intense and full.

"What was that? Hayden, Bette, are you ok?"

I mouth to Hayden: *What the fuck?*

He points to the headphones. They've come unplugged and we're not muted.

"Shit," I say with my pussy stuffed full of his glorious cock.

Hayden grunts out, "We're fine. There's been a strange thing going on today with the internet."

"You're together in the same office?"

Hayden thrusts up into me and I brace myself on his shoulders.

I throw my head back as I move without thought. I can't hold back. I have to fuck this gorgeous man.

Hayden grits out, "You're all great and things are perfect moving forward. Ok, bye." He leaves the meeting and slams his computer closed. Then he puts his hands on my ass and gets me moving at a much faster pace.

"Make me come, you hellion. I can't contain myself around you."

My new orgasm is already at the base of my spine. I'm bouncing on top of him. We're staring at each other.

"You're so good at fucking me. You're the best at it. I promise I'm clean... Fucking you bare is the best thing I've ever fucking felt in my whole life. I've never fucked anyone like this."

"Never?" I can barely breathe, as I'm about to lose it.

"No, you?"

I grin. "Never and I need to feel you from the inside, hot and fast. Come, now."

"Christ, Lizzie. Fuck me, Bette. This is so fucking good." He calls me both names. I like it. We're slamming together. The meeting is still droning on my computer and he grips me hard as I feel him pour himself into me. Just as his cock jerks inside of me, I lose it. I squeeze him so tight as it ripples through me. I keep coming in more intense ways and it's incredible. It won't stop, so I clutch onto him and bury my head on his shoulder as we ride the end of our climax.

I hold his face and we say nothing. What started as a game took a serious turn and I won't survive if we don't make it. I will never love a man like I love this one, but I'm terrified to tell him that.

HAYDEN

We're sitting on our couch, her feet in my lap. We tried to work. Neither of us are interested, so we're sipping whiskey and wine and watching a movie. I don't know what's happening, I just like watching her watch. Her face is so expressive, as if it's an interactive sport. I'd love to see her at a sporting event—a wave of sadness overtakes me. She never saw me play football; fucking bastard stole that from me. I squeeze her feet and pause the movie.

"Where's Kris? You never mention her. Are you two still friends?"

She tries to move her feet, but I have ahold of them. She sits up a little. "What are we doing?"

"I want to know what happened when we were apart. I know there was pain on both sides, but did you ever go back to Europe? Dance on a table? Was Kris in your wedding? Where did you meet that guy? Where is she now?"

Her voice gets quiet. "Kris was my maid of honor. It was a couple months before she was diagnosed with bile duct cancer. It's rare. There's not a lot to be done, nothing works."

I pull her arms up and to me. She scrambles onto my lap.

"I'm so sorry. That was callous of me to say. I'm so sorry. Oh my God. Are you ok?"

"I'm not fine at all. I'll never get over it. I often thought it was extra cruel to lose both of you."

I pull her closer. "If it matters, you never lost me. I was just lost." Tears flood her eyes. "Do you miss her still?"

She wipes her tears. "Every day. I talk to her a lot. I have to, or she'll get lost, too."

I hold her close. We stay like that for a long time.

"Lizzie, I was trying to fill in the blanks, not upset you."

She smiles. "It's ok. She's the other piece of me that helped me become Bette. She gave me the strength to pull myself up. She got me off the path I was rapidly descending."

"What was that?"

"I didn't have a sport or a family to protect. I went a little self-destructive to work out the pain of losing you."

My heart aches even more. "There's nothing I can do about all of that. I would if I could."

"I know. Can I ask you questions, too?"

"Of course, I'm not sure there's more to tell."

"How did your mom adjust to moving to Philly?" She moves her legs out and snuggles onto my chest. Message received, let's talk about me for a while.

"She liked not facing the neighborhood at first. We all reunited with her sister. Eventually, my brothers and I kicked in to buy her Boston house back. She missed it too much."

She sits up. "The house?"

"Robbie thought it would do her good. She never connected with the townhouse crowd in Philly. She longed for the Southie neighborhood. Every time she'd hear a new family moved in, she'd moan about who was going to make them welcome to Southie cannoli and lasagna. She splits her time now between my auntie's house on the Cape, Claire and Robbie's house in Philly, and the old house in the hood."

"Really?"

"We offered her paradise in Florida, but she won't go. She's happiest when she's soaking up the stoop gossip from voices around her."

There's a pause again as I trace circles on her arms and finally ask, "What are you thinking about?"

"How she'll react to me."

She squirms a bit and I lift her chin.

"If I'm happy then she's happy."

"Does she know about me?" She scrambles off my lap and onto the end of the couch. She pulls her knees up and rests her chin on them. I stare at her and shift so I can face her.

"Claire has a very big mouth. How's your mom?"

"Skeptical, but happy, I think. She's found a way to move on from my dad. She's a more complete person, but I don't want to push her."

"Why not, we nag our ma all the time."

"That's because you're boys and girls are different. We drop hints for a while before telling someone they might be better off. She has a boyfriend who is fine, I guess."

I lean over and kiss her. "Let's stop being mopey. Come on, I want to take you out."

"Like a date?"

"Exactly like a date. Do you want to double with Dax and Sophie?"

She already running to her room to get prepped. I'm sure she'll knock the wind out of me when she's finished primping. "They're in Boston."

"Are they for real?"

"As far as I know."

BETTE

I'm sitting at Buvette working, but so is he. Because we've determined we're unable to work in our hotel suite without fucking.

He passes me a stack of drawings. I'm letting him take lead on the tone since it was his idea. But he hasn't touched my words. He'll suggest tweaks, but I've haven't let him alter one comma. And he's totally fine with it. We're in the final stages of the pitch and it came together rather quickly. I had another idea we almost went with, but we decided his was stronger.

I look over and a dark hair falls in his face as he sips his coffee. I can't get enough of his face. I can't believe I get to see this all the time.

My phone dings.

MOM: I'm selling the house. Phil turned out to be a cheater. I need a massive change. Why do I pick men who devalue me?

BETTE: I'm so sorry. But why sell our house?

MOM: It's time, honey. But I'd like for you to come help me clean it out. I know you're in the middle of all the work stuff. And I wouldn't ask if it weren't important. There's a cash offer on the house and I have to be out of here in a couple of days.

BETTE: It's been on the market, and you didn't tell me.

MOM: I was moving in with Phil and didn't know how to tell you, so now I'm homeless because I broke up with him. And the house has to be vacated and I haven't touched your father's office. I thought you might want to investigate things. I was going to take all his stuff with me in boxes to Phil's for you later.

BETTE: Mom, this is a conversation. I'll call you in a minute.

Hayden must have seen my face and frustration.

"And I thought only I could give you that level of frustration. Is it a new frenemy you have a secret past with?"

I laugh and sip my coffee. "I have to call my mom. She sold our house and now she's homeless."

"Did she not know she'd need to leave the house if she sold?" He sits back, raises his arms above his head and laces his fingers together with his arms twisted, then stretches. He's so bendy.

"I don't know. She's all upside down since Phil cheated on her, apparently. And I don't know what I can do from here." He scoots a chair closer to me and covers my hand with his. Then he kisses me. It's slow and sweet. His lips are lush with a hint of wild. There's no desperation, simply affirmation.

"What was that for?"

"Because I can."

"Do it again."

He draws me closer to him. Our kiss is more than tame but less than carnal. There's a warm liquid sensation running through me. It's like spilled warm honey oozing comfort into all my rough spots. I'm in so much trouble. I already love him. It's going to slip out of my mouth and I'll be mortified when I say it first. We'll be uneven because no one survives the uneven love. The unreturned I love you weighs heavily on a couple, and I can't have that. I'll say nothing.

He pulls back from our sensual kiss and pecks my lips once more, like an exclamation point on the moment. My mouth pulls up at the corners and my biggest smile claims my face.

He holds my knees. "I've got this. Go. We have our concept. I have art to finish and we can work on it remotely. I'll head to Boston to see Ma and Auntie J. I'll visit, catch up with Dax, see my house, and finish up there. We can have work calls without avatars and personal calls without clothes."

I laugh but it's a bit hollow. I don't know if I can step away from a project, but he's making a compelling case. I have to try and trust him even though I've spent the past couple of years with my back up.

"I'll be right here. You're not losing me again. I know we don't talk about it because we're scared, but after the announcement, I have something I need to show you."

"Bad?" I panic.

"Very good. I'm not going anywhere, no matter who gets this job."

I grin. "Me neither. And after all we've learned about my dad, I really want to see what he did and said—"

"About how I'm THE best boyfriend. I'm sure there are lots of writings and emails about how I'm perfect for his daughter."

I laugh. But then there's a pause. I know it was meant to be playful. But I can't help but roll the word off my tongue. "Boyfriend?"

"You prefer paramour?"

"Most definitely not."

"Manfriend?" He grins and I mirror it. "Lover?"

"Bleck. Not lover."

He tickles my stomach for a moment. We're sitting so close in this restaurant. I can't imagine what people think.

He raises a finger at me. "How about you just call me yours?"

"I introduce you like that?"

"If you like." He nods and I roll my eyes.

"Hello, everyone—" I gesture to him "—this is mine."

"Exactly. And this—" He holds my face and I lean into his touch "—is mine."

I totally am.

There are three large PODS and one is partially filled with furniture from our living room. The door is open because my mother trusts everyone. Funny, I trust no one. He did that to both of us.

"Mom, I'm here." I step into the house and the smell knocks me over. I haven't been here in four years. I meet her at my aunt's beach house on the Washington coast usually.

My mom comes rushing around the corner. Her new honey blonde hair bouncing on her shoulders, more lines around her deep green eyes, and her figure stick straight a touch frailer. She looks almost hungry, but maybe it's just an underlining desire for more of everything in life.

I don't know how to help her, but I want to. She throws her arms around me and begins to cry. I hold her. Somehow, I know these tears aren't for Phil the boring cheater, but for everything that's happened in this house. The tears are for remorse over the things done to me and the moments I had to witness. He was cruel to us, kind to others, but complicated. And now I want to know the depth of all he did.

I kiss my mom on the cheek and she wipes her eyes. “Do I have mascara running?”

“No. But why do you have mascara on to clean out the house?”

“There are movers coming back later to move the big stuff into those PODS for storage. And they’re kind of attractive.”

“MOM.”

“I am on the market. Come with me. I have iced tea and you have tea to spill.”

“How do you know that phrase?”

“I’m not that old. And Andy Cohen uses it a lot on *Watch What Happens Live*.”

“Fair enough.”

I drop my stuff in my old room. There’s a certain light that only exists in California. It’s brighter but also laced with almost a sepia tone. It’s like nostalgia is built in. A constant wanting of things to have been better or seem better than they are. I’m a California girl and nowhere on earth makes me more relaxed or myself, but the memories of it always seem better than the reality. Perhaps that’s anyone’s childhood. I’m here at the house they bought after the rift. But it’s all my stuff in this room I almost never used. Like a memorial to a girl he created and I never really was. But then again, you grow beyond, but never really move past your beginning.

I follow her into the dated dark-cabinet kitchen with the beige countertops and white appliances. It’s a study in contrasts and I hope the new owners gut it. Gut the whole house, light some sage, and start over. This house deserves joy.

"Mom, why don't you move to Hawaii or someplace super different?"

"OOOH. I love that idea. I rented a condo on the far side of town that will be ready for me in about a month. I'm staying with Aunt Ida in the meantime."

"You'll kill each other."

"Most likely, but what are my choices," she says resolutely. She slices lemons in perfectly pretty wedges and places them on the rim of the glass. She's always made things better. Always added a little something special. I forget to notice sometimes.

"Stay at my place in Chicago. I'm in New York now and probably staying if I get the job."

"When you get the job. I know this Danny/Hayden person is special to you, but you still deserve that job."

"I do. And we're both dealing with possibly being unemployed or elated. But we'll figure out the aftermath of it all together."

"That serious?"

"Yes."

"Careful giving away everything too soon." I get her warning. I'm sitting in her warning. She sold a house to move in with a man who was cheating.

"I'll think about Chicago. I do love the ballet there."

I nod and my phone dings.

HAYDEN: How's your ma?

BETTE: Coping. How's your ma?

HAYDEN: Busy cooking everything in Boston. I'm headed to yoga and then a bike ride just to work off Italian mother breakfast.

BETTE: I miss you.

HAYDEN: You have no idea how much I miss you. I've gotten so used to you being around again. It's torture to be apart now. Let's never do it again. All visits to our mothers can be done together. Got it?

BETTE: Deal.

HAYDEN: Now, if you'll excuse me, I have to go find some lube for my poor overworked cock. He needs you, but until you can make time for him, I'm just going to have to jerk off for the billionth time today.

BETTE: It hasn't been that long.

HAYDEN: Billionth and one.

BETTE: You just came?

HAYDEN: The very thought of you...

BETTE: I'll call you later and maybe we can work through some of your cock's issues together.

HAYDEN: Thank you. He'd like that.

HAYDEN

I'M DRUMMING ON THE TABLE ON THE BACK DECK OF MA'S BOSTON house with my pencil. I do it when I think. My mom steadies my arm. The brief is done, but I'm itchy about it. I know one of us will be the new VP Creative Director, but I'm not so sure what that job is anymore or how it matters.

My ma asks while wiping her hands on her apron, "Tesoro, my darling, what troubles you so? Come to the kitchen." You'd think this kitchen would trigger us, but we've both worked hard to make it a place of warmth and growth. We did throw out all the furniture, though. And she painted the room a cheery yellow, like she always wanted to.

My mom speaks as if she's a grandmother. Soft and genteel. Even though she'd cut a bitch to protect her own. She's endured more than all of us, but her heart remains open. I want to give her everything. And my brothers have tried, but she wants her simple life in Philadelphia and here, where she still cooks arancini for the block parties. There are only a few extravagances she allows. Really good chocolate, high-end baking dishes, and travel to see her boys play their sport. She also accepted a suitable car. We tried to get her a dreamy car, but she wanted a reliable Honda Accord so she could drive between Philly and Boston without worrying. As if a Mercedes wasn't reliable.

I know she loves having one of us around and that's all I've been able to offer that the other two can't. They have more money than they know what to do with, but I can give her time. During season, Claire travels with Robbie, so I go to Philly and make pasta with her or take her to a quilting thing. Claire works part-time for the team in their events department and does charity work the rest of the time.

Ma's formerly dark hair is now streaked with silver and pulled into a very familiar bun. Her dark grey eyes are the ones that tempered my father's blue in all of her children.

I scratch my nose with my pencil. "Nothing. Everything. She's everything and nothing right now."

"What does that mean?" She smacks the back of my head.

"MA!" She may talk genteel, but she's anything but with us sometimes.

She straightens the tablecloth, then folds the tea towel she just used to wipe the clean pots dry. "This girl needs to be cherished. She's fate's present. How—after all these years, your wish comes true—can you doubt it?"

I cross my legs. I'm uncomfortable talking about how I feel right now because I'm not sure. Away from her, I'm crawling out of my skin, but then again, I'm remembering the man I built in her absence.

"It's the stupid job, Ma. The one that could define our careers. And one of us will get nothing."

"Except each other." She dusts my cheek.

I grin at her. The logistical problems have been gnawing at me for days. She's my person and I don't want to screw it up by competing for a job that means nothing compared to what we could have. But then again, it's who I've been for the last six years. And who she's been for almost five years. I don't want to give up something like this for her and vice versa. I'm afraid there will be resentment on one side.

My mother's up and stirring and mincing. She's still listening. I sip her sweet wine, which is repulsive, but she loves a good Lambrusco.

"I know, we say that. But after it all goes down, how will we feel about each other? If it gets nasty in the competition or interviews, can we write it off as business and move on with the personal?"

My mother wipes her hands on her apron again and sits. She's making saltimbocca for me for dinner. It's Law's favorite. She's missing him, so do I.

I can't shake a radical thought I've been having. It goes against everything I'm saying and I think I am, but it might work. The more I think of the job, I wonder if my obsession was about the job or beating her. There's a lot more meetings with the new job and I hate meetings, unless I'm eating out the perfect pussy.

I'm grabbing drinks with Dax and Tony later. I need to talk through this insane idea I have. One that will shape my future and hers. Dax won't like it, but he'll help. Tony will love it because he still has no grip on reality. He's been through two wives searching for adventure. Each leaving with a tidy sum and no remorse. He loves excitement and to be challenged. I just got an invite for wedding number three. When I told him to stop marrying bimbos, he scoffed and yelled, "To adventure!"

My idea will put a strain on Sophie and Dax's relationship, so I need to check in with him before I go through with it.

I sip and wince at the wine again. I say in a loud sigh, "Oh, Mama."

She turns her head to the side and purses her lips. I laugh. "You only call me 'Mama' when you're in trouble. Are you in trouble?"

I stand up and walk around to get the blood flowing. The pitch is done. The boards are set, but I still can't help but feel something's not complete. It's not right. "I'm going to be in trouble for a long time, but I think I know what I have to do."

"Will you be the boy I raised when you do this?"

"I will."

"And you love her, do you not? I see it. It's like when Robbie would talk about Claire long ago. Your eyes do a swoony thing."

For a second my mind goes to her. I snap back to my ma and understand what she means.

She says, "Swoony. Now, I need grandbabies. Is she ready for that?"

"MA! We're barely in a relationship. We're hanging on by a thin thread and a promise."

She continues, "What's wrong with Robbie's penis? Why is there no new baby?"

I choke on the sugar wine. She turns back to her sauce and I quickly FaceTime my brother.

"Ma, say that again."

She leans back from the counter. "What is wrong with Robbie's penis? Or is it Claire's—"

She's interrupted by Robbie screaming, "MA! Knock it off. Jesus."

She smacks me with a tea towel, then takes the phone and looks at his face. "Where are the babies?"

"Stop asking. I might be retiring, but we have to figure

some things out." Ma tosses me the phone and starts to dance around the kitchen in a sort of jig, flinging her tea towel in a circle. She's giggling and singing in Italian. I get every other word, but it's not clear.

"What the hell are you doing, Ma?"

Robbie says, resigned, "She knows. But how?"

"Knows what?" I'm so confused.

My mama scoops up the phone and twirls it around. "You all have a tell. I taught you all to look for them. That's why you all clean up in the poker. But your brother just lied to me. His Claire is taking care of the new baby in her belly right now."

I yank the phone back. "True?"

"True. We're shy of three months, so don't fucking tell a soul. And do not tell Claire you know. MA! I have a tell? Does she know it?"

Ma yells, "Yes. I gave it to her as a wedding present."

I say, "What is it? And what's mine?"

She leans to the phone. "I will never say a word. I take it to my grave. And only your wives can know. You let that little firecracker know there's a prize if she sticks around."

Robbie asks, "Lizzie?" I nod. "How's it going?"

"Too good." I grin.

"Sometimes too good can be everything."

I roll my eyes and hang up on him. It's what we do.

My ma asks, "When you do the thing you have to do, will it hurt? Neither of you should have any more pain because of what that man did. Both of those awful men."

I grin at my mother whose past pain wins all the contests.

I push the chair back from the table and pull the bowl from the sun porch where the focaccia dough was rising. I flour the counter and plop the dough in the center and begin to knead. "I'm going to have to break some hearts to accomplish this. I hope I can put them back together in the aftermath."

She leans her cheek over and I kiss it. And then she smacks my butt.

"Go. Do your thing. Trust yourself. And draw me a nice picture. I need a new one for my living room. A great big one. Maybe a painting this time. Mio caro artista." She pinches my cheek like she's an old-world grandmother. She's so beautiful and young. She's only fifty-three. She didn't see anything except him for the longest time. And now she's settled into an existence like her mother before her. That of an old neighborhood Italian sage.

"Hey, Soph!"

She stands in one of Dax's tank tops that hangs to her knees. She still doesn't trust me.

"Heard from Bette?" I ask.

"Don't you call her Lizzie?"

"Not sure what your deal is, but people usually like me."

She turns away without saying a word. She's tough. Dax lopes around the corner and kisses her before he gets to me.

I nod in her direction. "She live here now?" Dax shrugs. "You cool with that?"

"I want her here. If that answers all your questions." I lean on the doorframe as Dax sits down on his hall bench. He's like Mr. Rogers. He has inside shoes and outside shoes.

He looks up at me as he slips on his Adidas. "You really want to do this?"

I texted him my plan. My face settles into a resolute

grin. "I think it's the only way. It will be a hell of a surprise. She's going to be so fucking pissed. I would freak the fuck out if she did this to me. I'm so glad I get to do it first."

Dax laughs. "That's for fucking sure. Like a killer prank. Hell, you'll outdo the ping pong balls. You'll go out on top with the penultimate prank."

"I might regret it for a long time, but in the end it's what's best for me and ultimately her. I can't pull this off without you."

Dax stands and slaps me on the back. "Cool. I think it will be fucking awesome. Pull the rug right out from under her."

I embrace my friend and partner. "Let's go to the office."

BETTE

HAYDEN: That was some good cyber fucking. Thanks, my lady. I'm so fucking excited to see you tomorrow.

BETTE: I miss you.

HAYDEN: There are things to be said. I want to tell them all to you.

BETTE: And I want to hear them. Sorry, this took so long. I think we're in really wonderful shape for the pitch. I'm so proud of you.

HAYDEN: You have no idea how impressed, proud and grateful I am for you. I'm more pleased with fate, but you're a close second. And I have a surprise for you.

BETTE: I don't always love surprises.

HAYDEN: I'll take my chances.

BETTE: Until tomorrow.

HAYDEN: Night firecracker.

I'm lying here in bed, but it's only, like, 2:30 p.m, emotionally exhausted. I'm so happy to be leaving here tomorrow having been surrounded by all the proof of my father's deceptions. There were messages to my teachers from kindergarten through Berkeley. There were developmental timeline charts and lists of books to feed me if I mentioned a subject. The worst were the emails to school friends declining playdates I never knew about. I thought I wasn't invited to anyone's birthday parties but he wanted me focused and friendless. I'm going to break his last remaining hold over me and gather a gaggle of new friends.

He was a monster and we'll never know why. We had a bonfire with all his precious shit. His legacy is gone. We dumped his computer with his unpublished dissertations in a river. Because fuck him. We were gaslit for decades but we're free now. My mom's getting propped up by her new abuse support group. I went the other night and it was weird to call it abuse. Therapy is my next stop, but I'm so glad I told him to fuck off while he was alive.

Hayden is my cosmic "fuck you" to my dad and my cosmic gift from Kristin.

Sophie's warnings creep at the edges of my mind. I did give in to the inferior idea for our pitch, but it's still good. It eats at me a little. But it's ok. It's ok if I don't get the job, as long as I have him. And I think he feels the same.

I pull up my texts and there are, like, seven from Sophie. And four missed calls. I haven't talked to her in a couple of days.

"Where the fuck you been?"

"Finding out my life is a lie," I say, referring to my father's shit.

"Good, then this won't be too much of a blow," she says, but it's not funny or cheeky.

"What are you talking about?"

I roll over onto my pillow.

"Baby doll, he's a lie, too. I hate it, honey. I hate to be this person. I heard things at Dax's house and I bolted."

"To Chicago?"

"I'm at Logan right now.

"Did Dax tell you things? Does he think you're broken up?"

"I don't give a fuck what he thinks. I gotta go with chicks over dicks on this one. Even though his dick is perfect. But that's a tale for another time."

"SOPHIE. Focus. Tell me."

"Hayden came over. He and Dax were talking about pulling the rug out from under you. And how it's the ultimate prank. They didn't go into details."

I sit up, pull my knees up and rest my chin on them.

"I heard Dax say, 'You're right. She'll never see it coming.' And Hayden said, 'I can't pull this off without you.' Then they said something about going to the office. I'm so sorry."

"You think he's going to pitch something else and cut me out?"

"That's where my mind went."

My eyes fill as my entire soul explodes. She was right. She was fucking right. I'm never going to survive this. I whip my fingers around in a circle and say it out loud.

"Double it."

"Double what?"

"The amount of therapy I think I'm going to need." I let a cry slip.

"Honey."

I stand up, sobbing, but cradle the phone between my ear and shoulder. I throw my things in a bag. I have to go now.

"I gave him the job. I fucking handed it to him. I played right into his lap. Another man controlling my life. Shit. This can't be real. He has to care about me a little. What's he planning to do? What did he say back to Dax?"

There's a long pause.

"Are you sure you want to know this?"

"I've spent a lifetime being kept in the dark and I won't do it again."

"I'm so, so sorry. He said, 'She's going lose it. I would. I would freak the fuck out if she did this to me. I'm so glad I get to do it first.' I wrote it down so I wouldn't forget it. What can I do?"

I'm shellshocked. And pissed at him and myself. Fuck. Fuck. I start throwing things. I only have soft things in my room so it's not very effective, but still, I throw them hard. Then I pick my phone back up. Steel forms in my back as I slide another wall into place. If there's anything I've taught myself over the last ten years, it's how to focus. Everything else can fall away when I go after something I want, and right now, I want to destroy him. And get that job.

"Fuck him. I'll cry later. I need you."

"You got me."

"I'm going to send you a pitch idea and some rough drawings I did to get the point across to Hayden. I need you to work it up tonight so I can pitch it tomorrow afternoon. I'll go before him. We're only supposed to have one pitch, so his will never see the light of fucking day."

"I got you."

"I'm jumping on the first plane to New York, call you when I land."

"Dax has called like ten times but I'll sort this all out later. I have an ad to draw."

"Throw it in my personal Google Drive, not the work one. And I'll print and mount it in the morning."

"You sound a bit manic."

"Oh, I am. I'm a fucking mess, but I don't have time to fall apart."

"You're super screwed up in the head."

"That, I am," I say.

"But I love you."

My eyes fill with tears. I'm so happy to have her. "I love you, too. Thanks for having my back, Soph."

I quickly turn off my phone, I have to compartmentalize this. I pack the rest of my stuff and try to block out the betrayal and pain.

How can I hate and love someone so desperately? I wanted to trust myself and him. I want to believe this isn't him, but a lifetime of being wrong about everything has taught me my gut is bullshit. Never trust my gut.

Oh God, this hurts so much. Everyone says time heals all wounds, but it's healed shit for me. Now I have to validate myself again and do the only thing I can control. I wipe my tears and get ready to go to work.

HAYDEN

We've been apart four days. Four days of me working towards our future. The one I planned, the one that's evolved, and the one it's time to claim. I can't wait until this fucking day is over and we can be on the other side of this. She flew in early this morning and I haven't seen her yet. She told me to meet her here but I'm dying to see her.

I can feel that this job is mine. I've already talked to Eva and Rinaldi and it's all set. I don't want it to get ugly or complicated. I've waited a lifetime for this moment. I see it and taste it, and I won't let it slip away.

Finally, she breezes into the conference room. She's stunning in a coral dress that highlights everything good about her. I can't help but smile at what's about to happen. I don't lose. Our work is killer, but my pitch is the final deft blow to all of this. Her light floral scent fills my soul and I reach for her under the table. She keeps her attention on the West Coast idiots in the midst of their pitch. She tenses at my touch. I quickly scribble on a scrap of paper.

"Breathe. We got this."

She nods curtly. She's fucking stressed. It's cool to see

this killer instinct up close. In high school she was lying in wait, but over the past couple of years, I've seen what she's become. I've been on the losing end of her wrath. These assholes have no idea what they're in for. They finish and there's light applause around the room.

I squeeze her knee again but before I can stand up, she up and in front of the room holding a presentation. I don't move. Not sure what's happening.

"Hello, everyone. My name is Bette Miller and it's a pleasure to be here." She doesn't mention me, and Eva and Rinaldi look to me. I smile and nod, and everyone's attention returns to her. She reveals the artwork. It's not mine. This pitch isn't ours. I slide the one I've been working on back into my portfolio. I don't know what the fuck is happening.

She keeps talking and they're eating it up. She's dazzling in the room. She's dazzling in any room, but I don't understand what happened. She's killing it but I'm not part of it. I sit back in my chair and stare at her. She's avoiding eye contact.

She's lost to me in this moment. She played me. I'm sick to my stomach. I haven't trusted anyone since her, and now I can't trust her. She's stabbing me in the back right in front of me. The balls on whoever this person is are so much bigger than mine.

I can't catch my breath. I feel my cheeks and they're burning. I can't be here for this. Fuck Bette Miller. Somehow, over four days, and specifically the last twenty-four hours, Bette eliminated all traces of my Lizzie. Or a future for us. I take an envelope out of my jacket pocket and slide it into the portfolio. I stand and everyone looks at me.

"I've had an emergency come up, but you're all in the best hands possible. Proceed, Bette."

I barely get the words out before I'm rushing to our office. I know what's going to happen. I resigned this morning to make way for her. I don't lose, but I didn't want to know who they picked. I didn't think our relationship could survive, so I bowed out before either of us could get hurt. I slide the portfolio onto the sideboard in what is now her office and sit behind the desk.

My plan was to wait and talk to her, but I'm not sure I can handle hearing her. I'm numb and seeing red because she's hurt me in a whole new way. I reach in my pocket and shove my keys into the top drawer of the desk. I won't need them again.

I'm going ahead with my plans and leaving this shit behind. Jesus. This hurts more than before because I'm a spectacular fool. She played the player and I never saw it coming.

I pick up a pen but have no idea what to say. I'm staring at the door, waiting for this wave of fury and nausea to subside. I'm so fucking pissed at myself. And beyond furious at her. What the fuck?

HAYDEN: I'm still going, but she played me. She had a different pitch I wasn't a part of. Watch your back, brother—it had to be your girl's art.

DAX: What did you say to me?

HAYDEN: She won at any cost. I'll call you when I get somewhere.

DAX: Sophie did the art?

HAYDEN: Not sure. I think so. Did you see her working? Because it sure as shit wasn't mine. Way to go out with a whimper and not a bang.

DAX: Sophie bugged out. She went to Chicago before I even got back last night. This fucking sucks, man. Who the hell is this?

HAYDEN: When you find out, don't tell me. I need to walk

the fuck away from all of this. After this fucking meeting, I'm coming back to Boston then I'm gone. Can you fix the thing with Sophie?

DAX: The thing? She's THE thing. But now I don't know. Did I get played too? Shit, were we conned hard by some Windy City wenches?

HAYDEN: It appears so. Well, I don't know your girl at all. Turns out I didn't know mine either. Consider this fucking closure.

DAX: I'm flying to Chicago.

HAYDEN: If you think so. Watch your heart. Call me in the morning.

DAX: K.

I shove my phone in my pocket. I unzip the portfolio and roll up my recent non-work drawings. I sling my bag over my shoulder and the door flies open.

Her face is beaming and beautiful. This might be the most painful moment of my life. Not my dad or finding out I'll never play ball again. More painful than the phone call from her father a decade ago telling me she doesn't love me. This will be the moment I change and morph into someone else.

She throws her hands up in the air, then they settle on her hips. "Enjoying my office, are you?"

And it's all over except me getting the hell out of here.

I go numb looking at her hair falling across her face. Her smile is pure, but I don't know a damn thing about this woman.

"Congratulations. You deserve it. Especially with all that hard work behind my back."

She turns cold. "Look who's talking." She's itching for a fight, for some reason. I'm not feeling up to giving her one.

"I don't know what you're talking about. I have to go."

She's blocking the door and I don't want to touch her. I can't handle it.

Her voice is unlike any I've heard before. "You were going to fuck me over, so why not beat you to the punch?"

My entire being deflates. I'm surprised I'm still upright. I need to get away from her. She didn't trust me when I trusted her. Fuck, this is painful. Someday, I'll probably rage and attempt to ruin her life like a cartoon villain, but for now, I need to nurse my own gaping wounds.

I push past her and she tugs at my elbow. I look down at her. "It was strange to watch you become someone else. I didn't like it and I'm glad I don't have to see it again. I don't know you at all. Good luck with your job, Bette."

"You have to resign, you know."

Maybe I can hurt her a little bit. Dripping with all the sarcasm I can muster, I say, "Oh, I'm resigned. I'm resigned to the fact that I wasted a decade pining for a woman who never existed. And the fucked-up part is, I'm going to miss missing her. I'm going to mourn Lizzie because she was only ever a fantasy. Because Bette never deserved fucking anything."

"What the hell are you talking about?" Her back is up.

I take another look at her as I fracture inside. I wish she weren't so damn beautiful. Her soft light skin playing off her hair. Those stunning delicate bright-green eyes, capable of a cruelty I didn't think possible.

"Bye."

"That's it?" she says.

"Yup. That's it. I'm sure you want another fight, but you won't get one from me. You won. Not fair and square, but you won. I have to go."

She moves behind her desk and sits down. "I'll see you later. We have dinner, don't we? I need to figure out all the shit that just happened, aside from me winning. But we can talk. I need to talk." She's wringing her hands and I know she's trying to stop herself from having some kind of emotion but I don't fucking care.

Rage surfaces to salvage the last shreds of my dignity. "Talk? You think I'm ever fucking speaking to you again? Your delusion knows no bounds and neither does your fucking ambition. Which one of you was the act? Lizzie or Bette? My money's on the witch in front of me, being the real you."

"Come on. I only did what you were about to." She thought I was going to betray her. Why the hell would she think that? "I just got to it first."

Oh God. I have to get away, but not without sending her running to her therapist.

"You've lost touch with not only reality, but humanity. Why don't you fuck off and take some time to examine who you want to be?"

"Why don't you?"

"Oh, I'm fine. I know who I am and I'm completely at peace. In fact, by leaving here I will have no problems sleeping tonight. You, on the other hand—enjoy your hollow victory."

I walk away as she yells after me. She's still yammering on when I get to the stairwell and don't look back. There's nothing left here for me. She ruined all the things. Us. My work. And my dumbass faith in fate.

BETTE

I'm in our hotel suite and there's a bottle of champagne from work and some flowers from my mom. I pop the cork and drink from the bottle. I scream, "Woo!" And there's no answer.

"Hayden, I'm home!"

I need to know why he's so angry when I was only trying to take care of myself. I hope he's cooled off. He said some nasty things to me but I was making sure I didn't get screwed over. He doesn't get to be angry. He's the reason all of this went down like this. My heart is hurting as well as my pride for trusting him in business, but I need to figure this out. We can't end like this. We have to get through this, when he admits he was wrong.

SOPHIE: Congratulations! I'm glad it worked out.

BETTE: Thank you. I'm so excited. We're on our way, baby!

SOPHIE: Are you sure you're happy?

BETTE: This is why I've worked my ass off for the last five years.

SOPHIE: Ok. Dax wouldn't take no for an answer so he's

flying here. And when I told him you got the job, he said Hayden was really confused.

BETTE: We put them in their places. We rule. Boys drool.

SOPHIE: I'm going to listen to Dax.

BETTE: Is that what you want?

SOPHIE: I don't know. I think so. How is Hayden?

BETTE: He'll be fine. I'm not sure I will be if he doesn't come clean and apologize. I'm so pissed about what he did and hurt that he did it behind my back.

SOPHIE: You do know you just did the same thing?

BETTE: Stop being my conscious. I want to get past all of this. I've shoved the pain of his betrayal down so I can address it with him. I want to be rational when we talk about all this shit. And I won't apologize for getting to it first because if I didn't take care of myself, who else was going to do that? I would have been sitting there looking like a fucking idiot and feeling even worse.

SOPHIE: Look, I'm all TEAM BETTE, but girl, remember he was sitting there thinking the same.

BETTE: And that's why we'll talk about it all. I gotta go and face the music.

I put the phone down, take another swig of champagne, and walk over to his door. I knock on it. "Hayden, stop sulking and drink with me."

There's no answer so I bang, it slowly opens and the room is empty. It looks like it's been tossed by the cops. I start running from the closet to the bathroom then my room and back to the kitchen. I whip open the refrigerator to check for Greek yogurt, he's never without it. It's gone.

I put the bottle down and spin around, looking for any sign of him. All he left was his sexy-as-hell smell to haunt me. He ghosted me again. I know rationally he didn't before, but this time, the coward left. I flop down on the couch and pull my feet up under me.

I've already talked to my mom and Sophie. And he's not here which means, I have no one. I didn't even notice I've shoved everyone out of my life. Maybe Three-Date Tate will pick up.

Where did he go? I text on our work phone and my personal.

BETTE: We need to talk. Where are you? I need to know why you did that?

BETTE: You're really gone?

BETTE: Again.

I lay on the couch and the gloom creeps up on me. I thought I had a handle on it, but I feel it at the back of my spine and it envelops me without thought. It possesses me in such a familiar way, it's the same pain of being left by the one person I thought was meant for me. I don't understand how what I did was any different than what he was going to do?

I'm alone.

With my dream job.

I say weakly as I lift my fists on either side of my shoulders, "Yeah. Go you!"

I sit there for another minute or two staring at my quiet phone.

"Hey, Siri, I got a promotion!"

"I don't know what that means, 'I got a promotion.' Do you want me to search for it?"

No. I don't. "Hey, Siri, why am I alone?"

"Hmm... I don't have an answer for that, is there something else I can help you with?"

"Hey, Siri, are you happy?"

"I'd say I'm the software version of happy right now. How about you? Are you feeling happy?"

Fuck you, little robot. You're happy. I'm happy. Do not

ask me that again, little robot.

I say to her, "I guess."

Siri says, "That's great. You should write down everything you are feeling so you can remember it."

"Hey, Siri. Can you bring me fried chicken? That might make me happy."

"Here are places that deliver to your location." I push on one of them and get chicken delivered.

Where is he? I thought he loved me, and I know I love him. Even though he was going to undermine me at work, I love him. I don't know how to do anything else but love him. I should have told him or asked him about his Dax secret pitch. I should have been a better me but he should have been a better him.

Tears bubble up as I stand up and walk around trying to calm myself. But the tears come anyway because he's not here. He said things I thought were in the heat of the moment, but he meant them, like goodbye.

I sit down where I'm standing and slide to the floor. I curl up a bit to try and make the pain stop, but it's everywhere. My knees and shoulders hurt; it's permeated every part of me. He left me, doesn't really love me and probably played me. That's a bruising to my ego and heart that I'm not sure I can get up from this time. But what was his end game? What did he get by destroying me? I got the job or was that part of his plan?

I cry and I don't think I can stop. I'm shaking badly. I have the job of my dreams, how can it feel like nothing?

I wake up, peel my eyes open and I'm still on the floor. I'm a mess but I roll to the door. I need to hang the do not disturb but when I open the door I'm greeted by giant bag of cold chicken.

I sit on his bed.

"Kris! Where the fuck did he go? Did he run to Philly or Boston? I'm going to eat this chicken unless you give me some cosmic sign where to find him so I can understand. And I'll probably get sick eating floor chicken that's sat out all night. If you care about me at all, stop me."

I bite into the chicken and it's really good, so I chomp another piece, then head to the shower. I have to be the boss today.

It's been a painful week of pretending I'm thrilled and in charge. I'm not functioning well. The new job isn't a whole lot of creative and Sophie's barely talking to me. HR informed me Dax and Hayden both quit. Sophie didn't warn me but she's been bogged down in working remotely and now she's been saddled with Michelle Michelle as her new partner. I'm sure she'll quit.

I'm an island.

Every day I've left seven messages for him.

Today I left nine.

I pull my hat down over my face as I enter this insanely expensive hockey charity event: Meet the Flyers! I've come to Philadelphia hoping for answers. I'm standing in line to meet seven-time All-Star Robbie Danson. My head whips around at the sound of her voice.

"I liked you. I did. But you fucked up, girl." Did I?

I fucked up not talking to him, but I just tried to save myself by doing what he was going to do. I can't say that to Claire. I'm so freaking confused about the entire thing. I have to believe I did the right thing, but I need to talk to him about it. Step one in that plan is to freaking find him. I can't take this anymore. I don't want to be sad or devastated or confused, I can't go through another ten years without closure. Whether it's good or bad I need it.

"Nothing to say for yourself?" She tosses more attitude and it strikes me how much I like her. I try and contain my frustration at this situation.

"Hi, Claire, please back it down a bit. If I have it my way, we're going to be family, so I'll refrain from saying things I'll have to live down for the rest of our lives. I suggest you do the same."

She huffs, then crosses her arms and hardcore glares.

Robbie steps to me and he's a wall of muscle and brute energy. His hair is cropped short but the exact shade of Hayden's, and although I can tell he's broken his nose a couple of times, he's definitely his brother. He's also scary huge. He grins, lifts my hat, and musses my hair.

"Of course, baby bro fell for someone who can step up to my girl. It's not easy. She doesn't take shit from no one, but here you are in her face, backing her down. You're spunky."

I nod my head and the man fills my entire horizon. I can't see past him and I'm pretty sure this is the largest chest I've ever seen. My words explode out of me. So much for keeping it together.

"Ok. I'm spunky. I'm only spunky, or bold, or ballsy because someone kind, loving, and grounded believed in me a decade ago. He told me I was more and I believed him.

I might have taken it too far and become extra. Now I want to go back to just being more and not extra"

Claire yells from behind her giant husband, "Work for it BeLizzie. We can't give up baby bro that easily."

"Please believe me when I tell you, I want him. I want to talk to him and tell him a lot of things I never got the chance to say I don't have anything without him. Get it? I'm sorry you've had to deal with him or us, or whatever the hell this situation is, but I need to find him."

Claire pops up over his shoulder, jumping to be seen. "Tell him that."

"Where is he?" I yell, throwing my hands up in the air.

Robbie grins and answers dismissively, "Yeah. We don't know that."

"Then why the hell did you just make me beg your forgiveness?"

Claire pokes her head under his arm and looks at me. "It was kind of fun. I wanted to make sure you were worthy of him. Don't fuck with our little brother, got it?"

"Got it. But where the fuck is he?"

"There's only one person who knows. Don't get me wrong, he'd kill for us, but he only confides in Dax. I have an idea, but it isn't our place or story to tell."

Robbie says, "You should also know Law's ready to fly here and yell. He's more bark than bite, but his bark is pretty fucking awful. I'll tell him it's cool."

He signs my hat:

Don't fuck it up, firecracker—Robbie Danson.

I left eleven messages today.

Look at Claire and Robbie, and the way they have each other's backs. Or how they all have Hayden's back. I thought he had mine, he let me feel safe and protected and then he cracked it all open for this stupid job. The job that I'm not so sure is worth any of this.

A couple of restless nights and more floor chicken and I'm ready for a different life. Not the one I'm creating without him in a mess of confusion of old take out. I finish the most important email of my life and I've barely sent it when my phone rings. I have over nine months of vacation I've never taken, and I just requested three months of it, effective immediately.

"Hello, Eva."

"Bette, I've just received the most disturbing email of my life."

And then there's a knock at my office door. Rinaldi storms in with Eva right behind him on the phone with me. She speaks into her phone instead of to me in person. "I'll be unable to speak to you unless it's this way."

I keep the phone to my ear. They're wearing circus tents. Literally red-and-white wide-stripe jumpers that bell out at their knees.

I look at Rinaldi but speak in my phone. "I barely pushed send and Vancouver Bob can handle things for the next twelve weeks."

It's a fucked-up thing to get a new job and then leave it for three months, but miraculous things happened the last time I spent three months doing something completely out of character.

Eva screams into the phone, "Don't speak to me. Speak to Rinaldi!" I put the phone down and repeat everything I've just said to him. Then pick up the phone again to speak to her.

She says, "We'll take it under advisement. I need to hum." And she does, loudly. She's humming Lady Gaga's "Born This Way" for no real reason except it's like fucked-up hold music.

Rinaldi steps forward and touches my sleeve, then the top of my head. He rubs the space between my brows as I look into his lovely dark eyes. Eva's now chanting and Rinaldi leans down and whispers, "Go, my lamb. Go with all the blessings I have. She will never forgive you, but I always will. Do what you must." Then he presses his lips to my forehead.

Eva stops chanting nonsense and says into the phone, "He opened your third eye. Do not waste it! Tell him to meet me at the door."

I turn to Rinaldi. "Thank you for understanding and for the third eye thing. Eva will meet you at the door."

He nods, then turns and takes two steps to join Eva at the door.

She says into the phone, "Goodbye, Bette Miller."

Goodbye, indeed. It's probably time to let Bette Miller go. Goodbye, Bette Miller.

BETTE

I DON'T SLEEP SINCE HE LEFT, SO I WRITE TO KRIS. IT'S BEEN awhile since I've practiced this particular form of journaling and religion. She always manages to answer me in some way, and I need her because I'm starting to not recognize who I am again. I take out paper and a pen; she always insisted we write, not text or email. She wanted a physical thing to hold onto and I guess I need that now.

Kris,

I'm the boss and I hate it. My mom says it will get better but this is a woman who stayed married to a man she didn't truly love for like forever. Where's Hayden? I'm taking a couple months off starting next Monday and either my shredded heart heals or I actually learn to knit. He's just gone, and I can't move on or even really start. I haven't unpacked my office to avoid places we were together so I work in the conference room.

I could have called him out on his shit and talked about it all. Instead I barreled through and it's unlike me not to consider all the possible outcomes. I was so shocked and hurt by what I heard he was going to do and then when I put it all into business perspective, I thought we were even.

It's been a month without him, and it feels like a year. It's been six years without you, and I still can't believe it. It's just so weird that you're dead and he's missing.

Wish you were around.

XO

Lizzie

I toss everything in the top desk drawer and my breath catches. I quickly get up, lock the door, and fall apart with his Eiffel Tower key chain clutched in my hand. He really did leave me, he's not thinking things over or playing hard to get. That slim piece of hope that I was using to exaggerate the situation is gone.

I put the key chain with mine in the zipper pocket of my wallet and attempt to compose myself. I run to the bathroom to splash water on my face but when I get back, my door is open. Dax is rifling through a portfolio on the sideboard that I hadn't paid any attention.

"Can I help you with something?"

Dax whips around and the contents spill onto the floor. I'm shocked and confused why he's here.

"Hey." I kneel next to him and help pick things up. He snatches some papers quickly, and I notice they're pencil drawings of me and I realize it's Hayden's portfolio.

He reaches silently for the picture and I clutch it to my chest.

"Please tell me, where is he?"

"Can't."

I don't relinquish the drawing. I lean towards Dax. I'm desperate to know what happened. "Why was he in a rush to leave?"

"Think."

His economy of language is staggering. He gathers the rest of the spilled papers and boards. It must be their presentation I never saw. I didn't realize it was here all along. I flip it over to see what they were going to pitch before I usurped the opportunity. My face falls and my body goes limp as I realize in an instant my entire life is a lie. I might just have trust issues a little more severe than previously observed.

"You ok?"

I'm pale, numb and cold. I've turned into a selfish and horrible person. Damn, that is not where I thought Bette would end up. I got to pull this back. I have to fix this. I run my fingers over the presentation boardthey're ours. It's my words, his art. The one we tweaked and fussed about; it's our true collaboration.

"Where's your pitch? The other one?" I say frantically. He shrugs. "You don't know where your pitch is? The one you worked on together behind our backs. Where is that fucking pitch?" Oh God. This can't be happening.

He cocks his head to the side and raises an eyebrow. "There wasn't one."

I'm the biggest asshole in the world.

"What are you saying to me?"

"Pretty clear," he says, nonplussed.

"Be more clear! Sophie told me she overheard the two of you talking about a whole new thing and it was the ultimate prank."

He rocks back onto his butt. "Fucking Sophie." He blows out an exhale.

"Watch yourself," I warn.

He pins me with a stare. "I want her. But that doesn't seem to register with her."

I sit down, too, and lean against my office wall.

Dax scratches his wrists and says, "That's why she did

the art, you asked. She wouldn't say anything, then asked me to leave Chicago."

I say to him, "Give her a minute."

"Same."

I wipe my lips, then clasp my hands together. "I can't because all of this is my fault. This time the blame sits squarely on my unfeeling and confused shoulders. I don't trust easily."

"No shit."

"Neither does Soph."

"Again. No shit." He tucks his hair behind his ear. "I haven't known her long, but I am irrevocably in love with her."

My heart flutters for them, then thuds for me. I don't think he'll help me, but I'm going to try. Even if Hayden never talks to me again I at least need to apologize. I have to tell him how I fucked up our forever and I'd like it back.

"Dax, where is he? I went to see Claire and Robbie."

"I know." Then he shakes his head and arranges the papers into the portfolio and zips it. He gestures with his chin towards the boards. "You can keep those."

I laugh and a sob comes out.

"No. Please don't." His face softens.

"Please tell me where he is. I have to make this right, this isn't me. I have to fix this with him and for me." My heart and body ache.

He gets up, then pulls me to standing.

"You've never met the real me. Please help me." I extend my hand. "I'm Lizzie. Nice to meet you."

He grins. "Go back to the beginning."

My tears stop as I hit a wall of confusion.

"Huh?"

"It's all I can say. And if he knew I betrayed him like this, he'd kill me."

"You betrayed him with a cryptic riddle that I'm going to need the guy from *The Da Vinci Code* to help figure it out. We're going to need that twisty code thing or his sidekick volleyball to help."

"Cryptex. And those are two different movies." I shrug as he heads to the door and turns back to say goodbye.

"Tell Tony I said hi."

"I will."

I push my luck. "And tell Hayden I'm sorry and I'm hopelessly in love with him."

"I won't."

"You're a fucker, aren't you?"

"Yup."

He's almost out the door and I have a couple more questions.

"Hey, Dax." He nods. "What was the ultimate prank?"

He shuffles his feet and then turns back to me. "He resigned before the pitch; he wanted you to get the job." And chucunk, my gears grind to a halt.

"Was that my surprise?" I can barely get the words out.

He scribbles on the back of one of Danny's pictures of me. I mean Hayden.

"Go here. There's something you'll need."

"Thank you."

"And you're not an asshole, just lost."

He closes my door and I stare at the beautiful drawing of me laughing. I miss him. No matter what happens in my life, I miss him. And I had him and decided to fuck that up, too. I turn the picture over and there's an address.

BETTE: Heads up, you heard wrong. They never did a pitch. They were talking about something else and Dax knows every-

thing. Sorry, thanks for being team Bette but it might be time to pull out Lizzie. I'm a mess. You?

SOPHIE: Huge mess. OMG. I'm so sorry. Sorry I filled your head with my skeptical male bullshit. Honey, please know I only did it to protect you. We fucked it all up, didn't we?

BETTE: For what it's worth. He loves you.

SOPHIE: How could you tell, it's not like he's chatty? Well, outside of the bedroom.

BETTE: I'm going to find Hayden to try and fix this shit. Dax gave me clue to find him. Thought he was being secretive. 'Go back to the beginning.'

SOPHIE: That's so Dax. Boston?

BETTE: No. But I have to go to Boston first to get something. I'm sure my love is in Paris.

I'm driving past rows of gorgeous Victorian homes. I didn't know what to expect of South Boston. I'm humbled by my ignorance as I turn onto a street with more modest brick homes. It's about five thirty and all the neighbors are on their porches and stoops having drinks and talking while kids run around the cars and street.

I park and observe the woman I assume I'm here to see. She's stunning with her similar raven hair but hers is threaded with the most beautiful silver. It's his face and I'm knocked out by this moment. I don't know why Dax would send me to meet Hayden's mother.

She sits back and sips what looks like fruit punch, and I lean on the car door and trying to look nonchalant. I don't know how to start.

She yells, "Come, Lizzie." She gestures me towards her, and I nod with tears streaming down my face. Because that's what I do with my days now, I cry like a baby all the time. She gestures again. "Come."

As I get closer, she notices me wiping my eyes and rushes off the porch and wraps her arms around me. She's short but strong and I rest my head on her shoulder. We're on her sidewalk and I let it all go while Hayden's mother holds me. I'm careful not to rumple his drawing.

After what seems like hours, but is only ten minutes, I raise my head. "I'm so sorry to do this, Mrs. Danson. I'm so embarrassed, I don't usually fall apart like this. Well, lately I do, I'm sorry. How did you know it was me?"

She pats my arm and pulls me towards her house. "It's Lilliana. I know you from the many pictures around my house, my dear. And you weep because of love. It's a kind of love I've never known, but you have for my boy. Come, bella. We eat, you talk, and I'll try to understand."

Within minutes, there's a full feast in her house. A professionally set table with intricate lace tablecloth, napkins, crystal goblets, and polished silver.

"We're eating at the good table. Don't tell the boys. I never let them do this."

I grin. "Because they're too old?"

"Because they're messy boys. But us girls deserve this bit of fancy." She notices the piece of paper beside my plate and beams with pride.

"Is that for me?"

"Sorry, to surprise you. Do you really want another picture of me?"

She laughs. "I'm partial to the artist, but you're not a surprise. Dax told me you were coming." Well, that explains the feast. "Now, my dear, you have a full plate of braciola, spinach and sausage tortellini, and some potatoes. Manga. Eat and talk."

Pasta and potatoes. I think I love this woman.

I devour all of it, as if I haven't eaten before. Christ, the woman can cook. I talk and talk, and she listens and laughs. She reacts like she doesn't know most of our story, but I know she does. And when I finish my meal and my stories, I sit back and sip some really sweet and cold wine.

"I have a flight out tonight to go to Danny and try to fix this, but Dax said you had something I need."

She places a platter of gorgeous small desserts and pours two small glasses of sherry, then rifles in a drawer and places what she found in front of me. "He disappears to heal his wounds. I give him that space, considering all that he gives back to his family."

I put my hand over my heart. I can't stop staring at a pink Eiffel Tower key chain, identical to the one I have, but the enamel is still intact. There's a key attached and I grasp it to my chest. It's too much.

"Thank you."

She moves her chair closer and takes my hand.

"Stop your guilt. He's cut you as well. Don't blame yourself for a man who ran away. He did not face you and tell you his heart hurt. He hid away from destiny and you without thought. You're both fools but he didn't face the magnitude of what you share."

I inch closer to her.

She pats my arm. "My mama and papa were fated like you two. For better or worse, you are destino. Whether you choose to do something about it or not, it will always live in your heart."

I stand and she hugs me hard.

She whispers, "You know where he is. You've always known. He's right where you left him." I squeeze her back.

I'm beyond tears and grateful but it's time to go home.

She packs up too many cookies. She's used to cooking for athletes.

I call my mom while heading to the gate and let her know, "Liliana said the right thing."

"Damn, I wish I did."

I laugh at her. "Mom, it's time for me to go home. I need it."

Mom says, "Ok. If that's what you think. I'll be here."

I slept hard the entire flight and chomp some cookies from my purse as I wake up.

The flight attendant announces, "Ladies and gentlemen, as we begin our descent into Charles de Gaulle Airport, we ask that you return your tray tables and seats to their upright and locked positions. Merci et bien venue au Paris."

BETTE

I DROP MY STUFF AND GO DIRECTLY THERE. IT'S LATE BUT I'M determined, and it knocks me out how powerful these memories are. I stand across the street and stare at the building. I'd blocked all of this out for so long and now it's creeping up, flooding me with warmth of our history. The house is more beautiful than any memory. The stone is somehow older and more regal, and the door cheerier than when we left it. A piece of me has always lived here, a protected and special part of me that only he could ever have. I need it back so I can protect and care for both of us with it. All those years with a hole in my heart—who knew it was here all along?

He steals my breath away as I stare at the massive windows of the top floor. Bette would bang down the door, and Lizzie would run away. I'm not sure who I am but I'm not ready to be told there's no hope. I watch him paint for close to an hour and fall into my bed around 2:00 a.m. amongst the life and energy of the Left Bank.

I've been here for three days, but I only come by the house at night. I don't know what to say yet, so I occupy my days with croissants and revisiting our past. But each night around midnight, I wander over and watch him paint from the stoop across the street. I've determined he's alone and that he's magnificent. He's like the best TV show.

I went to Picasso Museum yesterday and today I'm sitting on a white marble bench, staring at the intersecting lines and archways of the Lefuel stairwell. The one where our fate was sealed. Not sure what I thought coming here. I guess a part of me was hoping he's be waiting here for me in our past.

A security guard smiles as I snap a picture of the staircase. Despite my overly dramatic antics wandering around Paris, right here is where he became the only one I'd ever truly rely on besides myself.

I'm standing out front, near the light up pyramid sculpture thing, and I get fucking furious. I see what should have been, the conversation I should have had and then I roll my eyes at the superior attitude I flipped out to justify my terrible behavior.

The thoughts whizz through my brain like a montage of what I wish would have happened.

He would have been there for prom and I would have been on the sidelines of all his games and held him when he ripped up his shoulder. I would have supported him as he pivoted towards a new dream. I wouldn't have let him compromise his art for the sake of paycheck.

And he would have let me be the Lizzie I was supposed to be without having to become Bette. He would have held me as Kristin took her last breath and been my cheerleader when I let my past slide off my overextended back and enjoyed the moment I threw out the rule book. I would have helped him get his mother away from his fucking father, and he would have helped me break it off with my father sooner.

I may have become a person I could be proud of, but I never would have loved myself if Danny Danson hadn't loved me first. Did we need the separation in order to be together? Life working out the way it's supposed to and all that. Is that how does destino works?

I wander away from the museum, pull Kris' trench coat around me. I'm going back to my hotel to get the drunkest I've ever been.

I'm hoping to black out the things I did and said a month ago. Is that the way blackout drunk works? Eliminate the dumb shit you've done that ruined your whole life? Can you pre-select the blackout moments like a very specific mind eraser? We'll see.

Well, I drank and puked the minibar. And I've forgotten zero of the pain or the dumbass move I pulled. I brush my teeth and flip open a notebook to pray to the only thing that makes sense, Kris. She has to be out there somewhere. You can't be that bold and vibrant, then nothing. I believe she became a part of the whole and now it burns red fucking hot because she's there. It's been six years since she flamed this world and lit up mine.

Kris,

Hey, it's your favorite soap opera. What the fuck do I do now? The bathroom floor is cold on my ass through this white embroidered nightgown. I bought it because it reminded me of the ones we bought in France back when you were fucking alive.

You were the only other person on this planet who ever got me from the beginning.

You were big enough to handle me. Now, I'm a hysterical crier. I don't know what to do.

I'm going to peel myself off this floor and crawl into the fluffy good bed and hopefully pass out until things are fixed.

Miss you, bish.

Xo

Lizzie.

BETTE

I TOSS AND TURN AND THINK OF KRIS, BUT THE BED HAS A SHARP spot. Not flat or lumpy but sharp, and I keep waking up when I roll over it. Kris took every opportunity and chance, and I'm paralyzed by not taking a chance on the one thing I want in life. I fought for the wrong thing.

I say out loud, "I'm an embarrassment to your memory." I roll over and wince again. I turn the light on to eliminate the sharp thing and when I rip back the covers, it's like a beacon, daring me to follow—the Eiffel Tower key chain with one solo key attached.

"This is it, right? I don't care if it's three in the morning. I'm doing it." I stand up and step on something pointed. I hop around for a second, in fucking pain. I look down and it's my key chain.

I look up as if Kris is looking down. I flip her off. "I got it! Enough. No more pain. You're right. I'm going."

I'm a flurry of activity, grabbing my trench coat and cramming my feet into the closest shoes. It's only when I'm on the street I realize they're the painful but pretty Chanel heels and I don't have a wallet or my phone. But I don't need them I have the key to my fucking future in my hand. I know exactly where I'm going for the first time in my life.

I run as fast as I can. I hope he'll understand the urgency. Or he'll call the police and lock me up.

The streets are quiet and familiar. The sparkle of the streetlamps are lighting a path as if it's the only way to go. My lungs are starting to burn a little and I ignore the stitch in my side. I'm running and the shoes are definitely filling with blood, but it doesn't matter. All that pain is nothing compared to the pain of losing him. I'm ready to face this, whether it goes badly or not. My guts feel like this is wrong and scary, so it must be right. Because they've always been wrong.

I careen around the last corner and our house sits at the end of the block. It's the beginning of who we were supposed to be.

I cross to my spot and grin at his messy hair and my heart will never recover. He's standing in one place, painting in our dream apartment where he said he'd create a studio all those years ago.

I wipe my eyes and rush across the street, and this time my eyes are filled with joy, not sadness. I bang on the door and wait. I bang with both fists again. But I know the way back to him now, so I put the key in the door, and it creaks open. The dazzling foyer, the black-and-white harlequin pattern floor, gives me chills.

I ditch my shoes and quickly climb the gleaming white marble staircase. The key works again and I walk into the third floor apartment. His things punctuate the space and it dawns on me, he didn't just come here. His mother has a key, he's lived here for years, maybe.

My heart pounds as I enter the kitchen, and run my hand over the same giant kitchen island. I cling so hard to the idea that this is ours. I'm here and I'll never leave his side, if he doesn't run.

I climb the stairs quietly, not sure what he'll do. I push the door and it creaks open. His eyes instantly turn to me. He's covered in paint but doesn't seem surprised to see me. Did his mom tell him she gave me the key? The citrus musk of that boy I loved so long ago and the man of my dreams standing before me has me dumbstruck.

"C'est moi. Je suis rentré." I simply say *it's me and I've come home*. There's silence. I'm so anxious and breathless and my stomach is in knots.

My breath catches as I stare at him, barefoot in paint-splattered jeans and a grey Temple t-shirt that's seen better days. There's all the colors of the world speckled on his shirt and I can't help but stare at this fabulous, sexy man.

We stand facing each other for moment. His blue-grey eyes lighting up, then hardening like quicksilver to stone.

He leans back on the wall with the city light spilling over him. He's breathtaking.

"Took you long enough to find me. What can I do for you, Bette?"

I blurt out without any thought of what I was actually going to say, all my rational explanations gone, "I'm so sorry. I'm so, so sorry. I'm sorry."

He says nothing, so I keep talking as he places his brush down and moves a small table filled with a palette and paints to the side.

"All of that was neither Lizzie nor Bette. I was quickly becoming the worst parts of them. Let's call her Eliza."

His voice is gruff and low as he scolds me a bit. "No more names."

"Fine. I want to be the best parts of them. I want to be the best me and I can only do that with you. I know why you left, but you don't know why I betrayed you."

"Because Sophie overheard me and Dax plotting my resignation and surprising you with a trip to Paris but misunderstood all of it."

I slump a little but say, "Dax never gave you up and he forgave Sophie." Hayden's mouth pulls into a semi-smile and then I ruin it. "If you knew, why didn't you tell me? Why didn't you reach out to me?"

As he shifts his position to face more of me, he says, "Why didn't you just ask me about the pitch?"

"I have an answer for that. Not a good one. But an answer."

He rolls his wrists encouraging me to speak.

"Gut instinct."

"Your guts are dumb," he says.

"Yes. My guts had me sitting at the Louvre steps today instead of banging down your door. They guided me to a messy college life, a useless marriage, and running in terrible, tortuous shoes. Which my gut compelled me to buy in the first place."

He laughs a little.

His arms are crossed over his chest, but his eyes are warming a touch. "You and Soph didn't trust us. Your lack of trust destroyed me all over again. And you don't get the easy way out. You don't get understanding Danny telling you it's ok you fucked me over. I didn't know that person who did that."

My voice is harsher. "You did. You helped forge her. But you left and didn't even talk to me. You wrote me off for a mistake I made." He cocks his head. I nod repeatedly for a second. "A massive mistake, but still a misstep that could have been corrected in the moment. I may have become a self-doubting, destructive lunatic, but you did the one thing that scares me more than anything."

"What's that?" He clenches his fists at his sides and flicks his thumbs out of them. He has every right to be angry, I fucked up. But what he needs to realize is, he did, too.

"You ghosted me. You didn't stand there and face me and say, 'You're a self-doubting, destructive lunatic.' You abandoned me and although it was my father pulling the strings long ago, he wasn't pulling them this time. All the bad thoughts, like I wasn't worth anything or good enough to stick around for swamped me in a painful alone when you left. Because I did something for myself and didn't do as I was told, therefore, I don't deserve love."

"That's your father speaking in your head."

"Absolutely, so when Sophie told me that shit, I was triggered. And yes, I'm going to need to call your therapy guy. I haven't done a fabulous job working through all my issues on my own."

The humid fall air is so thick. I'm sweating beneath my nightgown, but my entire body is cold. I may have gone full Bette, but he went full Danny. He turns in a tight circle and stretches. He stares at dancing patterns of light on the floor. I walk over and lift his chin and I see his anger abating with each second that he thinks through what I said.

"Look up, don't hide, ever. An incredible man told me that once or twice."

I'm done hiding forever. Wow, maybe I am good at fixing myself. Nah. I'm going to need some therapy.

I move my fingers from his chin but he's still staring at me. "Bette was born in the ashes of Lizzie. But she was also all the pieces you saw in me when I didn't. But when I evolved into her, I forgot to bring Lizzie along as well. The good and pure parts or myself. I'm so used to things not working out, people dying, leaving, or the consequences of not doing as I was told, that I doubted everything around me. I even told you once, I've spent my lifetime not only waiting for the other shoe to drop, but expecting to be smashed by it. I'm burning all the shoes. Starting with the heinous ones I left at our front door. I'm not waiting for the bad thing to happen because I finally deserve the good."

"Our?"

I put my hands on my hips. "Don't even try that. This is my house just as much as it's yours and I don't care who you rented it from, it's mine. We were made here, this is where we became destino."

"Christ, you saw my mother." I dangle her key chain from my finger. I can't believe they didn't tell him I was coming. I have a chance and they believe it too.

"And that answers my next question, how did you get up here? I knew, hoped, you'd figure out a way to get to me. I just didn't realize my family would aid and abet you."

"Dax sent me to Lilliana." He smiles and roll his eyes at the mention of his mother.

"That tracks."

He puts his hands behind his head and expands his chest. I'm caught off guard for a moment when I think about licking him. But I also need him to know we're on equal footing. "I have more to say, but you're not going to like it."

HAYDEN

"I DON'T LIKE MYSELF VERY MUCH RIGHT NOW ANYWAY, SO FIRE away." Her eyes are telling me stories about my past and future and I can't get away from this moment. I'm out of sorts and time. I don't get to contemplate and try to lose myself in painting anymore. She's here, right in front of me, and I know there is no closure.

She steps forward, but I move away. She plants herself and squares her shoulders. It's adorable and she's perfect, and I can't get past the scary cliff we're on the edge of. A lifetime of making sure I wasn't a victim has led me to hiding from her.

Her voice is sure and somehow I know she's going to rip us apart so we can maybe heal and find our way back together. "This was our first test together as a real couple, and we both failed. You ran scared like Danny did after you thought I broke up with you. After the horrible world you lived through, you protected yourself by leaving. Boston College played in California your freshman year. You could have found me and asked why. And I went catatonic and then went about burning everything to the ground. I raged forward, like I did when I discovered my father's meddling orchestrated way too much in my life. I believed I wasn't worthy of your love, so screw it, I'd become someone else. I changed because of you and in spite of you."

Since the moment I smelled her soft vanilla and green grass scent coming up the staircase tonight, I felt whole again. I raise my arms in a stretch and my shirt lifts. She looks at the strip of skin above my waistband. "Eyes up here."

She smiles and meets my smirk. I can't help but take in her chilled nipples in the thin cotton nightgown. But is this all chemistry? I think it might be time to find out who we are beyond our past.

"Fuck. I did run from everything, especially you. Do you think we can ditch our histories and create a new one?"

She steps towards me and I move from victim to complicit. I say, "Perhaps we leave those people behind."

She nods. "Then who do we become?"

I'm done questioning or pretending I'm not completely enthralled with her and that she's standing in front of me, fighting for me.

I say, "Us."

Her eyes brim with tears as she manages to say, "What you're telling me is, we should probably never leave each other again?"

"Don't let each other out of sight, for safety's sake, of course." I push off the wall and move towards her, giving up the high ground and collecting her into my arms. My body relaxes into who I'm supposed to be—which is simply hers.

She collapses into me and I bury my face in her. We stand there for way too long as we let it all go. With every second we hold each other, another piece of our armor and our fear falls away. We're shedding it like a skin we no longer need.

I say, "There's nothing else for me but you. I love you, Lizzie."

She rubs my stubble. "I think I'm finally Elizabeth. I want to be whole. I want to be with you and the rest will come to me."

Complete and whole sounds good.

"I'm going to need to stay Hayden. But a different Hayden. I can't be Danny or Christopher. I don't know what you should call me."

"How about 'mine?'"

"That works. I love you so much. I'm sorry I ran and left. I think I was so used to the pain of not having you that I returned to something familiar. Like prisoners who get out and can't hack it on the outside."

"I'm like prison?" She raises an eyebrow.

"That came out wrong."

"Yes, it did. Fortunately you have forever to rewrite it." Her skin is soft, and her voice is a bit deeper as she speaks.

I kiss her lightly and say, "Many, many drafts."

She smirks, "Lots of late nights and long hours for us to get it just right."

"It will be our greatest work in progress. All of this wasn't you and I wasn't fair. I want to build a life with you, not in spite of you. You're the only thing that's ever made any sense."

I kiss her lightly and it's the reason for everything. That feeling of good bourbon or a job well done, the sunshine after a shit-ass winter, and the taste of everything good in the fucking world. She's all of it.

She says as she pulls back from our kiss, "You're here in our house. It feels like it's yours, but how is that possible?"

"I bought it four years ago with Robbie's help. I couldn't bear to have anyone in our home. Then it became the place I wanted to be all the time. There wasn't pain here, only the good memories. Only the inspiration for a life you told me I could have. I let myself deserve things here, so I bought it. I come here a lot. The apartments were rented out until recently, so it kind of paid for itself after a while."

She kisses my paint splattered cheek. Her kiss is sweet and sultry, and she clutches me closer. I take hold of her hair and the kiss.

"I love you so much. I love you with all the bubbly excitement and dark sarcasm in the world. I love you more than winning," she says.

"That's saying something."

"Can I stay? I have three months to spare."

"Hmm, I wonder what can happen in three months, Elizabeth?" I roll her newest name off my tongue, and it fits. She's beaming, gorgeous, a mess—and she's mine.

"I've heard that after three months, the rest of your life can be charted out and planned."

"But only if you're willing to see it through." I let her go and walk towards the door to go downstairs. I outstretch my hand and say, "Shall we?"

She takes it and we leap away from the pain and towards our home, together. We head downstairs and she crawls on my back like a spider monkey. I grab her and keep going. She's kissing my neck and keeps muttering softly, "Mine."

I reply, "Yours. And I always have been."

The end

Epilogue

A bit later

ELIZABETH

I ROLL OFF HIM AND FLOP DOWN ON THE BED. I'M COVERED IN sweat and we're breathing heavily.

"Jesus, you just fucked me like Bette."

I laugh and smack his bicep with little force. He rolls over onto his elbow and traces little circles on my stomach. I sigh.

"Hot or iced?" It's not Starbucks every day because we live in Paris and there's a place down the street that's our go-to café but he grabs my coffee every morning. Before I can answer, he kisses me deeply while thrusting an unexpected finger back inside of me to give me one last shiver of pleasure before we face our day.

I gasp and say on his lips, "Iced."

It's been warm lately and air conditioning in this giant old house isn't a thing that works well. We have window units, but currently our 'tenants' have them all. He kisses me again.

"I don't need it today if you want to stay here and do that tongue thing again."

He jumps from the bed. "Temptress. I have to stop on the first floor and fix the disposal in their kitchen."

My only job is to make sure he stops by unit Two before he leaves the building.

I spread my legs and he moans. "Elizabeth. You need to stop it."

I love that he calls me Elizabeth. I'm whole, so it feels right not to be pieces of my name. He's Hayden to me. He's the man he had to reinvent to save himself. He's overcome so much, and I love him more than both Lizzie and Bette combined.

We opened a small boutique agency over here with Eva and Rinaldi's blessing called Danzie. Danny and Lizzie combined. They sent a shaman as a present and it took us three weeks to get rid of the man. And a month to get rid of the smell.

We've populated this house with love and his art. He paints every day and I'm thinking about writing something other than local ad copy. If I find time between orgasms.

He throws on a Boston College t-shirt and running shorts. I'm always a little sad when his abs disappear. I hop up, too.

He puts his arms up. "No jumping. I can't see those perfect bouncy breasts and not want to fuck them."

I lift them up and thumb my own nipples and groan. "These well-used tits?" I shake them at him.

"Ouch. The sexy flair of that alone will cripple me. Or blind me."

I toss on a bra, a Flyers shirt, and yoga pants.

"Where are you going? You stay in bed."

Not today. I shuffle my feet into the flats I keep by the

door. "I have to check in on Two."

He crosses the room quickly. "Danny ok?"

"I assume so, but I wanted to see him after his big sleepover."

He takes my hand and we descend from our apartment down to the landing that brings us to what we affectionately call "Two." He opens the door and our brunette ball of two-year-old energy charges for his dad. Our 'tenants' and friends yell surprise as we step inside the door.

Danny's yelling, "Da, things are all sold. Daddy. Daddy, paint wif me. Paint more me." Hayden scoops him up and I kiss his cheek. Then I wipe a bit of jam and powdered sugar off his chin. I glance at Team Grandma, a banner, balloons, and then to our friends scattered around the room here to celebrate Hayden's accomplishment.

My life is full of people now. I can't stop making new friends and cherishing my old one. I still talk to Kris almost every day and she reminds me often, with a lost item, or a loud bird chirping, or an unexpected song playing, to be grateful. And to continue to build a full and open life.

Luc, the gallery owner, is holding up a check because Hayden sold out his first art show even before opening.

He paints with Danny almost every day. And yes, he's Danny Danson. Well, he's Danny Danson Corelli, since Hayden legally changed his name and so did his mom.

I kiss my mom on the cheek. "How did it go?"

She says, "Well, we had a swell time. Danny fell asleep a little early, so he's a bit full of energy today." I notice Hayden's mother is quickly shoving a box of pastries into the microwave.

Danny runs by yelling, "Soccer fútbol. I need da kick. Daddy. Kicking and running." We didn't mean to get him hooked on a sport, and we certainly didn't assign it, but he's a bit obsessed with soccer, or football, as it's called here. He calls it both. Things like that happen when you have ex-pats for parents. He's bilingual since birth and his nonna is making sure he learns Italian, too.

When Danny runs sometimes, I see the grace Hayden was gifted with. But if it turns out he wants to be a scientist, we'll cheer for that, instead.

My mom offers up as Danny zooms through all of our legs, "Or he's had too many pastries."

Hayden's mom throws her hands up. "It's our job to spoil him. He has shit grandfathers, so we have to play double duty." I kiss her on the cheek. They've babysat before, of course, but last night they took Danny for the whole night. I love that he has an entire house full of people who love him for exactly who he is. We've all been burnt by that in life and it's the one thing we'll never pass on to him.

We moved the mamas in when I got pregnant since they were both alone in their homes living half-lives. We wanted to see if Paris could do for them what it did for us and make them whole. We thought they could keep Paris in their hearts the way we do. The 'tenants' are busybodies who became fast friends by bonding over who had the worst husband.

Now they spend their days flirting with French waiters and planning their next European excursion. They're trouble and wonderful together and travel all the time, but each has their own floor. The first floor has extra bedrooms for when Claire, Robbie, and Law come over for the off-season. Robbie's coaching now. Law seems to be unlucky in love, but he's in the starting lineup for the Diamondbacks and sleeping his way through most of Phoenix.

Hayden spins Danny around and heads over to his mom who throws her arms around both my boys. My mother touches her heart and I tear up. Lilliana takes Danny, and Hayden rushes to me, taking my face into his hands. "I'm a real artist. I sold out the whole show."

"You've always been a real artist. We just have money now to pay to keep this monstrosity of a house functional."

He kisses me in our now familiar way and my heart is so fucking full.

My mom hands Hayden coffee. "We figured you could take one morning off." He gets all three of us coffee every morning and occasionally white hot chocolate for Danny.

I stare at this most perfect man and hand him a second envelope. "Another thing."

"Did I sell out another show? I'm good, but I should probably paint something before we sell it." He opens the letter. "You're firing me?"

"Yes. The agency is going in a different direction. Good luck." I cross my arms, but he pulls me to him.

"You finally figured out how to get the top job and fire me."

I settle my arms around his neck and he raises an eyebrow at me. "I've been playing the long game. Sophie is officially hanging a Danzie shingle in Boston so your services are no longer needed."

"All my services?"

I whisper in his ear, "You'll have to keep servicing Bette, Lizzie, and Elizabeth." He growls and kisses me quickly.

It's about to get a bit sexier when Danny runs over, and I scoop him up. "What are you doing, buddy?" I have more surprises for Hayden, but today is about his art.

"Mommy. Mommy. DADDY! I asploding wif secrets. I da big brofer." And so much for waiting. Hayden's face goes white as he stares at me. Everyone cheers a bit and I kiss my baby boy who is the embodiment of all we could ever want.

"That's right, baby, you're no longer the baby. You're the big brother. And that's something new your daddy learned about me today."

Danny squeals and leans back to see his father. "I de big brofer now, Daddy. Daddy no cry. Mommy, Daddy is sad."

My eyes fill as well. "No. I think your daddy might just be completely happy."

Danny squeals and I raise my chin to kiss this gorgeous man of mine.

Hayden kisses the top of Danny's head, then mutters against my lips, "Completely. Wanna see if Team Grandma can stay on longer and we celebrate all this good news upstairs for an hour or so?"

"Yes. My answer to you is always yes."

The End

Thank you so much for reading Hayden and Elizabeth's story!!!

Up next for the Boston Brothers series -It's Tony's turn to see if there's a second chance for him with the girl he probably doesn't deserve but will fight for her anyway.

A billion dollars can buy a lot, except love. That you have to gamble on. Available now **KEEP VEGAS**

AND

If you want a novelette staring Hayden's hockey playing brother, KEEP PHILLY is a newsletter exclusive story. Just click the title and you can grab it for **FREE.**

And if you'd like to review Keep Paris that would be much appreciated!!! Thank you so much for being here.

Hey Kel, What Else Can I Read?

I'm so glad you asked.

FIVE FAMILIES VINEYARD ROMANCES

Interconnected standalone small town, found family, series exploring the lives and loves of five winery families.

LaChappelle/Whittier Vineyard Trilogy

(Josh & Elle) Enemies to Lovers

Crushing, Rootstock & Uncorked

Stafýlia Cellars Duet

(Tabi & Bax) Friends to Lovers

Over A Barrel & Under The Bus

Gelbert Family Winery

*Meritage: An Unexpected Blend (*Nat & David)

Secret Baby, Reformed Player, Single Dad

*Residual Sugar (*Becca & Brick*)*

Close Proximity, Opposites Attract, Ex Military

STILL TO COME

SLATED 2024 (might be sooner!)

Pietro Family: A different kind of family story
(Poppy & Sal)
Mafia, Opposites Attract, Secret Life
(Pre-Order is Live)

Langerford Cellars: An epic second chance, funny, romantic suspense
(Sam & ___)

CHITOWN LOVE STORIES

Shock Mount & Crossfade : A Lyrical Romance Duet. Rockstar, love triangle with no crossover and happily ever afters all around.

Present Tense : A Lyrical Romance Spinoff Standalone Second Chance, Single Mom, Alpharoll

---

CARRIAGE HOUSE CONTEMPORARY CHRONICLES

Funny, steamy, smart novellas when you don't know what to read next. All set in the same Chicago Carriage House.

Follow Me - Second chance, forced proximity, rock star (Out now)

Sound Off: Musical enemies to lovers

For the Rest of Us - Holiday, M/M, marriage in crisis, one bed

Something Good: Age Gap, Nanny, Rockstar.

Side Piece: A workaholic romance

Instalove workaholics cheating on their jobs not each other.

EVIE & KELLY'S HOLIDAY DISASTERS VOLUME ONE

With Evie Alexander- Side by side interconnected completely bonkers novellas focusing on one trope and holiday at a time.

Cupid Calamity

Cookout Carnage

Christmas Chaos

Reading Orders & playlists at www.kellykayromance.com

Acknowledgments

Well, well, well, we meet again. THANK YOU, readers, who came out in force to love Bette/Lizzie & Hayden/Danny hard. I adore you.

I plucked some real-life stuff for the first part of their story. The plan to be together after Paris was stolen from my dear friend Eileen's life. Thanks, Leenie, for letting me pinch a small part of your life story.

This book was joyous to write and also a little painful. I lost my own Kris a year ago. There's not a moment in writing about her that I didn't feel her making fun of my silly choices with a sarcastic laugh, or hugging me from behind because she was so damn proud of me. And I do talk aloud to her quite a bit, but she has yet to stab me with a keychain. The story of how the boys meet the girls is 100% true and based on what happened to Kris and me in Paris, in high school, in room 666.

Three outrageous girls from Philly (not Reno) met up with Kris and me, and we moved around Europe like a little crew. The girls were assigned room 666 in Paris and took a phone call from Tony as he asked if we were possessed. They showed up, and we all paired off for the duration of our time in Paris. I never spoke to my "Danny" again after Paris, except for a couple of letters we wrote, but I hope he's well.

Also, I'm not done with those Reno girls yet. This is only the first book in the ***Boston Brothers: A second chance***

series **.** Tony and Makenzie are on deck in **Keep Vegas.** With Maggie getting her day in the sun as well in Keep Tuscany.

Thank you to Holly Smith and Samantha - Sam - Smith, who answered French questions at all hours of the night. And who sat with me and talked about Paris neighborhoods. Merci, lovely ladies. Xo

To the Librarians who were patient with me as I ran through the rough draft of this instead of working and who inspired a character or two. And to my tribe, both new and old, who support me without question.

Thank you, Eve Kasey, for being on the other end of the phone or a DM with encouragement or advice or just listening to me rant. You are the ultimate indie author cheerleader, and I'm glad to call you a friend.

A special shout out to someone who, when asked to take a casual read of my fledgling story, gave it light and shade. She took way too much time out of her busy author life to care deeply about my words. Thank you, Julia Jarrett. I owe you some wine.

Thanks to my work wife, Evie Alexander, who always helps me to remember to laugh at all the absurdity we're trying to accomplish in life and as indie authors. And for jumping down the Holiday Disaster rabbit hole with me. We'll have to think up our next insane project when you finish your next series!

Aimee Walker, this book was a shift to a funnier, yet more dramatic at times, book, and you were right there with me. Thank you for your excellent suggestions and edits. And pictures of your chickens, tiny kitties, and puppies. They brighten my day the way you brighten my life. You're a genius, and I adore you.

Chris Wheary, your mastery of the English language is

astounding. And your level of care with my words is unprecedented. I'm so grateful, thank you.

And the alpha/betas, Allison, Becky & Sandie, thank you for reading the roughest of drafts and still seeing the story. Bird, thanks again for being the voice in my head that says I can do this.

LORI JACKSON. She gets all caps for the kickest of kick-ass covers. Good Lord, I love this cover. Thank you for your genius! Can't wait to see what we do next!

Thanks to Wildfire Marketing and the fabulous Shauna for your help in getting the word out about this book.

And thanks to Kate & Brey for corralling some incredible women to read this book that I'm so proud of.

I got the opportunity to meet some of you in the past couple of months, and I'll meet more of you right when this book comes out at Shameless Con. Those of you who have only been online friends were better in person than I could have imagined. Danica & Nikki. I can't wait to meet all of you out there in Romancelandia. But I must say it's the highlight to meet any reader, even if you've never read my words but stopped by to talk to me about what I write. To chat with me about what your world looks like, it means the world to me. Thank you.

Chuckie Smallz, who's not that smallz anymore, I love you, and I'm inspired by and for you. There's so much good swirling around you, kid. Thanks for putting up with Mommy and her absurd ideas all the time.

And to the man who doesn't hesitate to say yes, when I suggest, let's move the couch to the other end of the house or possibly the other end of the country. Eric's answer to me is always yes. I love you, my brillz husband. (Our son would cringe at me using brillz. I live to make him cringe!)

About the Author

Growing up my best friend and I would write "dreams." We'd each pick a boy we liked, then we'd write a meet-cute that always ended with a happily ever after. Now I dream every day, although now it's a little steamier. I'm married to a writer, mom of a creative dynamo of an eleven-year-old boy and currently a little sleepy. I'm a klutz and goofball and love lipstick as much as my Chuck Taylors. Odds are I have a cup of coffee or a glass of wine in my hand right now.

Feel Free to Follow Me in the following places!